Secondhand Inertia

The Slater Ibáñez Books

That First Heady Burn

True Vermilion

The Dark Shill

A Stack of Sawbucks

The Hillside Roble

The Peroxide Pomp

The Incidental Twin

Brawl in Bardo

The Window-Shade Job

The Convenient Patsy

The Artisanal Grifter

Shrink in the Shadows

Project Chartreuse

From a Desert Playa

The Tired Canary

A Desperate Frame-up

Trail of the Blue Agave

The Saucer-Heads

The Satin Squeeze Play

Chiseler in Jade

The Eagle and the Weasel

The Mojave Gimmick

The Hapless Gonif

Secondhand Inertia

Subscribe to the Slater
Ibáñez Books newsletter:

slaternews.dagmarmiura.com

Secondhand Inertia

Secondhand Inertia

George Bixley

Published by Dagmar Miura
Los Angeles
www.dagmarmiura.com

Secondhand Inertia

First published 2025

ISBN: 979-8-89195-055-9

ETTA WAS ONE OF Slater's operatives, although she worked a lot more for his business partner, Max, than she did for him. Like lots of people with multiple jobs, for her the investigations were a part-time gig. She'd summoned him to the office to pick his brain, she said, probably because Max wasn't around.

Slater parked in the surface lot across the street from the century-old office building, now mostly small clothing factories, and hustled over in a break in the traffic. It was past lunchtime, so the day laborers had cleared out, leaving just a couple of sticky notes on the wall for gigs cutting or sewing or carting fabric for the businesses upstairs. Pulling open the scissor grate on the ancient elevator, he rode up to the ninth floor, and admired their names on the door:

SLATER IBÁÑEZ

MAXIMILLIAN CONROY

INVESTIGATIONS

Their suite was three small offices, one for him and one for Max, plus a front office with a desk in it. Etta had painted the walls and found decent furniture for them. It had made them look like a serious enterprise, the little rooms more than just a perfunctory place to meet clients.

Etta was parked at the front desk, and she sat back and greeted him as he walked in. Curvy, she kept her black hair short, today wearing gray trousers and a dark vest. The little plaster statue of Rey Pascual that sat on the desk was turned to face her. He knew she wanted Rey to be able to watch her work. A skeleton wearing a crown and holding a scythe at the ready, Rey had become the unofficial office mascot.

"What's with the clothes?" Slater said.

She frowned. "What's wrong with my clothes?"

"Have you got a meeting? You look dressed up."

"You look like you always do. Like you need to do some gardening after."

"Jeans never go out of style." Slater stepped into his office, and sat behind the desk.

"Thanks for coming in," she said, dropping into the chair opposite.

"Where's Max, anyway? He's smarter about this stuff than I am."

"In Vegas. On a case."

"I fricking hate Vegas."

"You hate everything." Etta raised her eyebrows. "So I'm running a case on my own. One that Max didn't have time for. It's a window-shade job."

"Right on." He hated window-shade jobs too, but he didn't need to say that, and reinforce her biases. Instead he jabbed a finger at her. "Do not undercut our business. Those are Max's bread and butter."

Etta laughed. "It'll be a while before I'm confident enough to go full-time. So I did the camera work, and got photos of my target in the act."

"Show me," Slater said, and sat up.

Pulling out her phone, she tapped at it, then handed

it across the desk. The photo on the screen was of a man and a woman on a bed, both totally naked. The woman had carefully coiffed peroxide-blond hair and sat with her neck arched, her eyes closed. The man was behind her, with a money haircut, his brow furrowed in concentration. Slater swiped at the screen, and saw there were several more in the same vein.

"These are good. You can see both their faces, and there's no mistaking what they're doing. How did you get so close?"

"A camera drone," Etta said. "They were in an upstairs bedroom and left the curtains open."

"Smart." He handed the phone back. "Which one of them is your target?"

"The male is married to my client."

"What do you need my help with?"

"It's ugly, right?" She waggled the phone. "How do I break it to her?"

"Have you seen Max do it?"

"I sat in on those meetings a couple of times."

"She hired you to confirm her suspicions," Slater said, "so it's not going to be a surprise."

"I get that. But I'm a little intimidated by this woman."

"Has she high-hatted you?"

"Not really," Etta said. "But she's rich."

"That's always going to be the client on a window-shade job. Nobody else has assets they need to protect."

"And here I was thinking it was about love."

"If it were, she wouldn't need hard evidence," Slater said. "It's about business. Your client doesn't want her offspring to have to share assets with the blond's. She'll save money if she divorces him before there are more people to inherit."

"That seems like a cynical spin on it."

"It's a realistic spin. It's also why you don't need to

worry about breaking the news to her. You're not going to hurt her feelings. It's only about money and power. Preserving her position in this new gilded age."

"The way she presented it to me was like she was afraid of emotional betrayal," Etta said.

"Saying that is her way to get power over you. To get you to be more sympathetic to what she wants. In time you'll find that that's typical rich folks behavior." He waved a hand. "If she gets all entitled and demanding, tell her the work you do is like flying first class. She's getting the best for her money, a comfy seat and warm macadamias instead of peanuts, but the plane arrives the same time for everybody."

"It seems to me that when Max delivers the news, he's compassionate with them."

"Compassionate is fine. But you can't sugarcoat it. You need to be clear and firm. I know you can summon that. Talk to her like you're the doctor, not the funeral director."

Etta nodded. "Got it."

"You know that red suit Max wears? It creates a vibe, like 'This is serious.' Wear whatever the lesbian equivalent of that is. You want her to pay attention, and pay your bill."

"I actually got most of the fee up front."

"So you're already on it. You don't even need my help with this."

"I do, though," she said intently. "It's my first solo job. Max usually gives them a file folder with a couple of sheets of facts, like a timeline, and printed photos. Can't I just show her on a screen and email them?"

Slater shook his head. "You want it to be more tangible than that. With printouts they can't just swipe them away. If she decides to delete the email with the images, she might forget to pay you too."

"I know Max uses a print shop in the neighborhood."

"It's on Maple. Print them big, like eight by ten. Ask

them to do a white border around the edges. That contains the image to the paper, so it doesn't feel like it'll leak off the page and contaminate her twelve-hundred-dollar manicure."

"Damn it." Etta got up. "Let me get a pad." She stepped out to the front desk, then came back a second later with a notepad in hand, and a pen with a tuft of purple doll hair stuck on the end. "What else?"

"The woman who runs the print shop will know what to do, but you can remind her to bump up the red and yellow tones in the images. You want them to be vivid and lurid, not blue and gray and cold. They need to feel visceral, not clinical."

"Vivid but contained," she said, making notes. "Got it."

"Get her to print them glossy, not matte."

"Why is that?"

"Max figures it makes them more real."

"And this print shop owner is discreet?"

"That's why he uses the place," Slater said. "It's a one-woman shop, but if she has someone else working the counter, ask to deal with her personally."

"Do you know her? Maybe you can introduce me."

"I've met her, but I don't know her name." He threw up his hands. "If you're going now, I can come with."

Following Etta out into the hall, he locked the office door, and they rode down to the street. As they rounded the corner at the end of the block, a guy on a BMX bike rolled up next to a tree planted along the sidewalk and stopped. Skinny, with a shaved head, he was wearing absurdly baggy shorts, and reached into his backpack, pulling out what looked like an electric pruning saw. That's definitely what it was, Slater realized, as he could hear the whir of its motor as the guy started it up, and leaned toward the tree.

"Is that a chainsaw?" Etta said. "What the hell is he doing?"

Slater quickened his pace and strode up behind him, reaching around his neck and notching his throat into the crook of his arm. The tang of homelessness assaulted his nose, the smell of vinegar and sweat and stale piss, and he started breathing through his mouth as he squeezed.

The guy flailed and swung the saw overhand, aiming for his head. Ducking to avoid it, Slater increased the pressure on his neck, pulling the guy bodily away from the tree and off the bike. The saw wasn't really that dangerous, unless you could aim it, as it had a short blade with a guard on it.

He clawed at his arm, and the bike clattered to the concrete. As he lost consciousness his body went limp. Slater held tight a moment longer, then let him slump to the sidewalk, and stepped back.

Etta walked over, looking down at him. "Is he dead?"

"He'll come around."

Picking up the saw, he took it to the gutter and propped it against the curb, then stomped on it hard. It only took a couple of blows until the housing broke apart. He flipped it over with the toe of his boot to make sure the frame for the chain was sufficiently bent out of shape to render it inoperable.

On the sidewalk, the guy was coming to.

"Hey," he snapped. "What the fuck?"

"This isn't your tree."

As he got to his feet, Slater saw he was breathing hard, a wild look in his eyes. Meth, he decided. Meth-heads had spunk like this. At least the fetty rats just went to sleep.

Slater jabbed a finger at him. "Do not come at me."

"You can't just break my stuff."

"We both know you stole that. You can't fuck up the trees."

The guy rushed at him, fists balled. Slater dodged his arm and landed a punch on his jaw, spinning his head. Dazed, the guy stumbled a few steps. Slater planted a boot on his butt and propelled him into the street. He tumbled between the cars parked at the curb and landed on the gritty broken pavement.

"If you come at me again," Slater said, "she's going to take your bike."

The guy got to his feet, swaying a little, and looked at Etta, then back to Slater. Turning away, Slater walked up the block. Etta dawdled behind him, watching the guy for a moment.

"He's going the other way," she said finally, then caught up and walked abreast. "Was that really necessary?"

"He was going to cut down that tree. It would never be replaced. The city's broke."

"Like I tell my kids, you should use your words."

"Yapping never fixed anything. It has to be force or the threat of force."

"I would have engaged him, at least," she said.

"It's completely meaningless to talk to somebody who's drug-addled like that. They need to feel it."

"He looked so high I doubt he felt anything."

Slapping at his sleeve, Slater waved his arm around. "I just hope I can get rid of that smell."

"So you just squeeze until they pass out?"

He had to suppress a grin. This was the part where it got real, after the mandatory moralizing and the high-tone talk. She wanted to learn how to do it. Slater paused on the sidewalk.

"You don't want to crush his windpipe, so you can't use a baseball bat or a stick or anything. You have to get the windpipe in the crook of your arm, right here." He held out his arm and pointed to the inside of his elbow. "Don't pull toward yourself. You squeeze sideways. Like when you flex. It cuts off the blood flow, not the air. Once he goes limp you hold on for another few seconds."

"He was only unconscious for a few seconds," she said.

"That's long enough to get away from the situation."

"Or to bust up his chainsaw."

"It was a pruning saw."

They turned onto Maple and walked to the print shop. As they stepped inside, onto the ancient grubby carpet in the small space in front of the counter, an electronic chime sounded. Through the doorway farther in he could see a couple of oversize machines—document scanners and industrial printers.

The clerk stepped out of the back and greeted them. In her thirties, maybe, she was wearing glasses, and had her dark hair bundled back.

"I'm Etta," she said, "and you already know Slater. Our office is around the corner."

"Monta." She eyed Slater. "You've been in with Max. He's a good customer."

"Max is our colleague," Etta said. "I need to get some images printed."

Monta raised her eyebrows. "Cheating cheaters and their cheaty cheats?"

Etta chuckled. "You know the drill."

"Email them to that address," she said, handing her a business card, "and I'll get started."

Pulling out her phone, Etta tapped at it, glancing at the card.

She really could handle this herself, Slater realized. He didn't need to be here.

"So what would you charge me to look into something that's not about cheating?" Monta said.

Etta glanced up from her screen. "That depends. What do you need to look into?"

"A friend of mine died out in the desert a while back. The coroner said the cause of death was an overdose. The thing is, he never did drugs. He'd been clean for years. It makes no sense."

"Were you romantically involved?" Etta said.

"Ages ago. But we're just friends." She waved a hand. "*Were* just friends. I still can't believe he's gone."

"People relapse all the time," Slater said.

"Flynn wouldn't do that. I know him. The coroner is part of the sheriff's department out there. You know what cops are like. They got their simple answer, so that's the end of it. File the paperwork and move on. Maybe you could just talk to people, see if there's anything more to it."

"You think he was murdered," Etta said.

"I don't know. I just wish I knew more about what happened. There is evidence that things didn't go the way the coroner says they did."

"I've got a lot going on." Etta tucked her phone into her pants. "I couldn't dedicate the time to a new case."

"What about you," Monta said, eyeing Slater. "Or Max. Is he around?"

"Max is out of town," Slater said, "but I'll hear you out."

"That's all I'm asking."

He put his hands on his hips. "I'm not going to do it if it sounds like there's nothing to achieve."

"Fair enough. My staffer will be here soon. Can I come by your office and lay it on you?"

"Sure. It's not far from here."

"I know the building," Monta said. "Your address is on your letterhead. I printed all your stationery for Max. What floor are you on again?"

"The ninth. Around behind the elevator."

"I sent you the photos," Etta said.

Monta raised her eyebrows. "Eight by ten, white borders, glossy finish, bump up the warm tones, I'm thinking."

Etta laughed. "You got it."

"I'll do them now and bring them with me."

As they walked out, the door chime sounded again, and they headed toward the office. Slater paused on the sidewalk to look at the tree. It was a fern pine, and well limbed up, not bothering anybody. That idiot had nicked the bark with the saw, but if he didn't go after it again, it would survive.

At the corner across from the surface lot, Etta stopped. "I'm heading out. You can leave those photos on the front desk."

"You don't want to listen to Monta? It might be something you could work on."

"It sounds like too much for me. I need to start with straightforward jobs."

"Don't underestimate yourself."

"I also don't have the time to get into it," she said.

"Doesn't middle school have spring break?"

"It's almost over. I used that time on the window-shade job." She waved a hand. "Listen, thanks for mentoring me."

Slater frowned. "It's business. I'm just trying to make some scratch, and keep my head above water."

She chuckled. "Well, thanks anyway."

TWO

A s Etta crossed to the parking lot, Slater went up to the office, and flicked on the lights. The statue of Rey Pascual was facing the front door now. Dropping into his desk chair, he leaned back and heaved his boots onto the desktop, eyeing the other office tchotchke, parked next to his computer monitor. It was a little statue of a naked guy standing with a horse. Inscribed on the base was his name, Pollux. It had been a gift from Pike, and the matching statue of Castor sat on his desk. One side of it was flat, and it was heavy, so they were probably intended to be bookends. Sweet Pike. Just thinking about the guy made his heart soar.

A while later came a knock at the door, and he got up to open it, and waved Monta inside. She was wearing a light jacket now, and had a brown satchel slung over her shoulder.

"Etta's photos." She pulled a bulky white envelope out of her bag.

"You can leave them here. She uses this desk."

"I like the art deco vibe," she said, looking around.

"That's all Etta's doing. The furniture, the paint job, even the light fixtures."

"I like this." Monta leaned down to examine the statue on the front desk. "It's not Santa Muerte."

"His name is Rey Pascual. He's the king of the graveyard."

"He's Central American, I'm thinking."

"I think so. The woman who gave him to me is Honduran."

She stepped over to look into Max's office. "This must be Max. I recognize that suit."

He'd left his brown jacket on a hanger on the front of the wardrobe that sat in the corner of his office, Slater saw, looking in behind her. He hated that suit, hated the way it looked on the guy, hated how often he wore it. It made him want to punch Max in the face. But that's how he felt about a lot of people.

"I'm in this one." He waved her over to his own office, and scooted the chair closer to his desk as she took the chair opposite. "Is Monta short for something?"

She met his gaze. "Montserrat. It's Catalan."

"That's a personal name?"

"Believe it or not. I don't usually tell people what it is. In high school I was known as Monster Rat."

"As a diss, that's not even very creative." Slater dug his phone out of his jeans and opened a blank note. "What's the dead guy's name?"

Her expression shifted, her brow furrowing. "Flynn. That's also a first name." Reaching into her bag, she pulled out her phone. "I can share a copy of his death certificate. Where can I send it?"

Rolling open the top drawer, he found a business card and handed it over.

Monta set it on the edge of the desk, peering at it as she tapped at her phone with her thumbs. "You're supposed to be able to order them online, but I had to drive out to freaking San Berdoo to get a paper copy. It felt like they were intentionally messing with me."

"When's the last time you saw Flynn?"

"In the fall. He was in town for a couple nights and stayed with me. He'd been working out there, in Twenty-nine Palms, at a thrift store. It's called Retread Me."

Slater tapped the name into his phone. "When did he die?"

"Not that long ago. Mercury was still in retrograde. Sometime in late January."

He sat back. "You're into astrology."

"I pay attention. Why does that matter?"

"It makes you less credible. You get that, don't you? It makes everything you say suspect."

"It doesn't rule my life. It's not like I'm Joan of Arc with the saints whispering in my ear." She waved a hand. "I'm not wearing crystals to make myself immune to microplastics."

Stifling a scoff, he sat up, and grabbed his computer mouse, and pulled up the death certificate, reading through it.

"The cause of death just says 'T40.'"

"It's a bureaucratic code," Monta said. "It means opioids. I talked to a guy in the sheriff's department who said it was probably fentanyl, based on the residue they saw on the smoking paraphernalia. It was near the body."

"What kind of paraphernalia?"

"A lighter, a piece of foil with scorch marks on it, the tube from a pen. Even when he was using, Flynn didn't do that. He was clean and organized. I can't imagine him burning anything to get high."

"What kind of dope was he into?"

She looked away. "Flynn was a pillhead."

Peering at the screen, he scrolled down the document. The address for the decedent's residence looked familiar.

He'd heard of that street, and that was Doris's zip code.

"He lived in Mount Washington?"

"Close," Monta said. "That address is in Cypress Park. It's where I live. Flynn was using it on his ID. He didn't know how long he'd be in Twentynine. I don't even know where he was staying out there. It sounded like a temporary arrangement."

Slater looked back to the document. "The location of death has the latitude and longitude. Why not a street address?"

"It's in the wilderness. In the national park. Some hiker found him. The rangers had to walk in and then helicopter the body out. It was nowhere near any roads."

"Did you talk to the hiker?"

"I talked to a ranger who'd been involved in the body recovery. She said they couldn't release the respondent's identity, but then off the record she also said it wouldn't matter anyway, because it was an anonymous call. It actually took them a couple days to go out there and check. She said because it was anonymous, they thought it might be bogus."

Watching her, he thought it through. It sounded a little suspicious. But then if he stumbled on a corpse, he'd likely do the same thing, since the idiots would try to pin it on him, or at the very least waste a bunch of his time. Not getting involved was a reasonable instinct.

"How did they identify him?"

"His wallet with his ID was in his pocket. Also he had a tattoo on his wrist. The deputy said his father recognized it."

"Is he around?"

"He lives in Mississippi, or Missouri, or one of those. I talked to him on the phone. He told me he handled it all remotely."

"Somebody checked the box that says autopsy performed," Slater said.

"The deputy wouldn't tell me anything about that. Just about the smoking kit. They decided it meshed with his record. He'd been arrested a couple of times for possession."

"What happened to the body?"

Monta took a breath. "Flynn and I weren't in contact all that often, so I didn't hear about it right away. By the time I found out, Flynn's father had had him cremated. It felt a little odd that he'd get involved. They weren't close. You can actually refuse to take responsibility and let the county bury the body. I just read that there's a couple thousand of those every year in LA. Unknown or unclaimed."

"That's a lot of stiffs," he said. "If there's any way to get somebody else to pay for it, I'm sure they push hard. They probably threatened to sue his father if he didn't pony up. Was his phone on the body?"

"I don't know. Nobody said anything about it."

"What evidence is there that the coroner got it wrong?"

"Flynn's not a junkie, and I know he's not a smoker. Not tobacco or weed or anything."

"So it's mostly your gut feeling. Or was it in his star chart?"

She frowned. "I had access to one of his credit cards. Our finances were still intermingled. The last thing he bought was a couple of granola bars and bottles of water. At a gas station in Joshua Tree. I drove out there and talked to the clerk. She said Flynn might have been with someone."

"She remembered him? You said you didn't hear about it right away. How long after was this?"

"A month or so. Flynn has a distinctive car. A mid-seventies GTO. People remember it."

"Sweet ride," Slater said. "What color was it?"

"It's kind of gold-brown. He spent a lot of time working on it."

"And the clerk described it."

"The color and everything. She wasn't sure, but her

impression was that he wasn't alone."

"Was it near where he died? Parked at a trailhead?"

"I have no idea what happened to the car," Monta said. "The rangers didn't find it. The one I talked to said he must have hitchhiked out there. She said people do that sometimes when they're on a through-hike."

"Do you still have access to the credit card?"

"It went offline, but I got some screenshots of the last few transactions."

"Share that with me," Slater said. "Which market? Who did you talk to there?"

"So you'll take the job?"

"You've already done a lot of the work. I can't promise results, but I can poke around. It's what I do."

She smiled. "The clerk's name is Rupinder. It's a family business, and there's two Rupinders. She's the younger one."

On his phone, Slater tapped it into a note. "Rupinder the Younger." He looked up. "I'll need photos of the guy."

Picking up her phone, Monta tapped at it, and he looked at the images she sent. In the first one Flynn was posing with Monta, his arm around her shoulder, his shirt open a few buttons. He had shaggy hair, that brown color that so many white dudes had, and a tightly trimmed beard, blue eyes, a toothy smile. The guy was fuckable.

"He was hot," Slater said.

She chuckled. "He thought so. I guess he was, for a *güero.*"

"I thought that word meant blond."

"It means white folks. You look like you should speak the language."

"So I'm told." He heard it a lot, as he had his father's Latin coloring, his black hair.

"I assume you'll need some money up front," Monta said.

"Two grand to start. We'll reassess in a few days."

She pulled her wallet out of her bag and counted out the C-notes, setting them on the desktop.

"I don't usually walk around with that much cash, but I figured you'd prefer that to a transfer."

"Always." Scooping up the bills, he got up, and folded them in half, and tucked them into his jeans.

She rose with him. "You're not going to count it?"

"Max trusts you with his business. I can trust you with this."

"I know this all sounds cut and dried. The coroner signed off on it, so as far as they're concerned, it's finished. I just want to know more."

"I'll see what I can do."

After she left, he took a minute to lock his computer, then texted Andy:

I'm on my way over.

KILLING THE LIGHTS, SLATER stepped out of the office and bolted the door, then went down to the street and across to the surface lot.

Parked along the fence was a maroon and cream Pacer, sleek and beautiful, and he used the key to unlock the door. It was a '78, and a new acquisition for him. It felt small compared to his regular ride, and low to the ground, and it had a lot of glass. It was fun to drive but he knew he didn't need to be collecting cars, cluttering up the garage like a damn hoarder.

Slater drove the few blocks to Broadway and parked behind Andy's building. Once he'd paid the attendant, he walked around to the front entrance and up to Andy's floor.

As he pulled open the door, Andy flashed that easy smile and waved him in. He had wild brown hair, and needed a shave, and as usual he was wearing a T-shirt and boxer shorts.

His loft was mostly one room, with a bed and a desk with an array of monitors, and it got good light from tall windows overlooking the square. As Slater followed him inside, he eyed the red mobility scooter parked near the door.

"Where's that gunsel you married?"

Andy dropped into his gaming chair. "At ELAC. He has a class."

"What's he studying? How to con your maid into taking care of your polo pony?"

"I think it's philosophy."

"Must be nice to be a man of leisure."

Andy frowned. "He's not that guy. He doesn't have a … maid or a horse."

"I know he's not grinding like I am. Playing my part to keep all this going." He waved at the room. "Is he trying to get a degree or something?"

"He's just interested in it. I'm actually glad he's … into expanding his mind."

"Plus it gets him out of your hair. It must be suffocating to have him around."

The front door opened, and Kyle walked in. The guy was lanky, and buff, and kept his hair in a natty style. Slater hated how his chinos fit him so well, how his shirt showed his pecs. His expression darkened at the sight of Slater.

"If it isn't the booze hag," Kyle said. "I wondered what that smell was. I assume it's last night's bathtub gin seeping out of your pores."

"You look as sweet as a whole bag of gumdrops, babe. I see your mom is finally letting you wear long pants."

"Are you high right now, or just hung over?"

Slater put his hands on his hips. "Andy said you're studying philosophy. You know there's a shortcut, right?"

"Is it something you found in the bottom of a bottle?"

"The ancients knew about it. You stare at your own belly button for seven days straight, and all the wisdom of the universe will blast out in a flash of blinding light."

"I didn't realize you were the esoteric philosophy type,"

Kyle said. "I think of you more as the angry drunk. The emotional wreck."

"That's interesting, because I think of you as the vapid high-fructose toothache."

"Dirtbag," Kyle said through his teeth.

Andy raised his voice. "Sweetness, I told you I'll handle him. Just let me … do that."

Slater frowned at him. "Nobody handles me. I don't get handled."

"Why are you here?" Andy demanded.

He huffed. "I need a coroner's report. My client was able to get the death certificate. I'll share it." He dug out his phone and tapped at it.

"I'm not sure those are … always public," Andy said.

He glanced up at him. "When has that ever slowed you down?"

Kyle folded his arms, planting his feet apart. "It sounds like your work is devolving into the macabre."

"I don't have the trust fund or the white privilege to insulate me from reality," Slater said, tucking his phone away. "I do what I have to do."

"You don't get to put that on me. You're about as Latin as a cucumber sandwich with a toothpick in it. With the crusts cut off, and extra mayo."

Slater squeezed one hand with the other, audibly cracking his knuckles. "I want to punch you in the face so bad right now."

"Slater, focus," Andy said. "I'll let you know what I … find. Now, get out of here."

"I don't have time for you fools anyway." He raised his voice. "So quit bugging me."

Walking out, he went to the fire stairs instead of the elevator, hustling down, moving fast to burn off the adrenaline. It seemed inevitable that he'd give Kyle a tune-up one of these days, but he needed to resist the instinct for as long as possible. He couldn't afford to lose Andy and his research skills. Why had he married that little shvantz?

Once he'd climbed into the Pacer, he drove to his house, a modern box set amid the mostly century-old houses not far from Downtown LA. It had been built by gentrifiers, and it was a little obnoxious, and out of step with the neighborhood. The fact that he'd bought it probably meant he qualified as a gentrifier too.

The magnolia near the end of his block had started to leaf out, he saw as he drove by, the greenery obscuring the dramatic white tepals that had started to drop to the ground. Farther along was a camellia he'd been watching run riot this winter, its flowers also dropping and gradually carpeting the street and the yard it was in. It was a weird one, with tidy and symmetrical pale pink flowers, far from the rough and scraggy look of wild camellias. Someone had bred it to look like that at least a century ago, when the massive tree had been planted here, in an era when tight and controlled flora was in vogue.

Pike wasn't back from work yet, as there was no sign of his rig out front. He rolled the Pacer into the garage and parked next to the Continental. Just seeing it gave him a twinge of guilt. His cars were hogging up the garage, and Pike had to park on the street. But logically it was the least valuable of the vehicles, and Pike didn't seem to care.

The bedrooms were over the garage, and above that was the kitchen and the living space and a deck. Climbing both flights, Slater grabbed his laptop and went out the French doors to sit in one of the loungers. It was still nice out, the late afternoon sun still blazing, the last of the spring warmth before May gray set in.

Monta had sent a lot of photos, and he looked through them, shifting the lounger so that the sun wasn't on his screen. Flynn didn't always have the beard, he saw. At some point he'd been clean-shaven. Monta looked younger in those pictures too. In one of the photos the tattoo Monta had mentioned was visible, on the inside of Flynn's wrist. He zoomed in on it. The image was grainy, but he could see it was a circle with a superimposed triangle. Inside them was another shape, but at this resolution it showed only as a fuzzy blue blob.

Next he looked up the coordinates of where the body had been found. It really was in the wilderness. No trails were marked anywhere nearby, and it was miles from the road.

He looked at it on a topo map, and then a satellite image. The landscape was hilly rocks and boulders. He knew what it was like, as he'd been there, in the northern part of the park. The boulder piles formed ridges with arroyos running between them. There were walking routes, he knew, but a lot of the terrain was either impassible or required scrambling on the rocks.

Eventually he got up and went inside to the kitchen. Pike was standing at the counter, munching on an apple. Built thick, his dark hair was brushed back. He was still dressed for the office.

"I didn't hear you come in," Slater said.

"I just got here."

He embraced him, and mouthed his neck and his jaw. "You taste like apple."

Pike chuckled and nuzzled his neck. "You want to eat?"

He murmured assent, then squeezed him tightly for a moment, inhaling the heady scent of his neck and his hair, then pulled back.

"There's a brewpub on Grand," Pike said. "It's not really hotcha, but we could eat there, and listen to the music after."

"Who's playing?"

"A blues singer. Ernesta. I kind of want to see her."

"If you want to, I want to."

"Even if Ernesta is terrible?" Pike gestured with his

apple. "What if she's an affront to the blues?"

"If that happens, you'll pay for it later."

"Oh, really." Pike stood up straighter, his eyes bright. "So you're a tough guy."

Slater leaned in to mouth his neck. "I'm going to demolish you anyway. Destroy you. Fuck you raw."

"Such delicate sentiments, petal."

Downstairs in the bedroom Slater put on a clean shirt, and Pike changed into a pair of chinos and a short-sleeved print shirt. In the garage they climbed into the Pacer, and Slater backed into the street, and flicked on the headlights in the looming gray of dusk. When they got to Downtown, he spotted a meter and pulled in.

The brewpub was crowded but they got a table, and sat adjacent, facing the stage at the back of the room. They ordered beer and the nachos to share. Once the server stepped away, Slater spoke.

"So I got a job today. It's out in the desert."

"How far out?"

"Around Joshua Tree and Twentynine Palms."

"That's not that far," Pike said. "What do you have to do?"

"This guy overdosed. His ex wants me to find out if there's more to it."

"You don't usually work that kind of case."

"It's not about how he died. She wants to know what happened before that. My only real concern is that she's into astrology."

Pike laughed. "What did she say about that?"

He waited while the server set down their beer glasses, and lifted his, and tapped it against Pike's.

"She said Mercury was in retrograde when it happened," he said, once he'd taken a sip. "As if that mattered."

"Lots of people are into astrology. It doesn't mean she's irrational."

"But astrology is irrational. It calls everything she says into question. Does she have legitimate concerns about this guy's demise, or is it all because Saturn's *I Ching* bubble quotient came up snake eyes?"

His eyes narrowed. "The *I Ching* isn't part of astrology."

"It's definitely part of crazy land."

"I think most people have both of those in their head at the same time," Pike said. "Rational and irrational ideas. Like religious thinking. It doesn't mesh with science, but even if you roll around on the church floor speaking in tongues on Sunday, you still go get your flu shot on Monday."

The plate of nachos arrived, and they dug into them. As they ate Slater could see the band setting up on the stage. A rail-thin man sat at the piano, and a woman sat at the drum kit. A minute later a guy with a trombone appeared, then another with a sax, and a guy with a trumpet. At first he thought they might be roadies, as they were dressed for yard work or a trip to the grocery store, but they were futzing with the instruments—these were the musicians.

"That seems like a lot of brass," Slater said.

"Ernesta must be going for a classic blues sound."

Eventually the band got settled, and Ernesta stepped out on the stage. It felt like the crowd knew who she was, as they applauded and hooted for her. She had wild Black hair, and like the band she was dressed casually, in jeans and a dark top. She raised a hand in greeting, acknowledging the applause, then leaned into the mike.

"You might be able to tell by the way I talk that I'm from Memphis. I've got deep roots in the Mississippi Delta. We all know the music that grew up there."

A woman at the side of the room called out, "Rock and roll."

Ernesta cocked her head. "Technically correct, ma'am. But I'm talking about something else."

Pike and half a dozen other voices called out, "The blues."

"Now, that's what I'm talking about." Ernesta waved a hand, and the drummer started into a song.

Some of her stuff sounded classic, slow and methodical and sad like the blues, and other pieces were more upbeat. She had a good voice with a lot of power in it. Slater sipped his beer and looked over at Pike. The guy was rapt, listening to her, his head bobbing with the music. He loved that about him, how present he was, how immersed he got. Slater didn't give a damn about blues music, but stuff like this was part of how Pike was a civilizing force in his life, how he made Slater a better man. Just looking at him right now made his throat hurt.

Ernesta took a break, and they finished the nachos, and then she came back and did another set. When they finally left it was dark and felt cold out as they walked to the Pacer.

"You enjoyed that," Slater said.

"You're right. Did you?"

"A lot. She sounds great."

Pike chuckled and briefly squeezed him around the waist.

———◦———

WHEN THEY GOT BACK to the house, and climbed up to the bedroom, Slater pulled off his boots and got undressed. As Pike dumped his wallet and his keys in the bureau drawer, Slater spotted a bulky ring sitting with his money clip and an old mechanical watch. He picked up the ring to look it over. It was gold, with scrollwork around the flat black stone.

"What's this?"

"My high school ring," Pike said.

"Why don't you wear it?"

"It's a little bulky."

"What's the stone?"

"Probably glass, or something nonprecious. It didn't cost a lot."

Slater slid it onto the ring finger of his right hand. "It fits me just right."

"I guess it makes you balanced. Gold on the left and gold on the right."

"I was actually thinking it'll leave nice bruises if I have to serve up some knuckle sauce."

"So it's practical too. I guess it looks OK."

Slater raised his eyebrows. "If you're not wearing it, I am. Until you revoke the privilege."

Stepping close, Pike grasped his hand. "So now you're just claiming my stuff."

"Use it or lose it, wise guy."

Pike met his mouth, and savaged his neck, then pulled back and started to unbutton his shirt. "There was chatter earlier about somebody getting demolished."

"That can be arranged." Slater waited for him to ditch his trousers, then pulled him onto the bed, caressing his skin and relishing the warmth of his body.

"You're hard." Pike grasped his cock. "You need to fuck me."

Reaching into the bedside drawer for the lube, Slater shifted next to him, pushing his knees apart, and massaged a thumb into him. Eventually he pressed into him, looming over his torso as he got into it. Pike pulled him in, mashing their mouths together, and Slater increased the pace, and started to pound him. He grunted as he came, straining into him.

He pulled up and squeezed Pike's cock, rock hard now.

"You should ride me," Pike said, and Slater straddled his pelvis, easing down onto him, then started rocking back and forth, kneading Pike's chest and his shoulders. Pike grasped his thighs, thrusting wildly, his body shuddering with a spasm as he came.

Pulling away, Slater stretched out beside him, catching his breath. He drifted off, with Pike's arm under his neck, but then started awake. He got up and went upstairs, pulling open the cupboard where they kept the booze, and tried not to look at the good stuff, Pike's scotch. He went through so much that his quotidian snort had to be the cheap-ass bourbon.

Pouring his ration into a tumbler, he took a slurp, savoring the heady fumes, then walked through to the French doors and stood to look out at the glittering lights of the city. Taking another gulp, he relished the burn in his throat, the warmth spreading from his belly. The feeling of satiety didn't last long, but right now it felt freaking great.

WHEN SLATER WOKE, DAYLIGHT was streaming in the windows, and his head felt clear. Obviously he hadn't overdone it on the applejack last night. Pike was already gone. Grabbing his phone, he saw there was a text from Andy:

I have your document.

Forcing himself out of bed, he took a quick shower, and got dressed, and trudged up to the kitchen. There was tepid coffee that Pike had left for him in the pot, and he slammed half a mugful, then grabbed a bagel to eat on the way.

As he climbed in behind the wheel of the Pacer, he felt a little guilty about ignoring the Continental, sitting there all sleek and cloudy blue and patiently waiting for him. He backed into the street, and waited for the garage door to roll down, then drove to Downtown and parked in the surface lot behind Andy's building.

Walking into the lobby he saw Andy waiting for the elevator, propped on his walking sticks, wearing a plaid shirt and dark green cargo shorts. He looked up as Slater approached and greeted him with that smile. Such a beautiful man.

"Did that cake-eater you married hock your scooter?" Slater said.

"I wasn't going far. Just to the … market for coffee."

"I know you like it Greek. Don't they deliver anymore?"

"I also wanted to see the damn sun. I spend too much … time indoors."

Slater stepped onto the elevator after him, eyeing the walking sticks. He didn't need them to go short distances, and Slater wasn't even convinced that they improved his gait. But he knew it was none of his business. He looked away as the doors rolled closed.

"So you were able to snag the coroner's report?" Slater said.

"You know it."

"Did you have to hack somebody to get it?"

"Don't ask me that."

When the elevator rolled open, Andy stepped off, and Slater followed him to his door. It took him a minute to get the key in the lock. His CP meant he lacked fine-motor control, and his movements looked like pure chaos, but eventually it happened, and he pushed the door open, and stepped inside.

Pulling his arms out of the cuffs, Andy propped the sticks in a corner and sat at his desk. It took him a minute to pull on his gauntlets, black plastic sleeves that served as an input device for his computer. Slater stood nearby as he settled in and studied the screen.

"I just shared it with you," Andy said finally.

He felt the notification buzz his phone in his pants, and watched as Andy pulled off the gauntlets.

"There's some gnarly photos in there, and lots of … doctor language. I can't translate it. You need a … medical person."

"You could have shared it without summoning me here."

He swiveled toward him. "But then paying me would be at … your convenience. This way you're here, and I can … demand payment."

Slater narrowed his eyes. "I think you just like seeing me."

"I admit I don't mind looking at those jeans."

"Is it because you need me to extract you from this? Does Kyle have this place bugged?" He put his hands on his hips. "Blink twice if you need me to get you out of here. I know people who can get you new IDs, get you set up in another city."

Andy chuckled. "My life doesn't … work like that. Like your seedy world."

"It would actually be easier just to rub out the problem. Say the word and Kyle can have a little accident. Maybe he forgets to wear his helmet and gets thrown off his polo pony. Why did he go riding so late at night? Or maybe he gets trampled in the stall. Horses can be unpredictable."

"Why do you think he plays polo?" Andy waved an arm. "The point of you being here is … cash money. You owe me five dollars."

"I actually run into lots of chiselers in my seedy world. You are undeniably a chiseler, son." Slater dug out his wad of cash, and counted out the C-notes, and handed them over. "Am I shelling out five yards for something you pulled off a public website?"

"If it were that easy, I'd only charge you … two hundred."

Slater watched him for a moment. "Bye, beautiful."

Walking out, he went down to the street, and climbed in the Pacer. When he rolled into the surface lot across from his office, the parking attendant waved at him. They didn't bug him because they recognized the distinctive vehicle, and knew he bought a monthly pass.

A couple of day laborers were in the lobby looking over the wall of schmatte-trade gig offers, and upstairs in the office no one was around. He flicked on the lights and double-clicked his tongue to greet Rey Pascual, silently watching the front door with his bony empty eye sockets.

In his own office he sat at his desk and stared at the computer screen as he went through the autopsy report. There were several pages of text, then a series of photos. Andy was right—it was stomach-churning to look at a corpse. Monta said they hadn't found it right away. It did look kind of decayed. He clicked through them quickly.

Thinking about it, Monta didn't need to see all this. He sent several of the photos, the ones of the face and the torso and the jittles, to the office printer, then made a copy of the file and deleted them. The photos that he left in the version for her included a close-up of one eye and the photo of the wrist tattoo.

In this image he could see the tat clearly. A circle and a triangle, and inside that was a sleepy-looking eye. He'd seen the image before somewhere, but what did it mean to this guy?

Pulling out his phone, he scrolled through his contact list. There was a medical student that he'd hooked up with once, back in the BP era, before Pike. He only kept phone numbers of the guys he might hit up again, and he knew he'd kept that one. Something with Matsu in it, he remembered. And there it was: Matsuda.

A familiar voice answered when he dialed: "Hey, Slater."

"I'm surprised you picked up."

"Oh, I remember you. The thing is, I can't really hook up. I'm trying to get my head on straight. I've been going to twelve-step meetings."

"That sounds awfully sad and boring. I'm not calling about a hookup. I need your input on something. You're in med school, correct?"

"I'm a resident now."

"I know that still means doctor," Slater said. "I need you to look at something."

"Do you not have medical insurance? The county has drop-in clinics. They're actually really good."

"It's not about that. It's for a case I'm working. I need you to look at some paperwork and explain it to me. I'll pay you for your time."

"What kind of paperwork?"

"You'll figure that out when we meet."

"I'm working in Hollywood," Matsuda said. "At Betreuen. Do you know where that is?"

He scoffed. "I may have heard of it."

It was a sprawling urban medical campus with a hospital and clinics and medical offices strung along a dozen blocks of Sunset. The company was even bigger than that, a conglomerate that had millions of customers in Cali. They set a time to meet, and Slater ended the call.

Setting his phone on the desk, he stared absently at the little statue of Pollux with his horse. He didn't really need stuff like that cluttering up the place, but he'd kept it at first because the guy had such great hair. He'd only got involved with Pike after Pollux had landed here. Pike must have had some inkling that it would be a spark for them. In any case it had worked, as their narrative complex had rapidly evolved into a raging inferno.

A knock at the door pulled him from his thoughts. Nobody came here without an appointment, and Max wasn't even around to be meeting people. He locked his computer and walked toward the front. Outside he heard a voice call, "Post office."

He pulled the door open a few inches. The guy was taller than him, and looked built. He wasn't wearing a uniform. Why did he recognize that ugly mug? Then it clicked: This was the cheater in Etta's window-shade photos.

At that moment the guy body-slammed the door, pushing his way inside, shouting at him, and threw a punch. Even though he was on the back foot, Slater managed to dodge the first blow, but the second one landed on his chest. Slater threw a right, connecting with his cheek. With the impact his finger hurt like hell. That was Pike's ring biting into his skin.

The guy pulled back, and Slater ducked and rushed him, aiming for his belt with his shoulder. That was muscle memory from middle-school wrestling: go low to destabilize your opponent. It knocked him off his feet, and as he lost his balance, he tumbled over Slater's back and rolled onto the floor.

Slater spun around and grabbed his wrist, dropping to one knee behind him and shoving his arm up his back. The guy yelped and tried to kick at him. He pushed his arm farther up.

"Knock it off, or I'll dislocate your shoulder."

He turned his head sideways, red-faced now. "Fuck, man. Let me go."

There was a red circle on his cheek where Pike's ring had made contact.

"How did you know who was investigating you?" Slater demanded.

The guy was breathing hard and didn't answer. Slater heaved on his arm, shoving it higher.

He yowled and shouted, "Stop it, you dick. I looked at my wife's phone."

"You know the damage is done, right? She knows about the blond. She's seen the photos. Coming after me is pointless."

"You blew up my life."

"You blew up your own life when you decided to fuck the blond." Pulling him to his feet, Slater frog-marched him to the door and shoved him into the hallway. "If you come here again, I'll break your fucking arm."

He bolted the door and stood listening. He couldn't hear the guy. His breathing gradually slowed, and he absently twisted Pike's ring. It still hurt, but it hadn't broken the skin. The thing had bit both of them. It wasn't as comfortable as brass knuckles, but it also wasn't illegal to walk around with. Maybe he'd turn it inside out when he needed to school somebody.

Digging out his phone he texted Etta:

> Your cheating spouse showed up at the office. He has a way to get into your client's phone. Tell her to change her unlock code and account passwords.

Scooping up the photos he'd sent to the printer, he tucked them into his satchel, then opened the front door and looked around. There was no sign of Etta's idiot ratfuck target. Locking up, he went down to the street and walked over to Monta's shop. The chime above the door sounded as he stepped inside.

Monta was at the counter, talking to a stocky guy with baggy pants and decent broad shoulders. They were speaking Spanish. She nodded when she spotted Slater, and they chatted a minute longer, and eventually the guy walked out.

"Does that guy owe you money?" Slater said.

"Why would you think that?"

"I heard him say *dinero.*"

"As in *envíos de dinero,*" Monta said. "Money transfers."

"You do that?"

"I'm no banker, but I help do that. A lot of people in this neighborhood are grinding for scarce resources."

"I guess Venus must be in opposition to their house of prosperity."

She frowned. "That's not how it works."

Slater gestured to a bundle of roses sitting on the countertop. "He brought you these?"

"It's not romantic. He's a satisfied customer. I think he works over at the flower market." She lifted them and held them to her nose. "They're not really scented."

"See how tight the petals are? They've been bred to keep the pollinators out. That also keeps the scent inside."

"I guess people don't want bugs crawling on their flowers."

"People are idiots."

"It's hard to argue with that," Monta said. "Can you give me a sec?"

She carried them into the back, and he heard water running. A minute later she returned with the roses in a glass vase and set them on the counter.

"I didn't want them to wilt."

"I'm not worried. You're paying me for my time." He shifted on his feet. "So I got a copy of the coroner's report."

Her eyebrows shot up. "You work fast. How did you manage that?"

"Do you know what plausible deniability is?"

"Not really." Her brow furrowed. "It sounds like legalese."

"It just means that if I don't explain my methods, nobody can make you tell them about it. All you need to know is that I obtained the coroner's report."

"That makes it sound like you did something illegal."

Slater placed a palm on his heart. "I would never knowingly break the law or act unethically."

She cackled. "I've known Max too long to buy that. I definitely want to look at that report."

"Can you print it out for me?"

Monta slid a business card across the counter, and he dug out his phone and sent the redacted version of the file to the email address it listed. Stepping over to the computer at the end of the counter, she pulled it up.

"It's mostly technical language," she said.

"I'm going to talk to somebody today to get it translated."

"Oh, gawd. There's photos."

"You don't need to spend time on those," Slater said. "Just print it all for me. My office printer isn't very good for photos."

He could see that she was breathing hard, staring at the screen. He snapped his fingers.

"Seriously—look away."

Monta stood erect. "I'm all right."

She clicked the mouse, and he heard the quiet whir of machinery in the back room. Stepping toward the printer, she returned a minute later with a sheaf of paper, and tucked it into a manila folder, and set it on the counter.

Slater leafed through the pages, then pointed to the tattoo in the close-up photo. "What do you know about this?"

"He got that fairly recently. After he moved out to the desert. I'm not really sure what it means."

"Is it astrological? Was he into that stuff too?"

"Isn't it on the back of the dollar bill?"

He frowned. "Are you kidding me?"

"Have you got a single on you?"

Digging out his wad of cash, he found one, and looked at the back.

"Fuck me dead. There it is."

Monta waggled her fingers for it, and he handed it over.

"The eye at the top of the pyramid." She looked at the photo of the tattoo again, then handed him the single. "It's not exactly the same as Flynn's. If it's on the dollar, I'm sure there's been a lot written about it."

He tucked the bill in his pants. "I'll let you know what the doctor says."

"Are you going out to the desert?"

"Not today, but I'm thinking I'll have to. You've been out there. Did you try to go to the site where they found the body?"

She shook her head. "I couldn't handle that."

"Fair enough." Slater jabbed a finger at her. "Do not go through those photos."

Walking out, he headed to the surface lot across from his office, and climbed into the Pacer. Flipping open his satchel, he fished out the photos he'd excluded from Monta's copy, not nearly as sharp as the ones she'd printed, and put them into the folder, then set the bag on the passenger seat.

The 101 was still moving, as it wasn't long past noon, and he headed toward Hollywood. The Pacer rode low, and at freeway speed it was a little unnerving to be so close to the pavement compared to the Continental. He exited onto Sunset Boulevard and cruised until he found Matsuda's building, revving the Pacer's engine to get up the ramp into the parking structure.

Climbing out, he looped the strap of his satchel over his shoulder and walked into the lobby. It looked to be medical offices, as there was a list of specialties posted next to the elevators along with their corresponding floor numbers. Stepping over to the desk, he spoke to the clerk.

"I'm here to see Dr. Matsuda. I know he works upstairs, but what office is he in?"

"Do you have an appointment?"

"He knows I'm coming."

"Are you a member?"

Slater frowned. "Of what?"

"Betreuen. Is Dr. Matsuda your primary care physician?"

"That makes no sense."

Her brow furrowed. "Excuse me?"

"Membership implies shared interests. This isn't a social club, toots. You're running a business. People pay you money to get help when they're sick. That makes them customers. Or am I missing something?"

Keeping her eyes on him, she reached for the desk phone. "Let me see if Dr. Matsuda is available."

He folded his arms and watched her as she murmured into the receiver. Eventually she set it down.

"You can go to section A on the seventh floor."

Slater threw up his hands. "How difficult was that?"

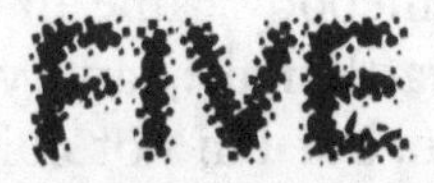

FIVE

WHEN SLATER GOT UPSTAIRS, he found the waiting room marked A, with rows of chairs and a dozen people sitting around. The TV mounted high on the wall was blaring an infomercial. It looked like he was going to have to sit here and wait.

But before he got settled, Matsuda walked out through a security door. Spotting Slater, he flashed that smile. The guy had a great head of hair, but it must have been a while since he'd seen him, as he definitely had more mileage on him now.

Matsuda waved him inside, and led him down the hall to a little room with an exam table and a desk. Slater stepped over to the window. It looked out at the Hollywood Hills, and in the distance he could see the dome of the Observatory.

"Nice view."

Matsuda sat on the rolling stool. "You're looking good."

Turning back, Slater gestured to him. "I like the white jacket. It makes it look like you know what you're doing."

"That's the whole point of wearing it."

"So you're not allowed to have sex anymore? What's up with that?"

He chuckled. "I think I'm an addict. I'm trying to get some clarity. I've been going to meetings."

"That seems like a waste, man. You're still hot."

"It's not like I'm celibate now," Matsuda said. "I'm just taking a step back."

"That's like if somebody came in here and said, 'Hey, doc, I got bit by a rattlesnake,' and you tell them, 'Well, I've got the antivenin, but I'm not going to give it to you, because I'm taking a step back.'"

Matsuda laughed. "Addiction isn't comparable to a snakebite."

"You're the one who's snakebit, if you forgot what your dick is for."

He pointed to Slater's left hand. "What's going on here? You got married?"

"Not quite. I'm involved in a fiery narrative complex."

His brow furrowed. "What's that?"

"Squares would call it a relationship, but it's more than that." Slater traced a random pattern in the air with a finger. "It's operating in multiple dimensions. Extending in directions you can't point."

"That sounds intense. What's he like?"

"I can't even tell. It's like looking at the night sky and trying to explain how the planets move around. He's the sun and the moon and all the stars."

"Nice." Matsuda absently swiveled the stool. "So what did you want to see me about?"

Slater slid his satchel around, and pulled out the folder, and handed it over. "Can you explain this to me?"

"It's an autopsy report," he said, flipping through it.

"I know that much."

He studied a couple of the pages before he spoke. "So the coroner out there didn't do a full autopsy. I'd call it a cursory examination. That means they look things over, take some samples, no cutting."

"Why didn't they do a full autopsy?"

"There was no reason to. They do one when the cause of death isn't evident. There's plenty of evidence that this guy OD'd." Matsuda flipped to the photos. "The blue lips and the blue fingernails mean he stopped breathing. They found mucus in his trachea, and pulmonary edema."

"What's that in English?"

"Fluid in the lungs. Opioids do all that, and the blood tested positive for opioids. The body had no signs of physical trauma, so they didn't need to cut any deeper."

"Does it say which opioid?"

"They don't usually name specific drugs," Matsuda said.

"Are they afraid of lawsuits if they get it wrong?"

"It's about funding. If you don't name the drug, the manufacturers will contribute to overdose prevention. If you name them, they clam up and play dumb. It's all a big game." He looked up. "It was probably fentanyl. That's what everybody's on. It's affordable and widespread."

Slater watched him as he studied the photos. "Those pictures are a little nauseating."

"I've seen worse."

"Why did they take a close-up of the tattoo on his wrist?"

"That's standard procedure. It's a great way to identify people. If this was the only photo of a tattoo in the file, it means he only had the one."

"Good to know." Stepping closer, Slater pointed to the page. "This line here, 'premorbid coloboma visible in the iris dexter.' What does that mean?"

"That's a defect in the colored part of his left eye. Lots of people have them. Usually they look black. 'Premorbid' just means it was there before he died. Not connected to what killed him. They photographed it." Matsuda flipped to the photo and held it up. "The cornea is cloudy, but you can see the defect."

"Gross." Slater squinted at the image. "I guess you have a strong stomach."

"It's part of the job." He tucked the photo into the folder. "Where did you get this?"

"It's public record. For a case I'm working."

"I thought you investigated car accidents."

"I investigate insurance fraud," Slater said, and took the folder. "Usually it's not about cars. Can I pay you for this?"

Matsuda frowned as he stood up. "No."

"Suit yourself. And hit me up if you ever get over your sex hangups."

"You could come to a meeting with me. They're quite sociable. Tons of guys are figuring out their stuff. There's one right here in Hollywood."

Slater scoffed. "What good would that do?"

Walking out, he headed down to the lobby, and into the parking structure. Once he was behind the wheel of the Pacer, he tapped at his phone, and found the photos Monta had sent him. When Flynn had been alive he was clearly blue-eyed. He zoomed in on some of the images, and couldn't get a close look, but his irises looked ordinary, with no visible dark spots.

In the close-up autopsy photo the defect was obvious. It looked like a brown eye, not blue, but that could be the lighting, or maybe how decomposition worked. Blossoms didn't hold their color for very long when they fell. Deep red faded to pink and then to gray.

As he nosed the Pacer out onto the boulevard, he phoned Monta.

"Did Flynn have a defect in his left eye?" he said when she picked up.

"What kind of defect?"

"Like a dark patch in the iris."

"I never noticed one," she said. "I think I'd remember something like that. It might have happened after I saw him last. Was that in those autopsy photos?"

"Don't worry about those," he said, and ended the call.

Navigating to the freeway, he cruised into Downtown, and parked across the street from his building. When he got upstairs and stepped inside, Etta poked her head out of Max's office.

"Guess who's back?" she said.

Slater stepped over and saw that Max was sitting at his desk. With mousy brown hair, he was a bulky guy, his gut hanging over his belt. He'd hung his suit jacket on the coatrack, revealing his sidearm and its holster strapped over his shirt. Leaning back, Max greeted him.

"You were in Vegas?" Slater said, and dropped into the chair next to Etta's.

"Not for fun. I was following up leads." Max waved dismissively. "So you got assaulted? You don't look any worse for wear."

"Dude tried to put the hurt on me," Slater said, "but he didn't know how to brawl. I overpowered him in a hot second."

The sound of a helicopter outside suddenly got louder, and rattled the glass in the window next to Max's desk.

Max frowned. "That's not PD."

Rising, he stood at the window, craning his neck. The view was mostly the brick wall of the building next door, but at the right angle you could see part of the sky.

"It's a Blackhawk," he said finally. "Your federal government at work."

"They're using military tactics to round up immigrants," Etta said. "Every time they do this half my kids stay home."

"Apparently they've got Reaper drones up there too," Max said. "At least they're unarmed."

Etta scoffed. "So they say."

The heavy thumping of the rotors subsided, and Max sat down.

"You're sure this visitor was about my case?" Etta said, eyeing Slater.

"I recognized him from your window-shade photos. It's the husband."

"Why would he come here?"

"Who knows?" Slater gestured helplessly. "Straight people are crazy."

"Rude." Max raised his eyebrows. "I happen to know some crazy gay people floating around this burg too."

"Are you mad at me for getting you jumped?" Etta said.

"Should I be? I'm stretched thin, Etta. I have so few fucks left to give."

"Nobody's mad about it," Max said. "This stuff happens."

"When did you report to your client?"

"Last night," Etta said.

"So he came here after that. I think dude just needed to punch somebody." In broad strokes he explained what had happened.

Max sat up, and folded his arms on the desk, and eyed Etta. "You should definitely tell your client that he can access her phone."

"I'll talk to her," she said.

"How did he find the office?"

"Probably because I invoiced her on company letterhead. Was that a mistake?"

"Not at all. It's one of the hazards of the job."

"Do you think I need to be worried about him?" she said.

"He assumed I was the one who took the pictures." Slater waved a hand. "I didn't correct him, so he won't be looking for you."

"It's completely pointless to come after the messenger," Max said. "He knows that. He's just lashing out because he can see his world imploding. The wife is the one with the money, I'm thinking, and he can see it being switched off."

"He won't show up here again," Slater said. "He'll have his hands full dealing with his wife and his girlfriend."

Etta nodded. "I'm glad you two see it the same way. So we're all comfortable with this work that we do, upending people's lives?"

"He upended his own life," Max said. "You're just the one who confirmed the client's suspicions. You did nothing wrong."

Slater eyed her sidelong. "You're good at this, and there's money in it." He raised his voice. "Suck it up."

Max laughed. "He's right. It's a little grubby sometimes, but you're not running a grift."

"Did you get paid yet?" Slater said.

Etta swiped her palms together like she was dusting them off. "She settled up last night. I'm done."

"Your first solo job," Max said. "Successful and paid up, complete with an angry spouse. That calls for a celebratory drink."

"Did she tell you she's using new tech?" Slater said. "A camera drone."

"I heard." Max rolled open the bottom drawer of his desk and pulled out the bottle he kept there.

"I figured why not bring the business into the modern age," Etta said. "A camera drone isn't even all that exotic. You two stumblebums need to be more agile."

Slater gestured around the room. "Says the woman who decorated this place like it's 1930."

She laughed at that, and Max poured a finger of scotch into each of the little tumblers, and Etta and Slater leaned in to tap their glasses together.

"Congrats, kid," Max said.

Slater savored the scotch, taking a long sip. It was delicious heady stuff.

"What about Monta?" Etta said. "Are you going to work for her?"

"I took the job yesterday. I'm not convinced there's anything substantial to dig up, but I'm already finding inconsistencies."

"Monta from the print shop?" Max said.

Slater explained her ask. "The only red flag is that she's into astrology."

Etta gestured with her tumbler. "What did she say about that?"

"Apparently Mercury was in retrograde when the guy bought it. The implication is that that somehow exacerbated the situation. So I'm concerned that she's a little nuts. But Pike says Jesus freaks still get their flu shots."

She frowned. "What does that mean?"

"You can believe your religion and still accept scientific evidence." He eyed Etta. "You do get vaccinated, don't you? Or do you ask Jesus to pray the flu away?"

"I'm Catholic. I'm not crazy."

"There you go," Max said.

"When I met you, you were working for free at the cathedral." Slater raised his eyebrows. "That actually qualifies as crazy."

"It's called volunteering. Most people see value in that. Humans actually tend to find altruism and being of service rewarding."

He waggled his fingers next to his head and spoke in falsetto: "Woo-woo."

Etta laughed. "You are such an asshole."

"So I'm told." He slammed the last of the scotch and stood up, eyeing her as he gestured to Max. "What he said about congrats and all that jazz. Same goes for me."

"Such eloquent words, Slater," she said. "You sound like Elizabeth Barrett Browning. I'd say you're getting soft."

He jabbed a finger at her. "You need to stick with the

work. Do not jump ship."

Setting the empty glass on Max's desk, he walked out, and went down to the street. It was a short drive to the flower market, and he pulled in at a meter and walked inside, scanning the offerings at the tightly spaced stalls. Spring meant lots of local stuff was available. He stepped into one of the stalls and spoke to the woman.

"Can you get me two of the tall vases?"

She nodded and walked into the back. From the buckets lining the space he chose an array of blossoms, cornflowers and gardenias and hollyhocks. The zinnias were pricey for some reason but he couldn't resist the colors, the vibrant red and fuchsia and magenta. He pulled several of those, until he had enough to fill both vases.

Once he'd paid her, he lifted one of them. "Can you help me with the other one?"

"Let me get my son." She stepped into the back and shouted, "Josué."

When Josué appeared, he greeted him and picked up the other vase. He had thick black hair, and a trim beard, and he was wearing a sweater despite the warm spring weather. Basically fuckable, he decided.

Slater led him out to the curb and opened the hatchback of the Pacer. The arrangements were too tall, so they loaded them into the back seat instead, setting the vases upright on the floor.

"What kind of car is this?" Josué said. "It's wild."

"It's a '78 Pacer. The most beautiful car ever built."

His brow furrowed. "If you say so. How do you keep it running when it's so old?"

"I've got a mechanic. And the word is classic, not old."

"You could pimp out the rims, like those lowriders."

"I like the original look of the wheels."

"*Entiendo.*" He raised his palm and turned to walk back into the market.

Driving to his house, Slater took the corners slow so that the vases wouldn't topple over. As he rolled up his block, he hit the garage door button, then spotted Pike across the street. He was inside the neighbor's fence, holding a colander and grabbing kumquats off the tree.

Nosing into the garage, Slater killed the engine, then walked across the street and into the yard.

"That's petty theft, son."

Pike chuckled. "Tilly said I could help myself."

He picked a kumquat from a branch and popped it in his mouth. As he crushed it between his teeth he closed his eyes to relish the flavors, sweet and bitter and citrus in one intense blast.

"They're good," Slater said. "She must water them."

"Don't you think you should wash that? It's been growing in the polluted LA air."

"I've been breathing it my whole life. I don't suppose eating a little of it will make things any worse."

When they walked into the garage, Slater hit the button to roll the door down, then stepped over to the Pacer and lifted out one of the vases, and handed it to Pike.

Pike wrapped an arm around it, shifting the colander to his other hand. "These are huge. You got them for Doris?"

"The woman is basically unhinged, but she did give birth to me. At least that's her story. I have no memory of that."

Slater lifted out the other vase and closed the car door.

"This is really thoughtful of you."

"The flower market was on the way. If I didn't take them, they'd wind up in the dumpster."

"It sounds like you were almost obligated to buy them," Pike said, starting up the stairs.

"Stuff is cheap at the end of the day."

"I believe you. But as much as you want to deny it, you're sentimental."

SIX

"I'T'LL BE A GOOD memory for her in case I get taken out," Slater said, following Pike up the stairs. "Maybe she'll remember that I'm not a total piece of trash."

"Let's not let that happen."

"People die. It's a thing. I had to go through an autopsy report today. It was nauseating." Stepping into the kitchen, he saw that there were dishes and bowls and utensils spread around on the counters. "You're busy up in here."

He set the vase in the sink, and filled it with water, then carried it into the big room, setting it on the floor across from the dining table. When he went back for the second vase, Pike was unbuttoning his shirt.

"I'm not sure why you want to bring her over here anyway," Slater said. "It's like those racoons in the yard. They look harmless enough, but if you get too close, or you bring them inside, you're in for a world of pain."

Pulling his shirt off, Pike hung it on a hook next to the Frigidaire. "So Doris is trying to mess you up."

"It's basically her life's mission."

Stepping close, Pike embraced him. "Thanks for getting flowers."

He ran his hands up and down Pike's bare back, and leaned in to mouth his jaw and smell his hair. It was the best scent in the world, sweaty and clean and pure Pike. Eventually he pulled back.

"She's always treated me like a beloved son-in-law," Pike said.

"It sounds like she's playing the long game. Laying an elaborate trap. Then one day"—he snapped his fingers—"*bam.*"

"You are so crazy," Pike said softly, and kissed him, then swatted his butt and moved away. He pulled an apron over his head and tied it at his waist.

"I like the clothing minimalism," Slater said.

"I don't want to get food on my shirt."

"You'd rather get me all turned on? I'd call that nervy, son."

"I'm almost done with this."

"What are you making, anyway?"

"Kugel," Pike said. "My mother uses egg noodles, and a lot of dairy, so I'm not sure what the veganized version is going to be like."

"It'll be great. Doris will say it's great whether she thinks it is or not." He tapped his temple with his index finger. "It's all part of the long game."

"Would Doris put onions in it?"

"No way. Hers is sweet. With sugar, and those blond raisins."

"This is a different entity, then," Pike said. "Savory kugel, with herbs and onions."

"She'll love it because you made it."

Slater leaned back on the counter, watching him work. "So I have to go out to the Mojave tomorrow for this case I'm on."

"I wish I could go with you. I have to be in the office."

"I figured. Can we swap cars for the day? I want to drive out to Lenny's land."

"It's your land now."

"It requires high clearance."

Pike glanced up at him. "I don't mind driving the Continental."

"You can use the Pacer too."

"I have mixed feelings about the Pacer," he said, pouring a yellowy sauce onto the noodles.

"That's weird, because most people either absolutely love it or absolutely hate it."

"All that glass. It's like being in a fishbowl. I feel vulnerable, and it draws attention."

"Grandstanding and showboating are a misuse of the Pacer's powers," Slater said. "Driving it is its own reward. People who need attention should audition for reality TV, not treif an automotive work of art."

Pike put the noodle mix into a baking dish, and sprinkled bread crumbs on it, then lifted it into the oven.

"In forty minutes we'll know what vegan kugel tastes like."

"You're the best, you know that?" Slater waved an arm. "I'm the only vegan, and you made it work."

"I want to impress Doris," Pike said, "but I love you."

Following him downstairs to the bedroom, Slater pulled off his shirt and dug in the closet until he found a linen one with long sleeves that Doris had given him.

"I feel like I should wash behind my ears, or get a haircut, or double-check my homework."

Pike had pulled on a blue dress shirt and was buttoning it. "You look fine."

"I do need to shave."

He went into the bathroom, and got into it, and was almost finished when the doorbell sounded.

"Fuck me," Slater muttered, then called to Pike, "Incoming."

He heard Pike hustle down the stairs, then the loud exchange of greetings. As he stepped out to the landing, tucking in his shirt, Pike was following Doris up the stairs. Petite, with some gray in her dark hair, she was wearing summery capris and a print blouse.

She embraced Slater, and kissed him, then pulled back. "You look so handsome." Taking hold of his hands, she examined the school ring. "What's this?"

"It's Pike's."

"It's pretty. I like the heft."

"Where's Albert?"

"He had to work this evening."

"I bet he was afraid he'd get assaulted," Pike said, and started up the stairs.

"He should be," Slater said, trudging up after them. "It's a very real possibility."

"He sends his regards," Doris said.

Pike was holding something, he saw, and pointed to it when they stepped into the kitchen. "What's that?"

"I brought a book I thought he'd enjoy," Doris said.

Slater frowned. "You don't need to butter him up. He already likes you."

"Good to know," Doris said, raising her eyebrows. "And not everything is a transaction."

About that, she was misinformed. But he bit his tongue. He needed to pick his battles with her.

"Educators know how to bring out the best in people," Pike said. "That's what book recommendations do. Doris knows I read."

He took the book from Pike's hand. "*The Razor's Edge.* It sounds stabby."

"It's not," Doris said.

"I look forward to it," Pike said, beaming like a goon.

He grabbed a bowl with the kumquats in it. "Come on in."

Slater set the book on the kitchen counter and followed them.

Pausing near the dining table, Doris spoke, her voice rising an octave. "Flowers. How lovely."

"Slater got those today."

"I love the cornflowers."

"That's why I snagged them," Slater said.

Walking through the big room, Pike gestured to the sofa and chairs. "We can sit in the groove area."

Doris laughed. "My generation grooved. Do people still do that?"

"I'm not sure what else to call it," Pike said. "There's the open quadrant, and then the lounge furniture in this subsector."

Doris paused in the middle of the big empty room. "You don't want to put anything in here? You could get a desk, maybe, and a fainting couch, or two little sofas facing each other. Get some houseplants. Maybe even a pool table."

"It needs to be empty," Slater said.

She frowned. "Why?"

"Does there need to be a reason?"

"It's symbolic space for our narrative complex to evolve," Pike said.

Doris raised her eyebrows. "Understood."

Walking over to the corner with the furniture, she sat on the sofa, and leaned down to touch the faux grass. There was a patch of it under the coffee table.

"I like the turf," she said. "It kind of works."

"That's all about this guy." Slater gestured to him.

Pike set the kumquats on the coffee table. "I thought it was more interesting than a rug. How about a gin and tonic?"

Doris smiled at him. "That sounds nice."

As he walked toward the kitchen, Slater sat in the chair opposite Doris, and folded his arms.

"It's hard to believe you used to groove," he said. "I guess in your day the hipsters went to encounter groups and freak-outs to do that."

"It's still my day, sweetheart." She reached for a kumquat. "Encounter groups were to offload your emotional hangups, and freak-outs were where you went to groove." She held his gaze. "Did I ever tell you I met your father at a freak-out?"

"That is such a lie," Slater snapped.

Doris bit into the kumquat, then covered her mouth to laugh. "It *is* a lie. I never went to a freak-out. But I knew people who did." She waved a hand. "Talking to Pike just now, I realize you've married your father."

He frowned. "What are you talking about?"

"Pike is a lot like your father. He has the same outlook."

"You're talking like a crazy person." Slater could feel his heart start to pound. He raised his voice. "Like you've read too much pop psychology."

"It's just an observation."

Pike came back and handed each of them a highball glass. "What are we shouting about?"

"I was telling him you're a lot like my late husband." She gestured up and down his frame as he sat in one of the other chairs. "You're solid, and connected, and optimistic. A mensch."

Pike briefly lifted his glass. "Doris, that is the highest compliment I've had in a good long while."

Closing his eyes for a second, Slater took a deep breath. But he just couldn't suppress it. "He's not my father," he shouted.

Pike eyed him. "She said 'like' your father."

"It's not a bad thing, sweetie," Doris said.

He threw up his hands. "And here we are, yet again.

Everyone else thinks it's perfectly normal to say something like that. Lo, I'm the crazy one."

Doris raised her eyebrows. "No one said you were crazy."

"Shrink," he said through his teeth.

"It makes me happy to hear it," Pike said. "I know you both cared about him a lot."

"So have you had to push through the protesters at your office?" Doris said, shifting in her chair and eyeing Pike. "Any skirmish lines interrupting your lunch hour?"

Pike sat up. "That's not happening where I work. There's a few different federal buildings around."

"Well, I'll be out marching on Saturday."

Slater took a breath. The conversation had already moved on. Why didn't either of them think that was an outrageous thing to say? He reached for a kumquat. It was glistening with droplets of water. Pike had washed them and put them in an earthenware bowl. He really did know how to do this stuff: entertain, relate to people, play nice.

"There's always protests," Slater said, "but it feels different this time. There were military helicopters over Downtown today."

"It's usually about protesting corruption and police brutality," Doris said. "This time the feds are sending the military after civilians. That part is unprecedented."

Pike gestured to Doris with his highball. "You said you were on a road trip?"

"We drove up the Central Coast. It's beautiful there."

And now the gossip. He knew they had a back channel, that they talked, that they compared notes. There was nothing he could do about that.

"That old croaker took you?" Slater said. "Did you go in that stupid little Boxster?"

"Albert has an SUV too. We took that."

"I've been to some of those towns for work," Pike said. "Mostly inland. There's so many wineries."

"You did go of your own free will, didn't you?" Slater gestured with the kumquat. "It wasn't some kind of hostage situation?"

Doris's eyes narrowed. "I'm not going to dignify that with a response." She eyed Pike. "It was a weekend get-away. We did some wineries, and some beach walks."

"I always thought you should move up there," Slater said, "now that you're retired. Get out of this crazy city."

"Get out of your hair, you mean." She waved a hand. "What am I going to do in some little town full of white people? All my friends are here."

They chatted some more, and finished the cocktails, and ate at the dining table. Of course Doris raved about the kugel. Eventually she got up to leave, and Slater moved the cornflowers from one vase to the other, and carried it out to her Buick. He dumped most of the water in the gutter, then loaded it on the floor of the back seat.

On the street Doris thanked Pike with an embrace, and then hugged Slater. "My beautiful son. Thanks for the flowers."

"Love you," he said, and kissed her.

Once she'd driven away, they trudged back upstairs, and he helped Pike clean up.

"What did I tell you about her reaction to the food?"

Pike chuckled. "You said it was good too."

"Just because it's objectively true doesn't mean she wouldn't lie about it if it weren't."

"Whatever the hidden motives, I'll take the compliment." Pike pulled open the dishwasher. "I'm just glad she isn't lumping me in with the feds who are abducting people off the streets. I know she's out there protesting it."

"She knows that's not what you do."

"So do you think it's true, that I'm like your father?"

"Fuck me. Why would she say something like that? Always with the tsuris." Slater took a breath, then gestured helplessly. "As much as I don't want to think about it, yeah, it's probably accurate. It makes sense I'd subconsciously try to recapture some of that connection. He left me when I was thirteen."

"That wasn't his choice."

Slater looked at him for a moment. "That's what he'd say."

Once they'd cleaned up, Pike rolled his shoulders, and stretched his back. "I'm wiped," he said, and headed down the stairs.

The book Doris had brought was still on the kitchen counter.

"Do you want your razor book?"

"You can put it on my desk," Pike called back.

Slater went down the stairs and stepped into the back bedroom. It had a bed in it, but Pike used it as an office when he worked remote. His desk was under the window, with a view of the neighborhood foliage and the rooftops. Setting it on the desktop, Slater saw there was another book here: *How Al-Anon Works*.

"What the hell is this?" he called out.

Pike stepped in, and Slater waved the book at him.

"Are you going to meetings?"

"A better question," Pike said, "is why is that upsetting to you?"

"Because the next step is me getting shanghaied into an intervention." He waved the book in the air. "You and Doris and fuck knows who else read me the riot act. You just know that croaker she's sleeping with will sign off on a 5150 hold. Then two burly guys in white coats step in and haul me off to rehab. Some hippie commune up the coast. Sisal and batik and patchouli. Is that what she was doing up there, scoping out the options? They'll keep me doped out and psychoanalyzed until I don't know which way is up. Once a month Doris will come to push me around the garden in a wheelchair while I drool on my straitjacket."

"That's not how rehab works."

He tossed the book on the desk. "And you'll move on to greener pastures. Like that dirtbag Davis."

"That is science fiction." Pike put his hands on his hips. "You know, I have the same fear. That you're going to get bored with me. Bored with our narrative complex when the inertia sets in. Then you'll throw me out on my ass."

He threw up his arms. "How could I get bored with the best thing that's ever happened to me?"

"I know you like variety. And I'm not going to do that. I'm not going to abandon you."

"So why are you going to Al-Anon?"

"Nobody tells you what to do. You'd clobber them. Extend me the same courtesy." Pike raised his eyebrows and spoke louder. "Don't tell me what to do."

"It's hard to do that when it's about me." Slater thumped his chest with his fist.

"It's actually not. It's about me. A way for me to get the tools to love you"—he spread his arms—"without telling you what to do."

Slater was breathing hard. He couldn't respond to that. He knew Pike had never been a control freak. It was a big part of why it worked so well. His voice broke with the lump in his throat.

"Fuck that."

Stepping close, Pike put his arms around him and squeezed. Slater shuddered with a sob. What was going on? Why did he lose control like this? It made no sense. He pounded on Pike's back with a fist.

"Stop that," Pike murmured, pulling away. "You'll give me bruises."

Slater rubbed the water out of his eyes. "Nothing makes sense," he croaked.

Pike met his gaze. "Want me to fuck you?"

"Are you going to report it in your Al-Anon meeting?" He chuckled. "Come on."

Slater followed him across to the front bedroom, and in a minute they were both undressed. Slater pulled him onto the bed, squeezing his cock, then pulled him into a kiss. Straddling him, Pike mouthed his neck and his jaw.

He shifted between his legs, and pushed his knees up, then probed him with a thumb. As he pressed into him, Slater winced at the intensity of it. He pushed harder, gradually building up to pounding him. He was sweating now, and a droplet fell from his hair onto Slater's chest.

"Is this better than that sicko Davis?" Slater demanded.

Pike pounded harder. "I never fucked Davis. He's not that guy."

He was breathing hard. "Am I hotter than Davis?"

"A million times. You know this."

With a hand on the back of his neck, Slater pulled him into a kiss, and mouthed his jaw, and buried his nose in his hair to inhale his heady scent. With a grunt, Pike's face contorted as he came, then sank onto his body.

A minute later, still breathing hard, he pulled himself up.

"Don't move," Slater said.

Still inside him, Pike grabbed his cock and pumped it.

Slater held his gaze, and ran a hand into Pike's hair, and shuddered as he climaxed.

Pulling back, Pike stretched out next to him and interlaced their fingers. A while later his voice roused him.

"You're always going to win that race."

"What race?" Slater mumbled.

"You or Davis. You're always going to mean more to me than that guy."

SEVEN

T HE ALARM SOUNDED WELL before dawn, and Slater scrabbled to kill it before it woke Pike. He got dressed and grabbed his faux leather jacket. It might still be cold in the desert. Upstairs he was eating some fruit at the dining table when Pike came up, wearing boxers and a T-shirt.

"You're getting an early start," Pike said.

"This way I can miss traffic."

"I'll make you some toast." He put a slice on a plate for each of them, and set out a jar of peanut butter, then sat adjacent. "I have some cop intel about the high desert. They patrol a lot more around Twentynine Palms, and less on the west side of the basin."

"Good to know," Slater said. "Do you have any idea why?"

He waved his spoon. "It's all based on data. There must be more incidents in Twentynine."

After they'd eaten, he got up and pulled on his jacket. Pike embraced him, running his hands around his waist.

"You look hot in leather."

"Faux leather. You'll have to report on it in your twelve-step meeting."

"I don't go to talk about you." He kissed him, then pulled away. "The high desert can be rough. You have to watch your back."

"I love you, you big mook."

Pike had a dumb grin on his face. "Always."

Down in the garage he went to the shelves and grabbed his day pack with the water bladder in it, then filled it in the sink back by the laundry machines. It was meant for trail running. He didn't do that, but he'd found it invaluable for walking around the desert. He grabbed a broad straw hat that he used for gardening, then walked out to Pike's SUV.

As he drove east the sun came up, and he pulled on his sunglasses. It was annoying now and then, when the freeway angled toward it, the glare on the pavement obscuring the lane lines, but eventually the sun was high enough not to be in his eyes.

Once he was through the Gorgonio Pass the land dried out in the Colorado Desert, and he headed north, up into the Mojave Desert, four thousand feet higher and with a very different ecosystem. From the main highway he turned onto a paved rural road, then onto back roads, and eventually the dirt road that needed the high clearance of Pike's SUV.

A dirt double-track ran along the edge of the property, and Slater stopped at the side of it and killed the engine. He didn't need to drive onto the land and do more soil damage. The tire tracks were still there from the last time he'd been out here.

As he climbed out he stretched his back and rotated his shoulders. He didn't even need his jacket as it was plenty warm in the sun. Grabbing his straw hat, he put it on his head, then set off along the tire tracks, and walked over the rise. The arroyo wasn't in view from the road, but it was only a few minutes' walk. The creosote bushes looked green. That meant they'd had some water recently. In dry times the tiny leaves contracted and looked black.

When he got to the arroyo, it looked like it had been running. There'd definitely been rain since he'd been here last. The elements were starting to erase the spot where he'd buried some loot on his last case. That was all done with now. Nature was smoothing it over, letting the land forget.

Slater sat on the gritty ground at the edge of the arroyo, leaning back on his hands. It wasn't windy, and there was almost no sound, with the nearest structures and human activity miles away. It felt good just to be somewhere so quiet.

He'd bought this acreage to help out a guy he'd met who needed cash. The twenty acres were undeveloped, and with no utilities anywhere nearby, and barely even a road, it seemed unlikely anyone would ever want to build on it. He probably didn't need to hang onto it, but inertia was easy, and the taxes were only a few hundred a year.

Some movement in the periphery caught his attention, and he turned his head to look. A lizard. Paused in the meager shade of a creosote, it looked chunky, and sort of white. He watched as it crouched there for a minute and looked around. It might be looking at him, he decided. It was hard to tell whether it was aware of him or not. A moment later it scuttled out of view.

Eventually Slater got up, and walked back over the rise to the SUV, and tossed his hat in the back seat, then climbed in. Looking at his phone, he saw that it had connectivity. He wasn't sure he knew that, that he could get a signal out here, but it made it feel less remote. He did a search, describing the lizard, and scanned the results. It was a horned lizard, probably, even though the photos of those looked a little different from what he'd seen.

Looking up, he saw a vehicle rolling toward him, from farther out. It was a red pickup, and it slowed as it approached, and stopped when the driver's door was next to Slater's. As the guy rolled down his window, he saw that he was bald, maybe in his fifties, and wearing sunglasses. He had specks of white stuff at the corners of his mouth, in sharp contrast to his rich dark skin.

"You're a long way from home," the guy said.

Slater frowned. "How would you know that, Miss Anne? I don't know you."

He laughed. "I know you're urban, with that attitude. This is all private property around here."

"I'm not out here to smoke meth or steal power tools. Some of this land actually belongs to me."

"Is your name Ibáñez? I saw the title change on that twenty with the arroyo. It's a nice piece of land." He looked around. "I guess that's this one."

"Do you live out here?"

"In a general sense I do. I live in Twentynine. I work on some of the parcels in this area that are in a trust." He held his hand out the window. "I'm Zeke."

Slater reached out to shake it. "What kind of work? There's nothing built anywhere near here. There's nothing to do."

"We're actually monitoring soil on several plots in the area."

"You mean the cryptobiotic soil?"

"We usually call them soil crusts," Zeke said, "but that's the idea."

"Why do they need monitoring?"

"Climate change is making things drier and warmer in the Mojave. The science people think it's stressing some of the components of the soil crusts."

"The fungi or the algae or the bacteria?"

He raised his eyebrows. "Some of the species of fungi."

"You're a scientist?"

"I'm a technician," Zeke said. "I work for the scientists."

"Do you spend any time in the park? The backcountry at the north end."

"I know it a little bit. I've been hiking in there for thirty years."

That was a good sign. Anyone who said they knew it like the back of their hand probably didn't. That kind of overconfidence was a red flag. Anyone who'd been there regularly for thirty years would know enough to realize their knowledge was incomplete. This guy was as savvy about that place as he was going to find.

"Maybe you could hike in with me," Slater said. "I need to visit a specific spot."

"Are you planning on harvesting rare plants?"

"You're asking me if I'm a thief."

"You seem to know a lot about the local fauna."

"It's a site where somebody died this winter. I need to look it over."

"Is it that backpacker who had a heart attack," Zeke said, "or the junkie who overdosed?"

"You seem to know all about the local death roll."

"This is a small community. People talk. I know some folks on the search and rescue crew. I used to help out with that myself." He shrugged. "It doesn't matter anyway. I don't know exactly where either of those incidents happened."

"I have precise coordinates," Slater said. "I figure if a junkie can walk in there, I can too. I just need somebody to get me there without me becoming vulture bait or coyote chow."

"I already have lots of stuff to do."

"I'll pay you for your time and expertise."

"Do you have any backcountry experience?" Zeke said.

"A little. I know how not to get sunstroke, and I have a water bladder backpack."

"What's on your feet?"

Slater popped open the door and stepped onto the dirt, and Zeke leaned out to look down.

"The boots are right for that kind of hike. Can you show me on a map where you want to go?"

Grabbing his phone, he found the location marker on the map, then stepped beside Zeke's window and handed it to him. He shifted his sunglasses up on his head and peered at the screen, then scrolled around.

"You have a good topo map, at least. This is where you can park." He pointed to a spot on the map. "There's an arroyo here to walk toward your marker. That'll be how the guy went in. I'd say it's about an hour's walk."

"So you'll do it."

Zeke eyed him. "Like you said, I don't know you. Why do you want to go there?"

"It's my job." He dug a business card out of his hip pocket and handed it over.

"Insurance investigator." He studied the card, then met his gaze. "So you're a flat-heel. The dead guy had insurance problems?"

"I can't really disclose the details."

"What's your company's budget for guide services?"

"How much do you want?"

Zeke chuckled. "Two hours hiking, plus drive time. A hundo?"

Taking his phone back, Slater nodded. He would have happily agreed to a lot more. "If we can take your rig, I'll pay you two."

"I've got a few things to do first. I'll meet you in an hour."

Once he'd told Slater where to be, and they'd exchanged phone numbers, he drove away. Climbing into the SUV, Slater fired up the engine, and did a three-point turn, and drove in the same direction. Once he was back on the pavement, he picked up speed, and soon turned onto the highway.

The gas station Monta had told him about was at the front end of a little strip mall on the main highway. It had a minimart behind the pumps and a string of retail businesses farther along. Slater pulled in, and fueled up the SUV, then stepped into the minimart. Nobody was inside except the clerk at the counter, sitting and staring at her phone. The wall behind her was a cramped array of tobacco products. She looked up as he approached.

"Are you Rupinder the Younger?" Slater said.

She cracked a smile. "I guess that's accurate. Who are you?"

He dug out a business card and handed it over. "This was the last known stop of a guy who went into the park and died."

"The one with the GTO." Rupinder looked up from the card. "I didn't know that was the man who died until I talked to his girlfriend. From LA."

"Did the deputies or the park rangers ask you about him?"

"She's the only one who came to talk to me. Why are you asking? This says you're in insurance. Is it about that beautiful car? Or do you do life insurance?"

"That's confidential," Slater said. "Why did you remember him so long after? A thousand people must buy stuff here every day."

"A couple dozen, anyway. It was the GTO. You don't see those every day. It was a '74. The last year they made them."

"How do you know what year it was?"

"The shape of the body. They changed it for '74." She traced the outline in the air with her finger. "The smooth slope and the tight trunk. Before that, the trunk was longer. The '74 was absolute perfection."

"You're a car whack."

"I wouldn't say that. I'm interested in classic cars. I don't have one."

"Do you remember anything else about the guy?"

"I noticed his ride," she said, "so I looked him over when he came in. I assumed he wasn't local because I'd never seen the car before. I remember he was a white dude. In his thirties. Not chunky, not skinny. Just a basic Anglo guy. I don't think I could pick him out of a lineup today if you showed me one."

"Did you talk about the GTO?"

Her brow furrowed. "Not in detail. I might have told him I admired it. I don't think we had a conversation."

"Was he with someone?" Slater said.

"The girlfriend asked me that too. If he was, that person didn't come into the store. There might have been somebody else around the GTO."

"Can you remember what they looked like?"

She shook her head. "I'm not even sure there was anybody."

"What are your feelings about the Pacer?"

"You mean the car?" Rupinder grinned and shifted on her stool. "They're beautiful. You know, they look like a compact, but they're not. They're just as wide as a full-size car. Although admittedly it has the short wheelbase."

He raised his eyebrows. "You say it's beautiful, but is it the most beautiful car ever built?"

She pursed her lips for a moment. "Close. Top ten for sure. Why are you asking me that?"

"I might have one to sell."

"I'm not in the market."

"You should be. You're a car whack. You should get a classic car. The desert air will prolong its life."

She chuckled. "I'll keep that in mind."

Walking out, he climbed in the SUV and drove to the

diner where Zeke had told him they'd meet. He had time to eat, he decided, and stepped inside, and sat at the counter.

There was nothing for him except fries and fruit, and he was finishing up when he saw Zeke's red pickup pull up in front. Rising, he paid at the register, then went out to Pike's rig and grabbed his gardener's hat and the water backpack.

Stepping over to Zeke's truck, he pulled open the passenger door.

"That's definitely the right hat," Zeke said, a grin on his face.

The interior was cluttered and dusty and needed to be detailed. As he climbed in Slater lifted a stack of paper off the seat and handed it to him. It looked like his mail, and he read the name on the top envelope.

"Ezekiel," Slater said. "You're named after one of my people."

"You're a fundamentalist?"

"Fuck, no. I'm Jewish."

Zeke laughed. "I suppose he was Jewish. The fundamentalists love the Old Testament. My people weren't fundies or Jews. I'm not sure what they were thinking."

Eyeing the rearview, he popped the transmission into Reverse, but then shifted back into Park. Slater looked over at him, and realized he was watching a woman walk out of the diner. Zeke rolled down his window.

The woman stepped up and greeted him. "Are you working today?"

"I'm headed into the monument to stretch my legs," Zeke said.

"Nice." She glanced over at Slater. "Well, have fun."

As she walked away, Zeke shifted into Reverse again.

"My neighbor," he said in a low voice.

"It's probably smart that you lied to her. I don't need my business broadcast all over town."

He glanced at him and frowned. "I didn't lie."

"You said we're going to the monument. That's not what we're doing. It sounds like a damn lie to me."

"I guess it's a park now," Zeke said. "That's an upgrade. It used to be the monument."

"How long have you lived around here?"

He laughed. "A while. Since before there was a national park."

When they drove into the park, its boundary was unmistakable, as the land instantly became wilderness. He could see why this was protected. The landscape was beautiful, with dramatic boulder piles, and Joshua trees everywhere. It wasn't that far from his twenty acres, but his land didn't have any of those. Clearly this part of the Mojave got more rainfall.

A few miles in, Zeke navigated into a parking lot, half full of cars, with pit toilets at one end. The land was flat where the road went through and where the lot was, and nearby the massive piles of boulders jutted into the sky. That's where Flynn had met his end, somewhere in that vast wilderness of pinky-tan rocks.

"It feels like there's a lot of people around," Slater said.

"This is actually quiet for spring. And you won't see any of them. They'll be on the marked trails and in the climbing areas. We're going the other way."

The guy was tall, Slater realized when they climbed out, and he was built like a linebacker. Zeke pulled a well-worn canvas backpack from behind the truck's seat, and tucked a couple of plastic quart bottles of water into it, and pulled it onto his shoulders. He put on a ball cap and watched as Slater donned the broad straw hat and strapped on his backpack.

"You said that has water in it," Zeke said. "How much?"

"Three liters. Whatever the hell that means."

He laughed. "Three quarts. Liters are the same as quarts.

That'll be plenty for a day like today."

"It's so useful to have two names for the same damn thing."

"I can tell you were never in the military. They're totally metric."

"So are drug dealers," he said. "And Europeans."

"This way." Zeke gestured and set off toward a trail.

Walking abreast, Slater eyed his feet. "Those boots are military. Is that your background?"

"These are sand boots. I didn't get them from the military, but I've been in. A long time ago."

A couple of people were walking on the trail ahead of them. They were dressed reasonably for the weather, in long-sleeved shirts and pants and hiking boots, but they were both carrying big black rectangles on their backs. They were positioned like backpacks, but from the way they moved, he could tell they had no weight.

Slater gestured to them. "What are those things?"

"They're for bouldering," Zeke said. "Foam-rubber pads with a nylon covering. They don't use ropes like rock climbers do. They put those on the ground in case they fall."

"Seriously?" he demanded. "A sofa cushion is going to mean the difference between a bruise and a broken bone? What if you miss the cushion?"

"I don't go bouldering, so I can't say how effective those are."

"I don't judge," Slater said, "but that's the stupidest fucking thing I've heard in a while."

Zeke chuckled. "That actually sounds a little judgmental."

"At least my head is still in one piece. Not smashed like a melon on these rocks next to a nylon cushion."

After a few minutes Zeke stepped off the trail onto an arroyo, and soon they were out of view of the parking lot and the trail, immersed in the piles of boulders. Zeke was right—out here there was nobody else around.

The boulders were weathered into smooth contours, some massive but most smaller, ranging a few feet to a few yards in size, and piled up in ridges. The gravel crunching under their feet was the same shade as the rocks, the detritus of their slow erosion. Touching the surface of a boulder as he walked past it, some grit brushed off under his hand. "These rocks are soft."

"It's called monzogranite," Zeke said. "It was a volcanic intrusion into a different kind of rock. That was even softer. It weathered away and left this. Everything wears away given enough time. Everything turns to dust." He waved a hand. "One day this entire planet is going to be dispersed atoms floating in the nothingness of space."

"You must be a blast at dinner parties, Zeke."

They walked in silence for a while, the crunch of their boots accompanied only by birdsong and the sound of insects. The calm was broken suddenly by a loud high-pitched whir from somewhere in front of them. He'd heard that before. It sounded a little like an electric leaf blower powering up, but some deep part of his brain knew what it really was, and made his heart start to pound. Zeke stopped short and took a step back.

"Rattlesnake." Zeke took another step backward and pointed to it.

Slater could see it now, coiled up on the arroyo, only a few yards ahead of them. It was the same color as the gravel.

"I would have stepped on it."

"That's what the rattle is for. She doesn't want to be stepped on." Zeke gestured to a gap in the brush lining the arroyo. "We'll go this way."

As they detoured around it, Slater eyed the snake again, unmoving on the gravel, and took deep breaths to dispel the adrenaline. "Do you run into them often?"

"In winter they're snoozing, but in summer sometimes you see them. Usually at dawn or dusk. She's probably out catching some sun at this hour because it's not really that warm yet."

"You seem awfully sanguine about it."

"There's no danger, as long as you listen to the rattle," Zeke said. "She's saying back off, so you back off. The old-timers would kill them. It's easier just to leave them alone."

"I can't argue with that logic."

EIGHT

SLATER FOLLOWED ZEKE AS he walked back onto the arroyo, with the rhythmic crunch of the gravel under their boots.

"So what are you hoping to find at this site that'll shed light on an insurance claim?" Zeke said.

"I won't know that until I see it. I'm trying to keep an open mind."

A while later the arroyo narrowed, and Slater walked behind Zeke. The quiet was broken by a hollow heavy clatter on the ridge of boulders on the right side. Slater shifted his hat back on his head and saw a group of big animals coming down the rocks. Zeke held up his arm.

"Bighorn sheep," he said under his breath. "Let them pass."

The creatures hustled across the arroyo a dozen yards farther up, elegantly hopping over it, six of them in series. Their footing was deft on the boulders, and a minute later they disappeared over the rocky ridge on the left. Zeke set off walking again, and Slater took a deep breath as he followed.

"That was intense. I can't believe anything that big can live out here. Where do they get water?"

"Most of the year there's rainwater that lingers in shady places. Between the boulders. They're called tanks."

"What do they eat?" Slater said. "Grasses and forbs only come out after it rains. That doesn't happen that often."

"Someone told me they eat anything green. Scrub oaks, nolinas, even cacti."

"They must be adapted to the place or they wouldn't be here."

"They're pretty rare." Zeke glanced back at him. "Like Black folks in the national park."

"This place is for everybody. That's the *national* part."

"In theory, sure. Lots of things are true in theory."

"Fifty percent of the people on this particular excursion are Black," Slater said.

He laughed. "I wondered if you had some Black in you, invoking the name of Miss Anne."

"My father was Latin, and my mother's white. She just told me that she met him at a freak-out. I'm not sure if I believe her or not."

Zeke stopped and turned toward him. "Show me your map."

Digging out his phone, Slater pulled it up, and handed it over. Studying the screen, Zeke pinched it, and scrolled around, then handed it back.

Slater tucked it in his jeans. "Are we on track?"

"This way."

They'd stopped where another arroyo fed into the one they were on, he saw, and Zeke walked onto it. It was narrower, and closer to the rocks, but the surface was the same crunchy gravel.

A while later the arroyo opened up, with an expanse of flat land between the rocky ridges. Zeke paused and pointed to a tall rock structure in the distance.

"What does that look like to you?"

Sucking on his water tube, Slater considered that. "It's like seeing things in the clouds. The four rocks on top are like knuckles. I'd say it looks like a fist punching at the sky. Or maybe a palisade."

"I like that. A giant fist. I call it punk rock, because to me it looks like a punk haircut. On the topo maps it's got somebody's name. I can't remember what it is."

"I'd bet cash money it's named after some white dude. Not the people who lived here first."

"I hear you, brother."

The arroyo hugged the rocks at one side of the wider landscape, and Slater walked a few yards behind him, looking at the boulder piles across the way, the scruffy piñons and showy nolinas growing in the space between, the paddle cacti and bright-red barrels. Zeke's voice interrupted his thoughts.

"Good morning."

A guy was approaching them on the arroyo, he saw. His face was dark, like he spent a lot of time in the sun, and he wasn't wearing a hat. The guy grinned at them, and met Slater's eye as he passed, but he didn't say anything. Once he was out of earshot behind them, Slater spoke.

"That's the first person we've seen since the parking lot."

"I'm not sure he was a person," Zeke said.

"The fuck are you talking about?"

"Didn't you pick up vibes from the guy?"

"What vibes? He didn't say anything. You can't blame him for that. I'm sure people come out here to be alone, not to socialize."

"It's more than that," Zeke said. "Something was off. Why wasn't he carrying anything? We're at least half an hour from any road. You have to bring water."

"Maybe he knows where the water is. Those tanks that the bighorns use."

"What did he look like to you? Describe him."

Slater thought about it. "A Latin guy who spends a lot of time in the sun."

"What was he wearing?"

"Some kind of shirt. Maybe jeans. Something light colored. No hat."

"See, I saw a Native American guy. He was wearing pants tied with a piece of rope. Like in the nineteenth century. I think he was a spirit being."

"Are you kidding me?" Slater demanded. "He just looked like a dude out on a morning walk."

"We saw different things because our minds filled in the blanks. Neither of us saw what he really was."

"You said Native American, and I said Latin. It's not always that different."

"I wonder if it was about us specifically. Like he was checking us out. Or maybe it was a message. Like, we're watching you."

Slater stifled a scoff. "This is my problem with conspiracy thinking. It puts you right at the center of everything. It's not some guy out for a walk. It's about you. Something is watching you, or there's a message just for you. The world revolves around you."

"I'm sensitive to these things," Zeke said. "That was no guy out for a walk."

"Should I hustle after him and ask if he's a ghost?"

"Not a ghost, a spirit being. And you'd never find him. He will have evaporated by now. Like those dusty whirlwinds." Zeke spread his fingers in the air. "Poof."

Soon the wide space between the rocks along the arroyo started to narrow. Joshua trees and scrub oaks were growing amid patches of soil crust.

Zeke paused and dug a bottle of water from his backpack. "What does your map say?"

Digging out his phone, Slater studied the screen.

"We're close. Two hundred meters that way."

"I thought you weren't a fan of the metric."

"I'm indifferent. It came with the mapping app. It's Russian."

Zeke took the phone and looked at the map, then zoomed in. Looking up, he surveyed the surrounding boulder piles.

"Got it," he said, and handed the phone back.

Slater followed him along the arroyo, in the general direction of the marker, and stopped when Zeke did at the base of a ridge of boulders.

"Show me again."

Slater dug out his phone and studied the map. "We're very close."

Once he'd looked at the screen, Zeke gestured to the boulder pile. "It has to be right up here."

He started climbing, moving from one to another. Slater watched for a minute, then followed him, but soon lost track of where he'd stepped. Looking up, he saw the guy was already much higher on the ridge.

"There's a technique," Zeke called down at him. "If it's too high to step up, look sideways. Then check the other side. If there's no options, take a step down and do it again. There's always another way to ascend."

Slater soon realized that Zeke was right. There wasn't a single trail or route to the top. It was more like playing a low-stakes video game, or solving a puzzle, and once he got into it, the climb was easier than it had looked from below.

It took a while, but eventually he got to the summit of the ridge, and stood next to Zeke. Digging out his phone again, he studied the screen.

"This is the exact spot."

He looked around. One of the boulders at the top of the ridge had a flat surface to sit on, and a piñon pine grew next to it. He could see why Flynn had stopped here. This was a high point above the arroyos on either side, with a good view of the rocky landscape stretching out in both directions, plus a tiny bit of shade under the piñon at the right time of day.

Thinking about it, no way had a random hiker stumbled on a corpse up here. It was too far from the easy walking on the arroyos. Flynn's demise had to have been reported by somebody who knew what had happened, somebody who'd been here with him.

"It's a beautiful spot," Zeke said, drinking from his water bottle. "There are worse places to be if you're going to buy it."

Slater pointed to the horizon. "What mountains are those? They still have snow on them."

"That's San Gorgonio. At Big Bear." He looked around. "It doesn't look like there's anything here."

"Just give me a minute."

Zeke stepped away, to the other side of the piñon, and sat on a rock.

On this side the flat boulder was like a table, or a bench. Flynn probably sat here for the view of the distant mountains. Slater sat and took it in. It really was a beautiful place, and not hard to get to for someone who knew the backcountry. You'd choose a place like this as the turn-around point on a hike, not as a spot to grease somebody.

He stepped down among the rocks on the side opposite where they'd climbed up. When he got down a few yards, he looked back toward the top, then looked around. A few feet away a spot of bright blue caught his eye, and he went over to it, carefully choosing his footsteps on the rocks. It was a water bottle, sitting on its side at the base of a boulder. It easily could have rolled off the flat rock up top and wound up down here.

Picking it up, he saw that it was empty, and had no cap.

It hadn't been here that long, he decided, as it wasn't weathered. Made of hard plastic, it had a logo on it, a clumsy drawing of a hand with fingers spread and a carabiner on the palm.

Slater climbed back up to the summit, and stepped over to Zeke, and sat next to him on the rock. "Do you recognize this logo?"

He looked at the bottle but didn't reach for it. "I'm pretty sure that's from the outfitter on the highway. It's near the turnoff into the park. They sell rock-climbing gear. Do you think it belonged to the dead guy? Your fingerprints are on it now."

"I don't need his prints. I already know he's dead." Pulling his pack around, he tucked the bottle into an outside pocket.

"Shouldn't you leave it where you found it, and tell the rangers?"

"Nobody cares anymore. The case is closed, the paperwork filed, the body cremated."

Zeke looked toward the mountains on the horizon. "Are you ready to head back?"

They got up and started to descend the boulders.

"How did you know you'd find something here?" Zeke said.

"I didn't. I just needed to look."

"I guess it makes sense the rangers didn't find that bottle. They came out to recover the body, not to clean up the garbage."

"Plus nobody had any doubt about the circumstances or the cause of death," Slater said. "They didn't even do a full autopsy."

"But you obviously had doubts. Or your insurance company did."

"That's all confidential, Zeke. Less chin music, more rock hopping."

Soon they were at the base of the rock pile. Zeke stepped onto the flat ground of the arroyo and waited for him. As he climbed off the last boulder, Slater's boot slipped on the gritty surface, grinding a little more gravel off it. Instinctively he grabbed at a bush at his side to stabilize himself, and managed to redirect his trajectory, and landed on his feet. The bush was a *Senegalia,* with sharp hooked prickles, and he yanked his hand away from the branch, but not before it pierced his palm in several places.

"Fuck me," he snapped.

Zeke stepped over. "What happened?"

"I cut myself on the *Senegalia,*" he said, and gestured to it.

"I've heard that called catclaw."

"That makes sense. The prickles look like a cat's claws. But it's definitely a *Senegalia.*"

"Those things are wicked. Almost everything that grows out here will cut you."

"It's not the plant's fault. I'm the idiot who grabbed it."

Massaging his palm, he could see the wounds. The one at the base of his index finger was oozing blood.

"It looks so green and lush," Zeke said. "It really is springtime."

"Those are drought deciduous. It has leaves because it got water recently. No water, no leaves, regardless of the season."

"Why do you know so much about plants?"

"I studied horticulture. But there's more money in going after lowlifes."

"Your card said you investigate insurance claims."

"It's all about fraud, Zeke. Lots and lots of fraud. Give me a second. I want to get some blood out. Less chance of it getting infected."

Squeezing the wound, he let a few drops of blood fall to the sandy earth.

"You're bound to this place now," Zeke said. "Sharing your blood. It knows you."

"Fine by me. As long as your spirit being doesn't show up and ask for more."

"I think it's mostly detached. Sometimes it's curious about us, but usually not."

Slater wriggled his fingers. "We can walk."

Zeke led the way, and when the arroyo widened, they walked abreast.

"Do you see spirit beings often?" Slater said.

"It never happened before. It's weird that it happened today. I've always had the sense that what we see isn't all that there is. There's more going on." Zeke waved a hand. "Like in the Middle Ages people weren't aware of radio waves. Now we use them routinely. We both have devices in our pockets that generate and receive them. We're swimming in radio waves. Maybe there's even more stuff we don't know about."

"Other radio frequencies we haven't been able to detect?"

"It's more than that. I think there's some life form, or some species. It's not human but it's intelligent, and it's living in the same place as us, just not in the same space."

"And we can't see them."

"Maybe we can, when they want to be seen. Like that guy on the trail."

Slater sucked at his water tube. "You're a complicated guy, Zeke."

"You never think about things like that?"

"Sometimes. When it comes and rattles my cage. Mostly I'm just trying to survive."

They walked in silence for a while, and Slater looked at his palm again. It wasn't bleeding anymore but it still hurt, the way bee stings and scorpion bites did long after the incident. There was likely some chemical the plant had evolved to leave a lasting impression, to remind animals like him not to come at it again.

"That ring on your finger implies you're hitched," Zeke said, gesturing to his hand.

"Not legally. Let's say committed. I'm deeply embroiled in a narrative complex."

"A narrative complex?"

"It's what you might call a romance, but there's more going on."

"That sounds complicated," Zeke said. "I guess I won't bother to hit on you."

"Seriously?" Slater eyed him sidelong. "You want a piece of this? I assumed you're the type to be married to somebody."

"Not at the moment. I know I'm not really attractive."

"I disagree. You're built like a freight train, and from what I've seen there's personality along with it. Plus you're wearing those fuck-me boots. All that adds up to smoking hot."

He chuckled. "But you're with someone."

"Listen, Zeke, I'm not going to make video reels shilling hair-care products with you, or pick out drapes at the drape store, or whatever it is you people do. But I will smoke you, if that's what you want."

"You people?"

"Normies. Squares. Whatever you call yourselves."

"Why would I be selling hair-care products?" He briefly lifted his ball cap. "I'm bald."

"Everything is monetized now. I'd be more surprised if you weren't selling something."

Zeke eyed him sidelong. "Have you ever been with a Black man?"

"A lot more of them than you have, I'd bet. You can save the mack for your hipster weekenders."

"Slater doesn't mess around. This feels awkward now."

He paused on the arroyo. "It doesn't have to be. You want me to smoke you?"

His eyebrows shot up. "You were serious. I definitely would."

Stepping over to a boulder, he grabbed Zeke's biceps, and pushed him back so that he was leaning on it. Holding his gaze, he groped his crotch through his jeans. The guy was getting chubby. Zeke sighed, and leaned toward him, and lingered in a kiss. His mouth was warm and taut.

Slater unzipped his fly, and pulled out his junk, then dropped to his knees and took him into his mouth. The guy was hard now, and he spent a minute working him. Eventually Zeke shuddered and came.

He stood up, panting from the exertion. "That wasn't awkward at all."

Zeke laughed and pulled him close, and kissed his neck, then unbuckled his belt and popped his fly. Pulling out his cock, he stroked it, then kissed him again. Absorbed in the intensity of his mouth, it didn't take long for Slater to climax.

Catching his breath, he rested for a moment with his head on Zeke's shoulder, then pulled back and buttoned his fly.

"How long are you in town for?" Zeke said.

"Not long."

He pushed himself up, and they started walking.

"I didn't anticipate any of this when I got up this morning," Zeke said. "Seeing a paranormal entity, then getting blown out here in the wilderness. Life can be pretty amazing."

"I wonder if your nonhuman intelligence was watching."

"If they were, I don't suppose they were overly concerned."

The arroyo didn't look especially familiar on the way back, but eventually they joined the trail that the boulderers with the cushions had been on, and soon came to the parking lot.

"There's your rig," Slater said. "You did it, man."

"You sound surprised. I'm not going to mislead you when you're paying me."

"What did we say, fifty bucks?"

"Two hundred."

"But with the discount for the blow job."

Zeke laughed. "There's no discounts, cowboy."

As they climbed into the red pickup, Slater pulled off his hat and then dug out his cash, peeling off two C-notes.

"Two yards for a morning's hike. I guess that's fair."

"You did find evidence," Zeke said, tucking the bills into the pocket of his shirt. "I'd say it was worth it."

NINE

ZEKE DROPPED SLATER AT Pike's rig, parked in the strip mall with the diner. It felt a lot warmer out now. The temperature swings were dramatic in the desert, and early afternoon was the hottest part of the day.

Tossing his pack and the straw hat into the back seat, he fired up the engine to get the air conditioning blowing. On his phone he looked up climbing outfitters, and found the shop with the carabiner logo, just a couple of miles up the highway.

Shifting into gear, he drove to the place. The sloppy logo was part of the sign mounted over the door. People were hanging around the vehicles in the parking lot. They were dressed for outdoor recreation, in Lycra and nylon and lightweight sports shoes in neon colors. Those weren't for trudging around the desert. Maybe for rock-climbing. This must be where they met to go on climbing excursions.

Slater stepped inside the store. It felt dark, and he pulled off his sunglasses. An array of rope in a range of colors lined one wall, and there were racks with backpacks and jackets, and stacks of the foam cushions he'd seen in the park.

When he approached the counter, a woman stepped up to it. She had sunken eyes and straw-dry bleached-out hair. Her name tag said CANDACE.

"Can I help you?"

As she braced her arms on the counter, he eyed the blue patch on her wrist. He knew that image. There was a close-up of it in Flynn's autopsy report.

"I like your tat, Candace. What does it mean?"

"I go by Candy." She looked at it and rubbed it with her thumb. "It's the all-seeing eye. From ancient Egypt."

"Why did you get that image put on your wrist?"

She frowned. "It's just a tattoo. What can I help you with today?"

Digging out his phone, he found a photo of Flynn. "This guy bought some gear here a few months ago." Turning the screen toward her, he watched her face. The unmistakable spark of recognition flitted through her eyes. "Do you remember him?"

"Lots of people buy stuff." She met his gaze. "I'm not here every day."

"You know him. I know you do." He raised his voice. "Sing, sister."

"I can't really say. It's supposed to be anonymous."

"So you've seen him at meetings. How long ago was that?"

"Look, if you're not shopping, I've got work to do."

She stepped around the counter and approached a woman who'd picked up one of the foam cushions. Slater watched her for a moment as she engaged with her customer, then walked out the door.

In the parking lot most of the sporty loiterers had already moved on, but a couple of men and a woman were standing here, all of them in their twenties. Unlike Zeke, with his sand boots and work shirt, they definitely weren't locals. The woman was wearing billowy harem pants and had magenta-colored hair. One of the guys was in capris and wearing a trilby, and the other was wearing bowling shoes. All three had the black foam blocks strapped on their backs. As Slater stepped out, one of them turned and bumped the bulky cushion into him.

"Careful, amigo," he said.

Slater shoved the cushion away. "I'm not your amigo, you racist fuck."

The guy stumbled and stepped back. He had shaggy black hair and untinted eyeglasses despite the bright sunlight. His eyebrows shot up. "I'm just saying."

"You don't expect pushback from brown folks, is what you're just saying. I'd punch you in the face right now, but your sofa cushion would break your fall. It's not worth the effort."

"It's not a sofa cushion," the woman said.

Slater eyed her. "Have you ever fallen on one of those?"

"I've seen people fall on them."

"Well, with any luck, your boyfriend here will miss and split his ugly hat-rack open."

He walked toward Pike's rig, then felt a palm on his back, and a hard shove. He stumbled and then turned back. It was the other guy, in the capri pants, blond with a scruffy beard, standing there with his fists balled.

"You should not have done that."

Slater lunged at him, and slapped him hard, left and right, a rapid kovac. Almost like he wasn't expecting it, the guy stumbled back, throwing his arms up in front of his face.

"Why do you make me do this to you?" Slater demanded.

Yanking his arm down, he landed another slap. The guy twisted away, then fell backward onto the cushion, hitting the pavement and holding his arms up in front of his face. Standing over him, Slater put his hands on his hips.

"You can't even get up right now, can you. You're like a tortoise flipped on its back."

"I'm calling the cops," the woman said.

"Go for it. Just remember that blondie here made the first move. The security footage will back that up." He gestured to the building's roofline. "That means he's the one who'll wind up in the hoosegow eating baloney sandwiches tonight."

Her brow furrowed, and she shifted on her feet.

Slater scoffed and walked away, pulling on his sunglasses. He hadn't actually spotted any security cameras, not outside, but those idiots didn't need to know that. He'd sown the seed of doubt, and that meant Magenta wasn't going to call anybody.

Climbing into Pike's rig, he pulled out onto the highway, and drove back to the diner where he'd met Zeke. Once he'd parked out front, he looked the place over. What was he doing here? There was nothing to eat. On his phone he found a place that listed a vegan burger on the menu, not far up the road, and drove to it.

Inside it was dark, and he pulled off his sunglasses. The cinderblock walls had high narrow windows with daylight filtering in. It wasn't busy, and he sat at a table.

When the server stepped over, he said, "Can you bring me the vegan burger? And some java."

He nodded and walked away.

There couldn't be a lot of twelve-step in such a small town, Slater thought, but when he searched for meetings on his phone, he found he was wrong about that—there were at least a dozen of them every week. Monta said Flynn had been a pillhead, so it was more likely he'd gone to narcotics meetings than the ones for alcoholics. There were a couple of those every day. Somebody at one of them would remember Flynn, and might know who he hung out with. Maybe somebody could explain why he had the same tattoo as Candy at the climbing store. It felt too specific to be a coincidence.

Tapping his phone screen, he found the entry for Reddy Kilowatt. It was the nickname he'd put in his contacts for Pike when they'd first met, out in the wildlands of New Mexico, on the chartreuse job. The guy had tased him that day. It was a dick move, but the nickname had stuck.

"Hey, forty-niner," Pike said as he picked up.

"Are you working?"

"I'm at my desk. I can talk."

"So I have to be here early tomorrow morning," Slater said. "I'm going to stay over."

"Do you have a place to sleep?"

"I didn't get that far. I guess I can crash in your car. Does the seat go flat?"

"Don't do that. Up there it's all about short-term rentals for the national park. I'll find you one. Just hang on."

He listened to Pike tapping at his keyboard, and sat back as the server set a steaming cup in front of him. Taking a sip, he savored the strong joe.

"This one looks good," Pike said finally. "It has a two-night minimum, but you can blow off the second night."

"Am I sleeping on somebody's couch?"

"You know I know you pretty well, right? I picked one with contactless check-in and no neighbors. You won't have to encounter any other humans."

"Can you live without your car for another day?"

"I don't need my car," Pike said. "The Continental works fine. The rear-wheel drive is actually optimal for doing street-takeover doughnuts and burnouts."

"Ouch. You'll mess up the wheel alignment. My mechanic will want to have a word with you."

"I'm going to try to work up the nerve to drive the Pacer. Embrace the fishbowl."

"Driving the Pacer is its own reward," Slater said. "You'll love it."

"I was stopped at a light this morning in the Continental,

and a guy on the corner gave me a thumbs-up. I think just seeing a classic car makes people happy."

"The Pacer will also spark joy in the world."

"I have to go. I love you, forty-niner."

"Forever, *mi vida*."

He ended the call, and his burger arrived. While he ate it he read the booking info Pike had sent. He could check into the rental soon.

After he'd eaten, and settled the check, he drove to a grocery store and bought a toothbrush. Next door to it he saw there was a discount clothing store, so he went in and bought a clean shirt and socks and skivvies.

The rental was away from the highway, on a dirt road, far enough out that it felt like the countryside. A little house with a corrugated fence around it, the gate was rolled open, and he drove in. The lock code Pike texted worked, and inside, the place was renovated and clean, with a lone bedroom, and a stacked washer and dryer next to the little kitchen.

Standing in front of the machines, he stripped down and threw all his clothes in, plus the stuff he'd just bought, and got it running, then went into the bathroom to take a shower.

While he was waiting for the laundry, he stretched out naked on the bed. The mattress felt comfortable. Pike had set all this up for him. Had he purposely chosen one with laundry, knowing he'd need it? Without his help, he probably would have just slept in the vehicle. The guy really was taking care of him. Like a father would. Was that fucked up? Why did Doris have to throw that grenade at him? He was happier not even considering it. The dryer dinged and stopped rumbling, and he pushed it out of his mind as he got up.

Once he was dressed again he sprawled on the sofa. The room got good light in the late afternoon. On his phone he looked up the all-seeing eye. It meant knowledge, and it was often shown capping a pyramid, like on the back of the dollar. Nothing he read about it said there was a connection to twelve-step. Candy had basically admitted she went to meetings. Why did she and Flynn both have a tattoo of it?

He looked through the listings of local meetings again. There was one tonight, an AA meeting, and looking at a map, he saw that it wasn't far away. It was starting soon. Even though it seemed unlikely that Flynn would have gone to that group, he could ask around.

SLATER FOLLOWED THE NAVIGATION app to the address for the meeting. It was a church, he saw, and it felt quiet, with just a couple of cars in the parking lot. The main doors were shut, but at one side a smaller door hung open. Climbing out, he walked toward it.

As he approached a woman stepped outside. Curvy, she was wearing jeans and a gray hoodie, and had her streaky blond hair tied back. She pulled the door closed and twisted a key in the lock.

"Are you here for the meeting?" she said when she noticed him.

"That's right."

"It ended a while ago."

He frowned. "I thought it was starting right now."

"You must have seen an old listing." She tucked her keys into her pants. "I'm Vi. Do you need to talk to someone tonight?"

"What's that?" Slater pointed to the book she was holding to her chest.

"My program book. I was leading the meeting tonight."

"I mean the logo on it. The triangle with the circle."

She flipped it over to look at it. "I never thought about

it. I know it's one of the symbols of program." She met his eye. "There's a meeting tomorrow at the recovery center. You should drop by that one."

"Got it," he said, and turned to walk back to the SUV.

"You've taken the most important step," Vi called after him. "You showed up."

Slater held up a palm as he climbed in behind the wheel.

On his phone he found a liquor store on the way back to his rental, and drove to it, and bought a pint of cheap bourbon. Vi definitely wouldn't approve of this, he thought, scooping up the brown paper bag from the counter.

In the same strip mall there was a bar, he saw, and he put the bottle in his vehicle, then walked over to it. Inside a few people were sitting around, and there was a ball game on the big TV. As he approached the bar, the guy behind it smiled at him as he stepped over. He had a ponytail and a patchy goatee. Basically fuckable, Slater decided.

"Do you do food?"

"Pub grub," the bartender said. "Burgers and fries and tendies."

"Can you bring me the fries? And a small of whatever ale you have on tap."

As the guy stepped away, Slater took a stool, and sipped at the beer when he set it in front of him, then munched on the fries. Both of them tasted a lot better than they probably were. It had been a long day.

By the time he drove back to the little rental, it was dark out, and he wasn't even sure he was in the right place until his headlights illuminated the corrugated fence. There were no street lights out here, making it feel even more isolated.

He was wiped out from all the hiking, and the high elevation, and the dry desert air. Cracking open the pint of bourbon, he guzzled from the bottle, not bothering to measure out his ration. He closed his eyes to savor it. It was just cheap applejack but the burn was so satisfying.

Stepping outside, he looked up at the sky. There was no sign of the moon, but a riot of stars peppered the expanse. So many were visible in such a dark place. He took another heady swig from the pint bottle.

A mystical entity out walking around in the backcountry, and a tattoo of a mystical symbol. He definitely had work to do.

TEN

▨▨▨▨▨▨▨▨▨▨

HIS ALARM SOUNDED EARLY, and Slater rolled out of bed. He looked in the fridge and opened the cupboards, but there was nothing to eat here. On the kitchen counter was one of those stupid pod machines to make coffee, and he set it up, and gulped at the scalding weak-ass ersatz java. He needed to get to that meeting, he saw, glancing at his phone.

When he stepped outside, the cold air hit, and he inhaled sharply. That happened in the desert, the big variation in temperature. Stepping back inside, he pulled on his faux leather jacket.

The morning narcotics meeting was at the same church as where the drunks had met last night. The schedule for this one clearly hadn't changed, as there were lots of cars in the parking lot. Inside the hall a few people were standing around, with most of them sitting in the circle of chairs that ringed the room.

Slater took a seat on the side near the door and looked over the crowd. They seemed ordinary, although maybe on average whiter and more blue-collar than they would be in LA.

Sitting at the lone table in the circle was a guy with a trim little mustache, wearing jeans and work boots, a notepad in hand. Basically fuckable, he decided. The guy greeted everyone, raising his voice, and the stragglers moved to sit down.

"I'll be leading the meeting today," he said. "My name is Paul, and I'm an addict."

Everyone in the room called back, "Hi, Paul."

He talked about some mundane group business, an upcoming conference and the meeting schedule, and eventually said, "Do we have any newcomers?"

Slater could feel a lot of eyes on him. He couldn't avoid this. Raising his hand, he used the same phrasing as Paul. "My name is Slater, and I'm an addict."

Many voices called back: "Hi, Slater."

"We have some shares today," Paul said, and a guy with shaggy graying hair and a leather jacket raised his hand.

"I'm Jason, and I'm an addict."

Slater joined the chorus: "Hi, Jason."

"I've got court in a couple weeks," Jason said, "so that's stressing me out. One bad drop and I'm back inside. But right now, I'm here."

Several people called back, "You're here."

"I'm trying to keep it real for my kids. That's the deal I made with their mother. I can see them as long as I stay clean. I know I need to be in their lives, so I'm here for them. I cannot go back to jail."

The group briefly clapped, and then a couple of other people shared their thoughts. It was actually interesting stuff, not perfunctory and superficial and boring like Paul's bookkeeping spiel. It was remarkable how frank they were, explaining their reality with no spin, no facade. In the *Theogony,* one of the classics that he and Pike had been reading, people regularly pissed off the Greek gods with their hubris, basically doing stupid things because they were overconfident. Listening to these junkies was the opposite of that. They were so real, relating their truth without any ego, or puffery, or bluster.

When the meeting ended, people started clearing out, and he approached Paul at the little table.

"It's good to see you." Paul flashed a smile as he rose. "Coming in is the most important step."

"Do you know a guy named Flynn?" Slater reached for his phone. "I have a photo of him."

He held up a palm. "Anonymous means anonymous. I can't talk to you about anyone in the fellowship."

"I get that." He dug his wad of cash out of his other pocket. "Would you talk to President Jackson about it? He's an awfully good listener."

Paul laughed. "Put your money away." He picked up his notepad and a ring of keys from the table. "It's good that you're here. This place can help you stay clean. Keep coming back."

The room had almost emptied out, and Slater walked out to the parking lot. Most of the attendees had already driven away, or were climbing into their cars. Why was everybody in such a damn rush? He needed to talk to these knuckleheads. Somebody needed to squawk. But it didn't feel like that was going to happen.

He paused to admire a motorcycle parked in the meager shade of a desert willow. It had beefy classic lines, factory pure, not modded and stylized into a chopper.

The guy in the leather jacket who'd spoken in the meeting walked up to him. Jason, he remembered.

"This place cleared out quickly," Slater said.

"People have to get to work." He gathered his shaggy gray hair in one hand and tied it up with a band.

"Is this yours?" He gestured to the bike. "It's making me chubby."

96

Jason laughed. "I'm thinking you ride."

"I can ride. Right now I'm in a cage." He gestured to the SUV, then eyed the bike. "I like the factory trim. It looks better than a custom job."

"I definitely don't need any more attention than I already get. Listen, do you want to ride this beast for a couple days? We could swap vehicles."

"I wish. The desert is motorcycle country, and the weather is perfect for it right now."

"I'm serious. You ride, and I'll drive the cage."

Slater frowned. "Why?"

"Without going into detail, someone I owe money to is looking for me. It's a small town. They know my ride."

He was telling the truth, Slater knew. The guy was rough, and he'd been on an involuntary retreat at the pleasure of the state, so he'd know how to spin bullshit. But this was real. He could feel it.

"The thing is, I don't know you. And I'm not sure how long I'll be in town."

"I don't know you either," Jason said. "I know you're clean right now, if you showed up here." He waved a hand. "It's just a day or two until I get this straightened out. If you have to leave town before that, call me, and we'll swap back. I didn't gleep it. My name is on the title."

"Is it a kick-starter?"

"It's newer than that. I keep it in good shape."

Slater pursed his lips and eyed the bike. "Will you let me photograph your ID? In case you disappear with my whip."

"That, I have no problem with," Jason said, and dug out his wallet.

Once Slater had snapped a picture of his license, and they exchanged phone numbers, Jason handed him the bike key, and Slater gave him the fob for Pike's vehicle.

"The key will open the saddlebags," Jason said. "Insurance and registration are in there."

"One other thing." Slater pulled out his phone and found a photo of Flynn. "Do you recognize this guy?"

Jason looked at the screen as he held it out, then met his gaze. "Do you need anything from your rig?"

This guy was hard. Like a brick wall. He knew the type. No way was Jason going to tell him anything if he thought it would make him a rat.

Slater threw up a hand. "So, nothing?"

"You should try on the helmet."

He tucked his phone away. The helmet fit well enough, he decided, pulling it on, and he flipped up the visor.

"Looking good," Jason said. "You need any help getting it started?"

"No, man. I'll be fine. But don't watch me." He waved him off. "On your way."

He chuckled. "Later, Slater."

Stepping over to Pike's rig, Jason climbed in and fired it up. He revved it a little before he dropped it into gear. That was something classic car people did. A technique you used with engines built before fuel injection. The SUV wasn't old enough to need it, but it meant the guy knew about cars.

As Jason pulled out, he turned to the motorcycle. He hadn't ridden in a while. Zipping up his jacket, he swung a leg over to straddle it, and pulled it upright. It took a minute to get comfortable. He went through it in his mind, and felt the clutch, and the throttle, and the brakes, and clicked the gearshift with his toe. Eventually he twisted the key and pressed the starter. The engine fired up right away. It sounded healthy.

Shifting into gear, he gave the throttle a gentle twist, and rolled through the parking lot. Turning onto the quiet street, he could feel his muscle memory kicking in as he shifted up. The clutch was firm. Jason wasn't lying when he said he kept it in good condition.

He stopped at a red light and planted his feet on the

ground. It felt good to be on two wheels. It was cold, and he probably should have considered that, but it was early in the day. It would warm up later.

Right now he needed to find breakfast, and he rode to a diner he'd passed earlier, with a big green sign out front. When he parked he left the helmet on the bike. Inside most of the booths and tables were occupied, and he took a stool at the counter, and turned over the coffee cup.

The server was a woman with wavy red hair and a riot of freckles, maybe still a teenager. She poured coffee from the carafe and said, "What can I get you?"

"Oatmeal. Hold the milk and the butter."

"Do you want it with oat milk?"

He sat up straighter. "You can do that?"

Her brow furrowed. "Do you know how many urban hep cats come through here?"

"I'm hep, granny," he said. "Set me up."

She laughed. "I'm not your granny, but I guess I asked for that." A minute later she came back and set down his bowl of oatmeal. "You don't look like a climber."

"You can tell I'm not local," Slater said.

"I haven't seen you around."

"I saw all the rock-climbing trash hanging out at that outfitter up the highway. It felt like the place was about more than just the equipment. Like they go there to groove."

"I don't know if they're trash. I know they drink a lot. You'd think if somebody was holding a rope that your life depended on, you'd want them to be stone sober, not holding a can of beer in their other hand."

He chuckled and started into his oatmeal.

Jason's explanation about why people were in such a damn rush to leave that meeting made sense. They had to get to their jobs at that hour. The timing of it was so they could hit a meeting before work. He wondered if the rest of them would stonewall him like Jason and Paul, the group leader. That guy wouldn't even look at a photo of Flynn. This whole twelve-step thing might be a dead-end.

That loud greeting. A whole roomful of people saying "Hi, Slater" in unison. It felt like twelve-step was actively shagging him. Pike was in freaking Al-Anon now for some inscrutable reason, and Matsuda had given up sex for twelve-step, and now he was hanging around NA meetings. It felt like a conspiracy. Unseen forces manipulating him. Like Zeke and his paranormal hiker.

The server stepped over and took his empty bowl. "Was it as oaty as you'd hoped it would be, daddy-o?"

"Even oatier. What's the damage?"

She set down the check and walked away. Peeling off a couple of bills, he tipped hard, then got up and walked out.

For a split second, as he pulled on his sunglasses, he looked for Pike's SUV. But he was on the bike now. It was out here waiting for him. Why had he agreed to this? It was so impractical. Sitting there on its stand, though, at that louche angle, it looked absolutely beautiful, and riding it felt almost as good as riding a man.

Pulling on the helmet, he zipped up his jacket and straddled the bike, then rode back to his rental. The place had a little desk under the window. He wished he'd brought his laptop. Instead he sprawled on the sofa and looked at his phone.

There was another meeting tonight, he found. Maybe after work people would be more likely to linger, and he could talk to some of them. Until then there was other stuff to do. On the map he searched for thrift stores in Twenty-nine Palms. He'd assumed there'd only be one or two, but there were actually a lot of them. There was more going on out here than it seemed. Checking his notes, Monta had said the one Flynn worked at was called Retread Me. It was a couple of blocks off the highway, and the hours listed implied that it would be open soon.

Rising, he went out to the bike, and pulled on the helmet, and zipped up his jacket, then started the big engine. He navigated to the highway and soon got to the stretch of open road between the towns. He really wanted to open it up, but that wasn't safe—he didn't actually have a motorcycle rating on his license. If he stuck to the right lane, and kept close to the speed limit, he'd be less likely to get pulled over.

He was getting comfortable on this thing, and even at the sedate speed limit, it felt good to have the throbbing engine between his thighs. He could understand why Pike was into it, even though he didn't have a bike anymore.

The thrift store was a big low-slung building on a corner, he saw as he pulled up. It was freestanding, with two other squat shops aligned with it on the same block. A couple of cars sat in the dusty parking strip along the street. He kicked down the stand and climbed off.

Leaving the helmet on the bike, he stepped toward the front door. A sign in the glass said HELP WANTED. When he stepped in, he was hit by that familiar smell, a sensory memory of places like this. It was idiosyncratic of thrift stores, sickly sweet with an acrid undertone. Why were they all the same?

It felt dark inside until he pulled off his sunglasses, and he looked around. There was a length of counter near the entrance, with the register and a set of shelves behind it, and a glass case below with some electronics on display. Next to the register was a bell with a hand-lettered sign in front of it that said RING FOR CHECKOUT.

A half dozen table lamps sat on the series of coffee tables and nightstands arranged tightly together under the front window. Stretching out on either side and filling most of the big room were clothes. In the middle of the room were low racks, and higher ones lined the walls on both sides.

Nobody was at the counter, and he walked farther in. Signs hanging from the drop ceiling segregated it into men's and women's stuff. At the back were shelves loaded with books, and cookware, and dishes. There was even a box stand with dozens of vinyl records in it. Everything looked worn and a little grubby.

After he'd done a circuit of the room, he walked back toward the front. A woman who'd been over at the shoe rack in the women's section was behind the counter now. Curvy, she was wearing a stretchy blue shirt that showed deep cleavage, and had her graying hair tied back. She was wearing glasses and a name tag that said LUANNE.

She eyed him as he approached. "How you doing, honey?"

"Did you know a guy who worked here named Flynn?" Slater said.

Luanne raised her eyebrows. "Flynn has moved on to his greater reward."

"You mean he's dead? I know that already."

"He worked full-time. I only came in when things got busy. Afternoons and weekends. Since he's gone home to Jesus, I'm here full-time."

"What kind of person was he?"

"Competent, I guess. He knew how to run the till." She leaned toward him, over the counter, and lowered her voice, even though no one was around. "I think he was a switch-hitter."

"What made you think that?"

"He'd flirt with the girls and the boys. Basically anybody who walked in." She stood up straight again. "Why are you asking about Flynn?"

"I wanted to know what happened to him. How he died."

"He fell off the wagon with the dope, I heard. Overdosed somewhere in the monument. They had to use a helicopter to recover the body."

"Did he ever go rock climbing?" Slater said. "Or that other one where they wear sofa cushions?"

"That's bouldering. I don't remember him talking about that. He was in good shape, so he could have been into one of those sports. My son Mike is about the same age. He couldn't climb a rope to save his life. He sits on his butt and plays video games."

"Did Flynn talk about twelve-step?"

"I remember he'd mention meetings once in a while," Luanne said. "Like, 'I have to get to a meeting.' I know he meant twelve-step. I think it was important to him. He didn't really gossip about it, though. I guess that's the 'anonymous' part." She waggled her fingers to put the word in air quotes. "There's just so much dope out there. It's like an epidemic."

"How long did Flynn work here?"

"You'd have to ask the owner. He's not around." She lowered her voice. "That man is a royal pain in the ass."

"When will he be back?"

"No idea. Some days he doesn't come in at all. I know he'll be here tomorrow. He said he has a meeting." She heaved a sigh. "I wish he was here more. There's only me right now, and I'm getting tired of the grind." Her expression shifted, like she'd just remembered something. "Why are you interested in Flynn, anyway?"

"Just curious," Slater said, and turned toward the door.

"I didn't catch your name."

He briefly turned back. "I didn't throw it. Don't work too hard, Luanne."

Outside it felt warmer, with the sun heating up his black jacket. He climbed on the bike, and started it up, and rode onto the quiet street.

Luanne didn't seem to know Flynn all that well, but at least the fact that he'd worked there checked out, and more significant, she'd confirmed what Candy at the outfitters had implied: Flynn went to twelve-step meetings.

He rode around Twentynine to get a feel for the place. It was a sizeable town, a lot bigger than the cluster of civilization near the park entrance, and it sprawled for miles. The vibe was a little dustier and low-income compared to farther west.

It was weird to be shagging a dead guy. Anything that was said about him was forever going to be secondhand. All he could do was compare versions of the stories people like Monta and Luanne told him and try to assemble some version of reality.

He rolled to a stop at a corner. Pike said the local cops focused their attention around here. He really didn't need to be in the middle of that. It was just asking for trouble. Crossing the intersection, he headed for the highway, and rode west, back to his rental.

ELEVEN

SLATER GRABBED HIS CLOTHES and his toothbrush and the pint bottle and carried them out to Jason's bike, where he stuffed them in one of the saddlebags next to the rear wheel. The bourbon didn't have too big a dent in it, he saw. He must have been tired last night. Back in the little house he looked around to make sure he hadn't forgotten anything. Pike had booked it for a second night, but he wasn't sure he'd need it.

Pulling on the helmet, he rode to the place with the burger, and after he'd eaten, checked his phone. He'd be on time for the evening NA meeting.

Twilight was setting in as he rode. It was at the same church, and more cars were here now than there had been this morning. Pike's SUV was nowhere in sight. That wasn't a cause for concern, he decided. Maybe Jason only did the early meeting.

As he climbed off the bike and pulled off the helmet, at the far side of the lot the beautiful lines of a classic vehicle caught his eye. He didn't even need to walk over and read the badge. It was unmistakably a GTO, and it had the distinctive short back end of the '74, the way Rupinder the Younger had described it. In the golden light of the end of the day the paint job glowed warm brown. It was such an unusual ride, and both Monta and Rupinder had described that color—it had to be Flynn's. But who was driving it now?

He walked inside and took a chair at the side of the room, between a bulky man in a plaid shirt and a woman with short hair wearing a delivery company jacket. The woman sitting at the table to lead the meeting was someone he hadn't seen before. As he glanced around the room at people getting settled in the circle of chairs, he noticed a guy sitting opposite the table, wearing a ball cap and chatting with a woman in shorts and a fleece jacket. Slater did a double-take. The shaggy brown hair, the thousand-watt smile. That was Flynn.

Watching him for a moment, he muttered, "Fuck me," and forced himself to look away before his intent gaze became obvious.

The woman sitting next to him leaned over. "Pardon me?"

"I didn't mean to say that out loud."

She chuckled. "I'm not worried about that. You're new, right? You seem tense. I know it's stressful at first. Just to show up. But you're here. That's the most important thing."

"So I've heard."

She held his gaze. "No one is beyond redemption."

One of the people at the table started speaking, and he briefly glanced at Flynn again. That was one hell of a redemption. The guy was back from the dead.

The woman at the table introduced herself as Gwen, and got the shout-back greeting. Slater chimed in with the group: "Hi, Gwen."

Only half listening to what she was saying, he eyed Flynn sidelong. Sitting with his arms folded across his chest, he was hotter than Slater expected. He was wearing a short-sleeved shirt that revealed his biceps and delts. The guy was totally fuckable.

He couldn't see the tattoo of the all-seeing eye yet, but it had to be there. Monta said he had it, and she'd recognized it in the coroner's photo. But that image was of the corpse from the backcountry, not this guy. If Flynn was revenant, sitting right here, who the fuck had they choppered out of the wilderness?

His focus shifted to Gwen when she asked the newcomers to introduce themselves. There were two others besides Slater. When it was his turn, he raised his hand. "I'm Slater, and I'm an addict."

"Hi, Slater."

A couple of people in the circle spoke about their lives, and Slater occasionally looked at Flynn. Was he seeing things? Maybe this guy was just a lookalike. So many white dudes looked like that, especially with the ball cap. Was his brain filling in the gaps, leaping to assumptions, making stuff up? But then he moved his arms, and Slater caught a glimpse of the blue design on his wrist. The all-seeing eye. He was sure of it now—this was Flynn.

A bone-thin woman on the opposite side of the room had the floor, and she was talking about her car. "You cannot live around here without a ride," she said. "Wheels knows what I'm talking about."

Flynn briefly raised a hand. "I do know."

Other people in the circle laughed at that, and the woman kept talking. Slater couldn't help but stare at him, and after a moment Flynn met his gaze, and flashed a wry smile.

As the meeting broke up, and people started to wander out, he rose and stretched, waiting to see what Flynn was going to do. Right now he was standing at the back of the room talking to a couple of people.

The woman who'd been sitting next to him spoke. "I'm Dani, by the way. With an *i*."

"Slater."

"Some of us are going to a restaurant," she said. "You should come. We call it fellowship."

"Who's going?"

She pointed to a woman standing near the front table. "Blanca there, and me, and Wheels so far. There might be some others."

"I can join you. Where are you headed?"

She told him the name of the place, and he walked outside. The sun had gone down, and beyond the reach of the floodlights on the side of the building was a void of darkness. As he climbed on the bike he saw a yellowy sliver of crescent moon near the glow at the horizon. That was either the last dregs of sunset or the light pollution of the distant metropolis. Either way, that had to be west.

It took him a second to find the headlight, and he flicked it on, then rode toward the highway. When he found the place, he parked and climbed off the bike. The neon sign in front said it was a bar and grill. These birds definitely weren't coming for the bar experience.

A lifted pickup with big tires pulled up in front, and Dani emerged. Another woman from the meeting climbed out the other side. She had Latin coloring, her black hair tied back.

Dani introduced her. "This is Blanca."

"Slater," he said, and looked behind her as the GTO pulled into the parking lot.

"You're on the motorcycle," Blanca said. "Is it scary to ride at night?"

"Not really. It has a good light."

When Flynn stepped over, Dani gestured to him. "This is Wheels, and this is Slater."

Flynn flashed that smile. "One of the newbies."

"I think it's just us," Dani said, and stepped over to the entrance.

It wasn't exactly a rug joint, Slater saw, following them inside, but it looked comfortable. The host put them at a booth, and Slater slid in opposite Flynn, followed by Blanca. The server stepped over, and they all ordered soft drinks.

At this range Slater could see the tattoo on Flynn's wrist. It was identical to Candy's, and identical to the dead guy's.

When the server left, Flynn turned to talk to Dani. Slater eyed Blanca, sitting on the bench next to him. She untied her hair and pushed it back, then picked up the menu.

Slater pointed to her wrist. "You have the same tattoo as Wheels."

"A bunch of us got them when we went to the state convention in Sacramento." She set the menu down. "The eye is from the dollar bill, and the circle and the triangle makes it look like the recovery symbol. But that's not the original meaning."

"So what does it mean?"

"I think it's Egyptian. I'm not exactly sure. For us it meant recovery. I did it for solidarity with the group. We were all doing it."

The drinks arrived, and he sipped at his soda water. "What's the tat on your other wrist?"

She held it out for him to inspect.

"A gecko?"

"It's more generic than that," Blanca said. "It's just a lizard. I study them."

"You're an academic?"

"I work for the feds. Up here there's a lot of federal land. The park, and the military base, and BLM land."

"On the map it's basically all a military base," Slater said. "Every square inch from here to freaking Barstow. What the hell are they doing with all that acreage?"

She laughed. "Whatever it is, they have to follow the laws about endangered species. I'm involved in that."

"I saw a horned lizard near here."

"Where, exactly?"

"A few miles north. Where the land flattens out."

"What time of day was it?"

"Early morning," Slater said. "An hour or so after sunrise."

"What color was it?"

"It looked white to me, but I guess it couldn't have been white. There's creosote bushes and catclaw growing there. Its coloring was lighter than those."

"What was it shaped like?" Blanca said.

"About this long." He held out his index fingers. "Its head was wider than its body, I think. It had spikes on its head, or maybe its neck."

"What part of the head or neck?"

He gestured to his own head. "Kind of on the back. Like they were pointing backward."

She nodded. "That sounds like a horned lizard."

Slater waved a hand. "All those questions to learn something I already knew."

"But you didn't know." Blanca met his gaze. "You had a hypothesis. The scientific method is to ask questions, and eliminate other possibilities. You still don't know it was a horned lizard, but it's much more likely than before all the questions. And you're not making any snap assumptions."

The server stepped up and asked about food. Dani and Blanca ordered nachos and cheese sticks.

"What's vegan?" Slater said.

Her brow furrowed. "I'm thinking nothing."

"Rats."

"What about fries?" Dani said.

"You're right." The server gestured with her handheld. "That would work."

He was getting tired of all the grease, but he threw up a hand. "Why not?"

When the server stepped away, Blanca took hold of his left hand, and tapped his ring finger. "You're married."

"Sort of. I'm entangled in a narrative complex. This is also his." He held up his other hand to display Pike's class ring.

"Is he an addict too?"

"He's a total normie," Slater said. "The guy is pure gravy. And when you dig into it, it's just more gravy. All the way down."

"Now I wish I'd ordered the steak au poivre." She waved a hand. "You're lucky. Two addicts together is a recipe for trouble."

Dani leaned across the table to talk to Blanca, and Slater sat back. Flynn was eyeing him now.

"Was this your first meeting?"

"I went to one this morning," Slater said.

"I'm sure everybody told you already, but that's the most important step."

"I have indeed heard that."

Flynn looked at his neck for a moment, then met his eye again. "I'm sure you'll augment the group gestalt."

The guy was totally flirting with him. That made this easy.

"I can definitely show you something augmented, Wheels, given the right circumstances."

Flynn laughed at that, his eyes bright. The guy was so vivid, such a spark. Why was he letting Monta think he was dead?

TWELVE

"IS GESTALT SOME TWELVE-STEP thing?" Slater said, and sipped at his soda water.

"It just means when the whole package of something is more than the sum of its parts. Like the group is more than its members."

"That sounds academic."

"I'm not that guy. I've been reading about lucid dreaming. It comes up in that stuff."

"Explain lucid dreaming," Slater said.

"It means you can kind of wake up inside your dreams. You're aware that you're dreaming, and you can manipulate what's happening as it unfolds."

"What's that got to do with a gestalt?"

"The idea is that your dream life is just as important as your waking life. If you can wake up inside your dreams, maybe you can integrate the experience more into the waking world. Both experiences make your life a gestalt."

"I met a guy who wrote on the back of his hand in Sharpie, 'Am I recording this dream?'"

Flynn leaned toward him. "That's totally about lucid

dreaming. You set up checkpoints in the waking world to look for in the dream world. If he looks at his hand in the dream, and the writing isn't there, he'll realize he's dreaming, and maybe he can get lucid."

"What are your checkpoints?"

"I read things twice. In the waking world the content is the same both times, but in the dream world it's not. Just now I read the description of the nachos twice."

"So are you certain that you're awake right now?"

Flynn laughed. "Ninety percent."

"Have you had any success waking up inside your dreams?"

"Once or twice. It's a work in progress."

They chatted some more, and ate the greasy food that showed up, then split the bill and walked outside. It felt cold out now.

Standing in front of Dani's vehicle, Blanca leaned in and gave Flynn a kiss on the cheek, then did the same with Slater.

"I'm riding with Dani," she said. "Good night, boys."

Dani waved, and they both climbed in the pickup. Slater zipped up his jacket as he watched her back out.

"Those two don't linger," he said. Maybe they'd picked up on the vibe between him and Flynn, and knew what was going to happen.

"I saw you leave the meeting on the motorcycle," Flynn said. "That looks like Jason's bike."

"I borrowed it from him."

"I wondered why you're not wearing leathers. You really should. The jacket isn't enough."

"Thanks for the advice, Pop." Slater gestured to the GTO. "Your ride is a total dick magnet. I'm getting a stiffy just looking at it."

He laughed. "I'm so conflicted right now. There's a thing in program where you're not supposed to hit on new people."

"Does that come with any tangible penalties? Incarceration, or a fine, or they'd eighty-six you from the group?"

"The point is that it might not be good for you."

"I'm the one who decides what's good for me."

Slater stepped close to him, and put a hand on the back of his neck, and met his mouth. The guy flinched but went with it, and grasped Slater's shoulders. His mouth was taut and warm. He explored it for a minute, then pulled back.

Flynn looked flushed, and took a breath. "Do you want to come over?"

"Where do you live?" he said, and dug out his phone.

He recited the address as Slater tapped it into his navigation app.

"It's the casita on the property," Flynn said. "The main house is on the left. My place is across the yard on the right. It's a few minutes' drive from here."

"Then I'll see you in a few minutes."

He walked over to the bike, and pulled on the helmet, and straddled the beast. There was nowhere to put his phone to navigate with a screen, he realized, and spent a minute memorizing the route. It wasn't complicated. A turn off the highway then two more turns. Tucking the phone away, he fired up the engine.

When he pulled up at the property, it was dark and rural, a lot like where his rental was, and it had a fence around it. The gate was open, and he rode inside, and killed the engine. The GTO was next to the casita, parked nose out, revealing its beautiful split grille.

There were lights on behind the curtains of the main house, and the door to the casita hung open. Flynn stepped into the frame and waved him in. It was like a studio apartment, with a bed and a sofa, and a bathroom and an open kitchen at the back.

Flynn closed the door behind him. "You're so damn beautiful."

Grabbing his biceps, Slater savaged his neck, and his jaw, and his mouth. When he groped his crotch, he found the guy was getting hard. Pulling on the sides of his belt, he ground his own woody into him.

"So what's your sex thing?" Slater said, pulling back.

"Do you want to fuck me?"

Pulling off his jacket, Slater unbuttoned his shirt, and sat on the side of the bed to untie his boots. Flynn was getting naked too. The guy wasn't cut, like a gymbot, but he had a solid physique.

As he ditched his jeans, Flynn said, "Are you on PrEP?"

"Get a condom anyway."

He dug in the bedside drawer, then climbed on the bed and ripped open the little package. "I want to put it on you."

Slater stretched out beside him, and kissed him again, and squeezed his cock. He could feel him getting harder. Eventually Flynn pulled back and rolled the condom on him.

Breathing hard now, Flynn shifted onto his back. "Does this work?"

"Family style," Slater said. "Works for me."

Moving close, he pressed a finger into him, holding his gaze. Flynn's face contorted.

"Oh, man."

Eventually Slater shifted position and pressed into him. Flynn screwed his eyes shut as he got into it, increasing the pace until he was pounding him. Shoving his arms under his shoulders, Slater lowered his weight onto his body, and buried his nose in his shaggy hair, inhaling the heady scent of his sweat as he came.

Taking a few breaths, Slater pulled back and grabbed his cock.

"Do you want to smoke me?" Flynn said.

He shifted down and took him into his mouth. The guy

was hard, and thrust upward, running a hand into Slater's hair, and soon climaxed.

Stretching out beside him, Slater folded his arm over his eyes.

"You can shower if you want."

He mumbled assent, and felt Flynn take hold of his left hand, and twist his ring.

"What's this about?" Flynn said.

The guy was going to be chatty, and he had to deal with it. This was for work.

Slater lifted his arm. "What does it usually mean?"

"You're married."

"Not really." He took a breath. "I never thought I'd be cut out for the double harness, but stuff happens. Now I'm deeply embroiled in a narrative complex."

"You mean a relationship? He doesn't mind you sleeping with other people?"

"He hates it," Slater said. "But he already knows I'm trash. I'm just afraid he'll figure out that I'm worse than that. A complete fraud. Then he'll throw me away like last year's tech."

"Is booze one of your substances? Because that's classic alcoholic talk."

Slater met his eye. "Your psychotherapy degree isn't posted on the wall. Are you allowed to practice in this jurisdiction?"

He chuckled. "I've known lots of addicts. It's a pattern." He caressed his chest. "You should come to more meetings."

"I would, but one of the members seduced me the first week."

Flynn groaned. "They call it the thirteenth step. It's kind of a no-no."

"I won't rat if you don't."

"That's the other thing. Confronting your addiction

is all about honesty. You don't really want to be keeping secrets either."

Slater sat up. "Can I sleep here?"

He beamed. "That would be fun."

"I need to check in with the old ball and chain." He got up and pulled on his jeans, then stepped into his boots and loosely knotted them. Flynn was watching him, his head propped on his elbow, a grin on his face.

"What?" Slater demanded.

"Do you even know how hot you are?"

"I'm not a right guy, Wheels. Remember that." He watched him for a moment, then walked outside.

The cold night breeze on his torso was startling, and he took a sharp breath as he pulled the door closed behind him. Opening the saddlebag on Jason's bike, he pulled out the pint bottle, then walked out through the gate to the deserted dirt road. The moon had set, and the stars glittered across the wide expanse of sky. Opening the bottle, he took a swig, then looked at his phone and dialed Reddy Kilowatt.

"Where are you?" Pike said when he picked up.

"In the desert. I'm looking at the sky right now. There's so damn many stars."

"Can you see Castor and Pollux?"

"I'm not sure."

"Let me check." A second later, he said, "Gemini is totally visible right now. Look in the northwest."

"Isn't Gemini from astrology? The fuck does that have to do with Castor and Pollux?"

"Gemini is one of the signs in astrology," Pike said. "It's also a constellation. Castor and Pollux are its brightest stars. That's why astrology is so seductive. Parts of it are real and observable."

Thinking about the directions, and the turns he'd taken to get here, he figured out where north was.

"I think I see them," Slater said. "They're kind of the brightest stars over there."

"Pollux is a little red, and Castor is blue-white."

"That's totally what I'm looking at."

"That's you and me, forty-niner. Blazing bright."

"I miss you. I have to stay over again."

"You're getting good leads out there?"

"It's coming together." He took another gulp from the pint.

"So I got up the nerve to take the Pacer to work," Pike said.

"Right on."

"I felt like a rolling museum display."

"You're beautiful. It's not wrong to let more people take that in. As long as they keep their paws off the merchandise."

"I stopped at a strip mall, and I overheard someone diss the car. He said, 'What's with the clown car?'"

"Slander."

"I didn't take it too hard," Pike said. "He looked like a middle-schooler. Too young to drive."

"That's like someone who's never played baseball saying, 'You don't play baseball very well.' They don't have enough information to know that they know nothing. They have no frame of reference to even understand the issues at play." He spoke louder. "The Pacer is the most beautiful vehicle even built."

Pike laughed. "Is that an objective measurable truth?"

They talked a little more, and he took another slug from the bottle. He was getting cold, and ended the call, and tucked the pint back in the saddlebag. When he stepped inside, he could hear the shower. As he stepped out of his jeans, Flynn came out of the bathroom, toweling his hair.

He looked Slater up and down. "Oh, man. Want to go again?"

"Not at this time."

"That's probably wise. I get up early."

As they climbed into bed, Flynn said, "Is that booze on your breath?"

"It's mouthwash. I don't have a toothbrush."

"You can use mine."

"Gross."

He chuckled. "You'll stick your tongue down my throat, but you won't use my toothbrush?"

He shifted Slater onto his side, and wrapped an arm around him, and notched his knees behind his. It wouldn't last long, Slater knew. They'd both get overheated. But for right now it felt really good.

THIRTEEN

W HEN SLATER WOKE, HE wasn't sure where he was. Bright daylight streamed in a wide multipane window at the foot of the bed. Outside was a palo verde, its bright yellow flowers showing. The smell of coffee was in the air. He heard the sound of dishes around the corner, and it all came back. Flynn was already up.

When he stepped into view, Flynn was wearing boxers and holding two mugs. He smiled when he saw that Slater was awake. Such a beautiful man.

"How do you take your joe?"

"Unless you have oat milk, just black."

"I only have normal milk."

He sat up and took one of the mugs, and Flynn climbed on next to him.

"What did you dream about?" Flynn said.

"Interesting question." He sipped at the joe. It was strong and rich. Thinking about it, there were snatches of something in his memory, some residue of his dreams, but nothing clear. "I'm not sure. It's gone."

"You should tell yourself before you sleep that you'll

remember your dreams. Then think about it when you wake up. Gradually you'll remember more of them. It's an effective pathway into lucid dreaming."

He slurped at the java. "I'm not sure my life is worthy of a cultivated gestalt."

"There's the alcoholic again," Flynn said. "The big ego with the low self-esteem."

Slater frowned at him. "Thank you for your assessment. Twelve-step is all about confronting your stuff, and being tits-out about it."

"That sounds accurate."

"So it's truth time, Wheels. That junkie who OD'd in the backcountry. Who was he? Why was your ID on him? Did you croak him?"

Flynn sat up in the bed, his brow furrowing. "What are you talking about?"

"Do not try to bullshit me, Flynn. You need to lean into your truth."

He took a breath. "How do you know about that? Are you with the sheriff's department?"

"I'm not anything to do with them."

"Then who the fuck are you?"

Slater set his mug on the bedside table and leaned over to grab his jeans. Digging out a business card, he handed it over, and Flynn studied it.

"Insurance investigator?"

"I look into lowlifes and deadbeats for a living."

"I'm not a lowlife."

"But you are legally dead."

Flynn frowned. "Are you working for Knox?"

"The fuck is that?"

He huffed. "Are you going to out me and blow up my life?"

"I'm not going to do anything until I get some answers. And if you don't have any, I will mess you up." He held his gaze. "Don't think that I won't. That sweet caboose of yours won't be enough to derail my resolve."

Reaching for the bedside table, Flynn grabbed his phone, and glanced at the screen. "I need to get to a meeting."

"Right now?" Slater demanded. "Can we sort this out first?"

"You could use a meeting too, what with tossing threats around." Rising, he pulled on his shirt.

Watching him, Slater took a breath. Maybe it would put the guy in a better mood. That seemed to happen to people afterward. He might be more inclined to talk. Pushing himself out of bed, he drained the mug and got dressed. Flynn stood waiting as he tied his boots.

"Where's the meeting?" Slater said, standing erect.

"Same place. You don't want to carpool?"

"I'll see you there."

Flynn followed him outside and locked the door.

He hadn't noticed last night in the dark, but besides the palo verde, there was a tall willow in the yard. Both of them were lush and exuberant. Somebody was watering them. The yard was cleared and sandy, and along the back fence was a row of evenly spaced agave pups. Those would do well here too with a little water.

Pulling on his helmet, he climbed on the bike, and rode out of the yard. On the highway he notched in behind a box truck moving close to the speed limit. Halfway to the meeting the GTO passed him in the left lane, along with lots of other traffic.

The parking lot was crowded when he pulled up, and inside he took a seat opposite where Flynn had sat. Flynn frowned at him, and pointed to the empty chair beside him, and threw up his hands, a tacit *What the hell?* That was probably a good sign. The guy wasn't trying to ghost him. He rose and crossed the floor to sit next to him.

The crowd looked different than last night. It skewed

older, maybe, and there were some office types among the blue-collar crowd. The woman who opened the meeting introduced herself as an alcoholic. It was an AA meeting. That explained the different demographic.

After she talked through some announcements, she opened the floor for shares.

Flynn nudged his elbow and whispered, "Go on."

The woman leading the meeting looked at him and smiled. That was a dirty trick, making him jump. Now it felt like he had to squawk or he'd look stupid.

"My name is Slater, and I'm an alcoholic."

"Hi, Slater."

"I'm not really sober. I mean, I am right now, obviously. I'm not a rum dumb. But I have bad habits." He huffed. "I work and I work till I'm half dead, and people tell me I'm getting soft. Maybe I am. Even so, I still manage to mess people up and let people down pretty effectively." Slater looked around the room. "I have to admit I appreciate the vibes in here. It feels like people are honest by default. I don't really see that anywhere else." He threw up his hands. "That's all I got."

People briefly clapped. That seemed odd. He wasn't saying anything significant or meaningful.

Some other alkies shared, and after the meeting, Flynn stepped over to chat with some of the group. As Slater walked outside, he fleetingly wondered if the guy might try to bolt. But it didn't feel like that's what was happening.

Eventually Flynn came outside. "Want to get breakfast?"

"Is this a fellowship thing with the other dipsos?"

He frowned. "No, man. You and me. We need to talk."

"Can we go to the diner with the green sign? I can eat there. It's on the south side of the highway."

"I know the place."

———·———

WHEN SLATER ROLLED UP to the diner, the GTO was already in the lot out front, and inside, Flynn was parked at a booth.

"It took you long enough," he said as Slater slid in across from him.

He flipped his coffee cup over. "I wasn't going to speed on someone else's bike."

He laughed. "I guess it would be pretty irresponsible to get it impounded."

"Says the man who's legally dead."

The redheaded server he'd met yesterday stepped up and poured java for both of them. "The cat came back."

"I heard this is where the hep cats come to groove," Slater said.

"Let me guess." She raised her eyebrows. "Oatmeal with oat milk."

Slater sat back. "Crazy, granny."

She eyed Flynn. "What says the cube?"

He frowned. "What?"

"She's asking what you want for breakfast," Slater said.

"A short stack and some bacon."

She nodded. "I can dig it."

"Why did you call her granny?" Flynn said as she walked away. "She's younger than you are."

"I ate here yesterday. She hit me with the beat lingo."

"What's a cube?"

"I assume it means very square. A conformist."

Flynn looked toward the counter. "She knows that tipping is discretionary, right?"

"She's just joking around."

"So why would Jason loan you his bike?" Flynn sipped at his coffee. "The guy is clean, but I'm pretty sure he was a gangster. He might still be."

"Jason's business falls under the anonymous category. As in none of your business."

He shifted on the bench. "How did you know about what's going on with me? Did somebody file an insurance claim that mentioned me? Is that why you seduced me?"

"Like you had no say in it. You're a damn dick hound." Slater waved a hand. "We're done talking about me. You need to talk about you."

Flynn took a breath. "I let it all happen because I needed to lie low. My former employer was trying to put me in jail."

Watching him talk, Slater sipped his java. The guy was already lying to him. He hadn't just let it happen. The cadaver had Flynn's ID on him. That implied intent and action.

"Your boss at the thrift store?"

"A guy named Knox. He owns the place."

"We're sitting in a public place right now," Slater said, "and you're going to meetings. How is that lying low?"

"Knox doesn't come over this way."

He watched him for a moment. "Why didn't you take a powder? Set yourself up in some other state? It would be a lot easier to avoid the thrift store owner. You could use the dead guy's identity to start a new life." He raised his eyebrows. "He's using yours."

"I thought of that. First I wanted to figure out why Knox set me up."

"You need to lay it out for me."

"It's not really any of your business."

Slater scoffed. "You don't get it, Flynn. If you don't talk to me, I'll go ask Knox what's going on, and tell him you're still breathing, and that I had your dick down my throat last night." He raised his voice. "Sing, brother."

He sat back as the server set down the oatmeal and a plate of pancakes. "I'll be back with a refill on the java."

Flynn started into his food and waved his fork. "Knox double-crossed me. He told me to rob the safe in the store when he was out of town."

"Why would you rob your own workplace?"

"Knox told me he had a tax problem, and losing the cash would help. He said he needed a write-off."

Slater dug into his oatmeal. If that was true, Flynn was either more gullible or stupider than he looked.

"It sounded like a reasonable idea at the time. It wasn't a whole lot of dough. Forty grand. I was supposed to keep twelve, and give him the rest."

"That's still a felony."

"I should have stopped when I saw the camera was running. Knox told me he'd disable it. In the low light you can still see the glow of the infrared lamps. I looked at it, and I saw he'd put electrical tape over the little light that shows it's working."

"And you robbed the place anyway."

They both looked up as the server poured coffee for them. She frowned at the silence before she stepped away. "Don't let me interrupt."

"He left the safe open like he said he would," Flynn said. "I thought maybe he'd delete the footage later. But then I figured out it was marked cash, and Knox had reported it to the bank, or maybe to the cops." He threw up his hands. "I was totally set up."

"What do you mean marked cash?"

"I owed a friend of mine some money, and I gave her a few of the bills. She runs a business in LA that helps people send dough overseas. So she handles lots of cash. She made a bank deposit, and the cops went to her shop to ask where she got a couple of specific C-notes. They were new and sequential, so it's easy to keep track of a whole rack."

"What did she tell them?" Slater said.

"She knew they were the ones from me, but she didn't tell them that. She said it could have been any customer for the last few months. I think they bought it. Her shop is in the Fashion District. Lots of undocumented workers in that neighborhood are her customers. They work in cash." Flynn waved his fork. "I'm just glad I didn't put any of it in the bank."

"If the cops knew about the C-notes, it means Knox reported the robbery. Did he name you, or show them the surveillance video?"

"I don't think so. If he had, they would have come for me. I think he was holding on to it for later. A way to blackmail me into doing stuff for him."

"Why would Knox do that to you?"

Flynn leaned toward him. "That's what I need to find out. It wasn't about his tax problems. He wanted me to go down."

"Did he ask you to do anything else," Slater said, "or tell you he was holding the video to pressure you?"

"Maybe that was coming. I don't know."

"Did you have a beef with him?"

"Not at all," he said intently. "We weren't buddies either. I didn't want to get too close to him. He's in one of those fundy churches."

Slater set his spoon down. "That actually explains a lot."

He frowned. "Like what?"

"Fundamentalists only have to act morally with other fundamentalists. If you're outside their little world, you're a sinner, so you can be used. Like cattle for beef, or forests for lumber."

"He never treated me like I was subhuman."

"If he tried to put you in the frame with the forty grand, he did."

Flynn looked at his plate and dug around with his fork.

"What happened to the rest of your cut?" Slater said. "The twelve grand in marked cash?"

"There are people in program who know how to move things around."

"You had somebody launder it for you," Slater said. That explained why he was able to coast for a while without working.

Flynn sighed and stuffed a chunk of pancake in his mouth.

"So why doesn't Blanca or Dani or anyone in the fellowship tell the cops you're still alive?"

"In the rooms I use my nickname. The cops put out my legal name. That's what was in the news. I guess nobody connected it to me, because nobody brought it up."

"So nobody knows Wheels is actually Flynn." Slater raised his eyebrows. "Who's the guy who died?"

He looked down at his plate. "His name was Ferret."

"You mean his nickname was Ferret."

"I don't know his real name. He was in program too. When word got out about a local junkie who died in the park, everybody just assumed it was Ferret. If you ran a survey of who do you think is most likely to overdose, Ferret would have been the top answer." Flynn shrugged. "He struggled."

"So the assumption people made was accurate. Ferret died."

"But his name wasn't really Flynn. I admit I helped lock down that version. I made sure I told people how tragic it was that Ferret relapsed." He raised his eyebrows. "That part was totally true."

"I know why they call you Wheels," Slater said. "That golden dick magnet parked outside. How did the wastoid get the nickname Ferret?"

"On the street somebody who's always trying to get fentanyl is called a ferret."

"What happened in the park that day?"

Flynn groaned and pushed his plate aside. "I was hiking with Ferret. We climbed up some boulders and sat on this rock. I was enjoying the wilderness, and the view. I wanted to sit for a minute and take a water break. Ferret pulls out a sheet of foil and a pen and offers me a taste. I tried to talk him out of it. 'Get with the program,' I said. 'Look at this beautiful place,' I said. 'You can see Big Bear. It's a natural high.' Ferret said that without getting high, it was all meaningless."

"It sounds like he was pretty deep into it."

"He was going to smoke no matter what. I didn't want to watch, so I went to walk around. I came back maybe half an hour later. I thought I'd have to drag him back to the car because he'd be nodding off. Fetty does that. Puts people to sleep. But he was sprawled out, and stiff, and dead." Flynn shuddered at the memory. "It's not like I could have done chest compressions or something. We were miles from nowhere. He was already cold."

"I know what dead means."

"Anyway, I sat there for a while, and thought about what to do. I'd just found out about the marked cash. It felt like Knox was coming after me. Like he'd give the video to the cops any day and I'd be locked up. It seemed like the universe was presenting an opportunity. So I put my wallet and phone in Ferret's pocket. He didn't even have an ID on him. I mean, at that point he didn't care."

"Since then, nobody has come looking for the guy?" Slater said. "Officially he's still alive."

"I think nobody reported him missing because he was basically on the streets."

That rang true, he decided. Monta had said two thousand bodies a year went unknown or unclaimed in LA. Some of them had to have family, even if they were out of contact or estranged or isolated. They might never find out what happened to a nickel rat like Ferret.

"That day I asked Ferret about his housing situation," Flynn said. "He told me he was sleeping on somebody's porch. He'd wait until the lights went off inside, then he'd crash, and leave again at dawn."

Slater gestured to his wrist. "Ferret had the same tattoo, in the same spot. It was part of how they identified you."

"How do you know that?"

"I saw the autopsy report."

Flynn frowned and absently rubbed it. "The all-seeing eye. Ferret came on that trip. A few of us got the same one."

"I saw Blanca's," Slater said. "Nobody knew you and Ferret were together that day?"

"I was at a gas station, and he wandered up. I think he was there to spare-change people. He hadn't been in the meetings for a while. I told him to come with me, that I was going into the park to take a hike and clear my head, and maybe he could do the same. I thought I was helping him. I didn't know he had a kit with him."

Slater dug out his wad of cash and peeled off a fifty. "Can you deal with the bill?"

"That's too much."

"She's beat," he said as he rose. "You have to tip heavily."

Flynn's brow furrowed. "Someone beat on her?"

"I mean she's a beatnik." He scoffed. "You really are a cube."

"Hold up." He waved a hand. "What now? I just spilled my guts to you."

"I'll come by your place later," Slater said, and walked out.

FOURTEEN

<hr>

IT WAS WARMING UP, and he left his jacket half unzipped as he pulled on the helmet and climbed on the bike. As he turned onto the highway, he saw that the fuel gauge read low.

A few blocks farther up the road he rolled into a gas station and kicked down the stand, not bothering to take off the helmet, as it had good peripheral vision. Once he got the pump working, he stood with the nozzle, filling the tank.

Slater turned to look when a Ranger Rover pulled up behind the bike, moving too fast. It stopped short, a few feet back, next to the adjacent pump. When the driver climbed out, Slater looked him over. Bald, he had a thick mustache, and was wearing a blue dress shirt with the sheen of satin.

The guy was glaring at him, he realized, and stomped over and struck Slater's shoulder with the heel of his hand. Slater let go of the nozzle and flipped up his visor.

"The fuck is wrong with you?"

His eyebrows shot up. "Who the hell are you? Did you steal this ride?"

Slater threw a fast right, connecting with his jaw. His

head spun, and he stumbled back a few steps. Grabbing the nozzle, Slater yanked it out of the bike's tank, splashing a few drops of fuel on the concrete, and held it toward him as the guy took a step.

"You want a high-octane bath, Butch?" he demanded. "I've got the vitamin G."

The guy's fists were balled, his face contorted with anger, but there was doubt now too, and he hesitated.

Slater waggled the nozzle. "I've got a lighter. We can have us a barbecue."

He jabbed a finger at him. "Tell Jason it's over for him. You hear me?"

Turning on his heel, he climbed into the Range Rover, and backed out, and punched it, roaring onto the highway.

"Idiot," Slater muttered, and shoved the nozzle back in the tank. Gas pumps didn't work like garden hoses. It had to be inside a tank before it would push fuel. It was probably a good thing the stupe didn't know that.

Once he'd topped off the tank, he hung up the nozzle, then dug out his phone and sent Jason a text:

Just got jumped at a gas station. White dude, age maybe fifty, bald, busted nose. Might have a foreign accent. Driving a black Range Rover with Nevada plates.

Tucking the phone away, he straddled the bike, but dug it out again when he felt it buzz in his pants. Jason had written back:

Are you OK?

Slater thumb-typed a response:

It was nothing I couldn't handle. Just giving you a heads up.

Jason replied:

Do you need me to take the bike?

He wrote back:

The bike is safe. I'm enjoying it.

Pulling out onto the highway, he rode east, toward Twentynine, and through the town. He knew the population got sparse farther east. The highway narrowed to two lanes as the streets gave way to open desert.

Some of the far-flung homesteads out here looked functional, and some were graffitied and decrepit, and a few were collapsed, and skeletal, and left to the elements. The landscape was beautiful, the classic Mojave, golden brown earth studded with creosotes and ringed by jagged distant mountains. It felt warmer here, and he zipped his jacket open to feel the breeze.

There wasn't much traffic. The next settlement on this road would be hours away, on the Colorado River, and most people headed east would be on the 10 or the 40, not on this back road. When there were no other vehicles in view, he opened it up and rode fast for a while. He loved the feeling of the engine, so calm and competent, and the speed felt great.

Flynn's story mostly had the ring of truth, and it aligned with what he already knew. The guy had downplayed his role in the misidentification, but at least he'd fessed up to making the identity switch. Slater had no way to verify what had happened in the backcountry that day. Flynn's version could be a crafted set of lies. There was no way to rule out that he'd greased Ferret for some reason. But he couldn't see a motive. Flynn wasn't living large on Ferret's bank accounts. He didn't even know the dead guy's real name.

He hated that Monta hadn't said anything about the cops chasing down the pilfered C-notes. It shouldn't be a surprise. Everybody lied to him. That didn't reflect on Flynn either, only on her. It wasn't really misleading, he decided. But why had she neglected to tell him that?

Eventually he turned around and rode back toward Flynn's place. The GTO was parked next to the casita, nose out again. It seemed odd that he backed it in. Most people would do the reversing on the way out. In daylight he could see the main house. It looked to have maybe two or three bedrooms, and there was a carport at one side.

Flynn must have heard the bike, as he stepped out the door of the casita as Slater was pulling off the helmet.

"Where did you go?" he called to him.

"What's it to you?"

Flynn frowned. "You know you hold my fate in your hands, right?" He glanced at the main house. "Come inside."

Slater followed him in and pulled off his jacket. "Do you have a lease here? Didn't the deputies come to look through your stuff?"

"It's an informal arrangement. The cops probably thought I was homeless like Ferret. The address on my license and for my bank stuff is my friend's place in LA." He threw up his hands. "So what now?"

"Do you want to smoke me?"

His eyebrows shot up. "Sure."

Slater started to unbutton his shirt.

"Leave the jeans on."

Flynn pushed him toward the bed, and Slater lay back, propped on his elbows, watching him. Pulling off his own shirt, Flynn climbed on with him, and unbuckled Slater's belt, and popped his fly. He was already getting hard. Flynn pulled out his junk, and took him into his mouth, and deftly worked him.

The guy looked up at him, and that sent Slater over. He put a hand in his hair to stop him as he climaxed. Catching his breath, he sat up and slid his hand under Flynn's belt, squeezing his cock.

"What do we do with this?"

"Let me get my pants off." Flynn stood up and ditched them. Hard now, he straddled Slater's hips, and stroked himself. "Just look at me."

Slater pulled his hand away and took hold of his cock, and stroked him, holding his gaze. Getting into it, Flynn bucked and thrust into his hand, and came with a yelp.

Rolling onto his back, Flynn was breathing hard. "Where did you come from?"

"I'm an Angeleno."

"That's not what I meant."

Slater started to button his fly. "Don't do that."

"Do what?"

"Get interested in me." He got up and went into the kitchen.

"I know you're already with somebody else," Flynn called to him. "The evidence is that ring on your finger."

Once he'd slammed a glass of water, Slater walked back and dropped onto the sofa, facing the bed.

"I'm trouble, Flynn. I do bad things."

He sat up and frowned. "What kind of bad things?"

"I spend a lot of time stalking lowlifes. Maybe I can look into your former employer."

His eyebrows shot up. "You'd do that? Why?"

"Because I believe your version of events."

"It's the truth."

"It seems like most of it probably is," Slater said. "The truth has this quality to it, this feeling. It's hard to describe. There's no distortions, no contradictions. It's usually not very pretty, but it is satisfying. It's the golden thread that stitches the world together."

"It's all true. Knox set me up."

"Full disclosure up front," he said. "Your pal Monta hired me to look into your demise."

"You know Monta? Is that why you're here? She filed an insurance claim?"

"It's not about insurance. She didn't believe you'd OD. She said you were good at staying clean."

Flynn watched him for a moment. "I wish you'd told me that. Are you really even an addict?"

"That part is totally true."

"What drugs did you abuse?"

"We're not talking about me, remember?"

He got up, and pulled on his pants, then his shirt. "If Monta hired you, why haven't you told her you found me? Or did you do that already?"

"I'm thinking she'd want me to help you out."

"I could use some help." Flynn sat on the side of the bed. "I don't really know what else to do. When I went off the grid, things just sort of stopped. I feel like I'm treading water." He gestured helplessly. "All I've got is inertia. What happened to Ferret is the ultimate version of that. Sometimes I remember the look on his face. Staring at nothing. He was chasing that high, and I'm the one who took him out there."

"He would have OD'd no matter where he was," Slater said. "No matter who he was with. The dope was more concentrated than he was used to. It happens all the time."

"It still feels like it's my fault."

"You need to smash that. You did nothing wrong."

"You don't know me," Flynn said. "You don't know what I've done."

"I know you said you asked him not to get high that day. I also know that no one is beyond redemption. Dani said that to my face."

"Ferret is."

"That was his choice. You're still here, and in twelve-step, so I know you're working on your stuff."

"Did you tell Monta that I'm alive?"

"Technically that's not what she hired me to find out," Slater said. "I'll have to give her some answers at some point. But it seems like that particular detail should be your call. Let me talk to Knox before you worry about that."

Flynn nodded. "The thrift store is called Retread Me. It's in Twentynine."

"I went in there yesterday. Knox wasn't around. I met Luanne."

"You went to ask about me? What did Luanne say?"

"She thinks you're AC/DC," Slater said. "She knew you were in twelve-step."

"So that's why you went to the meeting." He frowned. "How would she know who I sleep with?"

"She said you flirted with all the genders."

Flynn scoffed. "She's such a gossip. You know her kids are total deadweight. Her son blacked out his bedroom windows with foil and just sits in there. And her daughter won't even talk to her."

"Tell me about Knox."

"His wife looks totally churchy. The haircut, and the pinched face. A total Debbie Downer. She drives a Yukon." Flynn scoffed. "They've got a couple of rugrats. I think I saw the boy wearing guyliner. You know what that means. In his near future is a ticket to military school, or one of those camps where they try to brainwash the gay out of you."

Slater waved a hand. "Not the gossip, man. I need the dope on his business."

"He's basically a crook."

"I figured, since he got you to rob his safe."

"In the front window he has a sign that says the store benefits some charity. That's horseshit. It's just a regular store. He put up that sign so that people will donate free stuff for his business. He does some kind of importing too. At least he said it was importing. Cartons of stuff show up, and sit in the storeroom, and then people come and pick them up a few at a time."

"They're not retail customers?" Slater said.

"It feels like a wholesale transaction."

"What's in the boxes?"

"I'm not sure. I guess I should have paid more attention. I had to move them around once in a while. I never opened one. They weren't heavy. I assumed it was clothes."

"What else do you know about him?"

"I told you about the wacko church," Flynn said. "He's also very proud of his taste in shoes. He loves it when people notice them."

They talked some more, and then Slater got up and put on his shirt.

"You're going now?" Flynn said.

"Why not? Luanne said Knox would be around today."

"You'll come back here?"

"Unless I get popped."

"Can you give me your cell number?"

"It's on my card. Do you have a phone right now?"

Flynn winced. "It was Ferret's. I'm not even sure why he had one. The guy didn't have two dimes to rub together."

"That's the last thing people give up," he said. "You lose your housing first, then your car. Text me from that phone."

"Sure."

"Do it now," Slater said, raising his voice.

He dug in his pants and pulled out Slater's card. "You don't trust me."

"I don't trust anybody."

On his phone he tapped at the screen as he looked at the card. Slater dug out his own phone and saw a text from a new number. He'd written "Wheels." He stuffed the phone in his jeans and walked out.

FIFTEEN

<hr>

WHEN SLATER RODE UP to the thrift store, there were a couple of cars out front, and a dark-orange Wrangler parked along the side of the building. Luanne was behind the counter.

"Howdy, stranger," she said, and then, "I know you."

Slater paused in front of the register. "Is Knox around?"

"He's in the back. You can stick your head in. If his door is closed, just knock."

Slater walked among the racks of clothes toward the arched doorway at the back of the big room. It had saloon-style swinging doors, and a sign on one said DO NOT ENTER. He pushed through it. This was a stock room, he saw, with a garment rack loaded with empty hangers, boxes piled along the wall, and on the far side a back door with a crash bar and a lighted exit sign above it.

At one side was a half-open door with a sign on it that said PRIVATE. He stepped to the doorway. It was a small office, and a guy sat at the desk. This had to be Knox. The ring of thick dark hair around his head was too long, accentuating the bald patch on top. He looked a little paunchy, with sagging jowls. Fuckable in a pinch, Slater decided. Knox was wearing chinos and a dark-blue fleece, even though it was plenty warm out.

He swiveled toward him and gave him the once-over. "Can I help you?"

"I like those boots," Slater said. "Are they ostrich?"

They were freaking ugly, with upturned toes, the leather dyed a nauseating warm green color.

A smirk played on his lips. "They are."

"Are you the owner?"

"The name is Knox."

"I saw the sign in the door. What kind of help do you need?"

"Physical labor. Moving boxes around. Loading and unloading trucks. Also staffing the shop. That's mostly just running the till. People don't need a whole lot of help with the inventory."

"What are you paying?"

"What's minimum wage right now?"

Slater groaned. "There's so many jobs where I can sit on my ass for a penny-ante wage."

"Are you really that kind of guy?" Knox raised his eyebrows. "You want to sit around? You look like you can do the work. Will you pass a background check?"

"It depends what you're screening for. I can tell you I'm not a thief."

"Are you an addict?"

"Not in a way that would affect my work performance."

"At least you're not lying to me. You speak the language pretty well, so I'm thinking you're allowed to work?" Knox sat back. "It doesn't really matter, but if you're not, I won't bother with the tax forms."

"I was born here, you racist trash bag."

Knox didn't react. "I'm not racist. You just never know with you brown guys. So you want the job or not?"

"Let's see how it goes."

"Let me find the paperwork."

He scooted his chair sideways to the file cabinets against the far wall and rolled open a drawer. Slater knew this guy, knew the type. The *gantse macher*. This place was his kingdom.

As Knox dug in the vertical files, he looked around the room. Above the cabinets was a small window with bars on the outside. It didn't have a shade or curtains, but there was a pink-tinted layer of plastic film on the glass to cut the bright desert light.

On the wall facing the desk was a print of Jesus with his finger in the air, his heart outside his chest and radiating beams of gold, mounted in an ornate frame. Behind Knox's desk was a bookshelf, with a camera on top, aimed at the safe in the opposite corner. A small modern unit, the safe had a number pad and looked plenty secure. That heavy handle meant it had a multipoint lock.

He peered at the camera. It looked to be a consumer model, with the manufacturer's logo on the front. Mounted on a little stand, it had a wire trailing from it. He tried to commit the look of it to memory.

Knox turned toward him, handing him a sheet of paper and a pen. It was a basic tax form, Slater saw, and he leaned over the side of the desk to fill in the few boxes. In block letters he wrote the name of one of his aliases, John Slade, plus a Social Security number that he knew would pass a cursory check.

Standing erect, Slater handed him the form. "Are you Catholic?"

He scoffed. "Of course not. Why would you say that?"

"The Jesus print." Slater gestured to it. "The Sacred Heart thing is Catholic."

"Is it?" Knox frowned. "Someone donated that. Catholics don't have a patent on the lord." He looked down at the form. "John, huh. And here I was thinking you looked more like a Juan." He met his gaze. "Can you start tomorrow? The shop opens at ten."

"I'll be here," Slater said, and walked out.

Luanne was standing with another woman at a rack of long dresses, and glanced over at him as he walked through the shop. He raised a hand in greeting and headed to the front door.

Outside he climbed on the bike and rode back to Flynn's casita. The GTO was here, and Flynn pulled open the door when Slater knocked.

"So Knox hired me," Slater said, following him inside. "I start tomorrow."

"To work in the shop? Why would you do that?"

"So I can poke around his business, and see if I can figure out why he wanted to put you in the frame. Maybe he'll try to pull the same gimmick on me."

"I guess you don't mess around."

"You need to tell me what you know, and what to expect."

"Sit down." Flynn waved him to the sofa, and sat at the other end, facing him.

"When is he there and not there?" Slater said.

"That was never predictable. When he was around, he was always in the office. He never worked the floor. But he always let us know when he was leaving. He might not leave you alone there for a day or two, until he trusts you a little."

"He told me the job was about moving boxes and loading trucks."

"That's the wholesale thing he does in the back," Flynn said. "It's mindless. He had me unload his car, a couple dozen lightweight cartons, then load a few of them into other vehicles when somebody came to pick them up. It took a week or two from when the stuff arrived to get rid of it all. That didn't happen very often. Mostly I was working in the store."

"What's that like?"

"You have to run the cash register. Nothing is individually priced, but it's easy because there's only two or three prices for everything in there. Luanne will tell you how that works. Over the course of the day stuff winds up on the floor. The clothing. Sometimes Knox will come in and yell about it. 'Why is everything on the darn floor?' He doesn't swear because he's religious."

"So it's OK to be pissed," Slater said, "but not to say that you are?"

"I don't know the rules. I guess nothing makes Jesus angrier than cuss words."

"What happens when the clothes are on the floor?"

He chuckled. "You have to pick stuff up and put it back on the hangers. It's not separated by size or anything, so that's pretty easy. Knox won't trust you to get into the display case when you're new. It's right under the register. He keeps the valuable stuff in there. Real jewelry and the pricey electronics. He hides the key under the stupid *maneki neko* on the shelf behind the till."

"The fuck is that?"

"A statue of a white cat with its paw in the air," Flynn said. "You see them in retail shops. Sometimes they're motorized so the paw is beckoning." He curled his fingers and mimed the gesture. "It's supposed to attract good business."

"So the key to the good stuff is under the cat statue. What else?"

"He won't show you the bang-bang either, but it's in the very back of the cash drawer. You have to pull the tray out to get at it."

"Why does he keep a rod in the store?"

"In case he gets robbed. It seems unlikely. There's

nothing valuable. He's just a poseur."

"He has to be a little serious about it," Slater said. "It's hard to get a permit."

"It might be hard in LA. Out here it's not. One brief visit to the sheriff's station."

"Aren't you afraid of running into the guy? It's a small town."

"I spend my time in a different town," Flynn said. "And I look different now. When I worked there I had a beard. I make it a point to dress differently, and I wear a hat."

"I guess you managed to fool the coroner. You are kind of a generic white dude."

Flynn's eyes narrowed. "That sounds like an insult."

"No shade. Embrace your privilege, son." Slater rose. "I need to go to LA tonight, so I need the GTO."

"Why?"

"Jason has my rig. I can't ride the bike that far. It's too damn cold at night."

"That'll leave me stranded."

"I'll be back first thing. If you need to go to meetings, get a ride from one of the other wastoids."

Flynn groaned. "You know it's my baby. I spent years working on that car."

"I won't dent it."

He closed his eyes for a second. "Fine," he said finally. "It's got enough juice to get to LA, but you'll have to re-charge."

"You mean refuel."

"I mean charge the battery. I'll show you."

Flynn stood up and walked outside. Following him, Slater could see now why he backed in. A wall socket with a thick cable running from it was plugged into the GTO, under the license plate, where the gas cap should be.

"It's a resto-mod," Slater said. "You turned it into an EV."

"You didn't notice it was plugged in?"

Slater opened the driver's door. The wheel and the column and the gearshift looked original, but there were two wide screens built into the dash where the speedometer and the gauges should be.

"I can't believe you junked the engine and put in an electric motor."

"I didn't junk anything," Flynn said. "When I found it at the auto wreckers, it didn't have an engine. But it didn't need body work either."

"What's the range?"

"About three hundred miles. It should be charged close to that now. It'll show you on the display. It's better for the battery if you only charge it to eighty percent. You can control that on the screen."

Stepping to the back of the car, Flynn unplugged the power cable and hung it on a hook.

"You can charge it anywhere. Ask your navigation map for EV chargers. There's lots of them around."

"I actually have one in my garage," Slater said. "I put it in anticipating getting one of these."

"Right on. Let me get the key." Flynn walked back into the casita.

Slater stood there for a minute, staring absently at the car, then followed him inside. Grabbing Flynn's shoulder, he spun him around, and slapped him left and then right, a rapid kovac.

"Stop it," Flynn shouted, pulling away.

"You'll take it and you'll like it," he said through his teeth, and pulled his arm away to slap him again. "Why do you make me do this to you?"

"What are you talking about?" Flynn shoved him off.

"You lied to me."

Red-faced now, he held his hands up in front of him. "About what?"

"You said you met Ferret at a gas station." He raised his voice. "Why would you be at a gas station when you drive a fricking EV?"

"I needed to buy water, and I needed to wash my windshield. EV chargers don't have minimarts." He waved an arm. "And they don't have squeegees."

It wasn't just Flynn's word, he realized. Rupinder had seen the GTO too. She hadn't actually said he was buying gas. Slater had made that assumption.

"I can't believe you hit me," Flynn said.

"Open-handed."

"You're a lot of man, Ibáñez."

He waggled his fingers. "Keys."

Flynn scoffed and handed them over.

Walking out to the car, he climbed in. The start button was where the ignition should be, and he pressed it. The car made a soft noise and the screens lit up. Popping it into gear, he navigated to the highway. On the pavement it felt smooth, and when he punched it, it had amazing acceleration compared to a gasoline engine. Maybe this really was the future. He kind of loved this car.

On his phone he texted Svetlana, his Russian tech supplier:

Any chance you're around this evening? I can't get there during business hours.

Her response came a few minutes later:

I'm here until ten. If it's later and it's urgent, let me know, and I can return.

He wrote back:

I'll be there before that.

The desert highway merged onto the freeway in the low desert, and soon he was out of the Coachella Valley.

146

He could feel the air getting heavier and humid each time he crossed a mountain range. On the Reservoir Route, when he started the descent into the San Gabriel Valley, rain spattered the windshield, and he turned on the wipers. A while later it stopped again, but there was intermittent rain the rest of the way.

He hit traffic when he got close to Downtown LA, and it slowed to stop-and-go. The sky faded to gray and then to black. He needed to give Pike a heads up that he was in town, he realized, and dialed him.

"Where are you?" Pike said when he picked up.

"On the 10 by Downtown. There's so damn much traffic. What are all these yahoos doing out here, hogging up the freeway? Most of them are terrible drivers."

"Everyone out there is fighting a battle you don't know about."

"So why don't they do that somewhere else? Why are they fighting their battles in lane one?"

"The traffic reporter in the morning says *you* are the traffic," Pike said. "That means you."

"Stop that," he said flatly. "Listen, I'm going to be home tonight."

"Good to know. I'll clear out the rent boys."

"I knew it."

Pike laughed. "I'll see you there."

It was raining steadily when he exited onto the surface streets in Downtown. It seemed too late in the season for winter rain, too early for summer monsoon, but here it was, falling out of the sky. He'd been in the desert so long it felt weird to smell the humidity in the air, to see the wet asphalt glistening in the streetlights.

A digital road sign was parked at the bottom of the ramp, flashing the message "Curfew 8 p.m. to 6 a.m." Pulling in at a meter, he parked the GTO a couple of blocks from Monta's print store, then walked over. On this block the city had planted bauhinias along the sidewalk. They were still young, but a couple of them were flowering in delicate pink and white, with a smattering of petals on the concrete, taken down by the rain. They weren't native, and they were a little piggy with the water, but they were hardy. They wouldn't mind getting pissed on by all the homeless in this neighborhood.

He stepped inside the print shop, setting off the electronic chime. Monta greeted him as she emerged from the back and came to the counter. Slater put his hands on his hips and jutted his chin.

"Where's Mercury now?" he demanded.

Monta's eyes narrowed. "It just went into retrograde again. It might explain that look on your face. Why are you asking?"

"Did you know the GTO was an EV?"

"Sure. Flynn spent a lot of time on that project. That car was his baby."

"The last transactions on his card were at a gas station. Didn't you wonder what he was doing at a gas station with an EV?"

"Not really. There's other reasons to go to gas stations besides buying gas."

He took a breath. That actually fit. "Flynn gave you some cash a while back."

"He did." She raised her eyebrows. "How do you know about that?"

"He gave you C-notes."

"Why does that matter?"

"I'm asking the questions," Slater said. "You deposited the C-notes at your bank."

"It sounds like you already know this story. Where did you hear it?"

"I want your version." He raised his voice. "Sing, sister."

"I deposited the cash, and a day or two later—it happened really fast—a cop came in to ask me about it."

"A fed?"

"It was a local cop. He wouldn't tell me anything about it, except the serial numbers were from cash that was reported stolen."

"What happened then?"

She shrugged. "I never heard any more about it."

Slater raised his voice. "You told Flynn."

"Calm down. Yes, I talked to Flynn. He told me his boss at the thrift store had some loco scheme for him to rob the place. That's where the cash came from."

"Why didn't you tell me any of this?"

Monta huffed. "I didn't want you to think Flynn was a thief."

"But the boss tricked him into doing it."

"I didn't believe that. It sounded crazy. I can't believe he was that dumb."

"So you think he robbed the place on his own."

She gestured helplessly. "That's also hard to believe."

He stood watching her for a moment, considering that.

"Why all the questions?" she said.

"It's the scientific method. And you lied to me."

"It's not a lie. I just skipped over a detail. Who told you about this? And what have you found out? Did you go to the site in the park?"

He took a breath and rubbed his eyes. "I did. I also talked to some of his twelve-step cohort. I met the thrift-store owner."

"So what have you learned?"

"My research is ongoing."

"Are you here for more money?"

"I'm here to find out why you omitted part of the story," he said.

"The thrift store guy turned him in, I'm thinking. And if he reported the theft, he must have known it was Flynn."

"It looks like he reported the theft but didn't bring Flynn's name into it. I'm not sure why not. It might have been a squeeze play."

Monta frowned. "Meaning what?"

"The guy had evidence that could put Flynn in jail. Maybe he was going to use it to force Flynn to do something else. Something shadier. I'm going to dig into the guy, and find out what happened between them."

"So you're going back out there."

"That's where it all went down."

"Did anyone ever tell you that you're a little tightly wound?"

"Maybe my Jupiter got bogged down in Scorpio," Slater said. "I wonder if I need to call a cosmic tow truck."

"More likely you've got Mars in your second house."

"Well, that explains everything." He waved a hand. "So what does Gemini mean?"

She shifted on her feet. "It depends. If you're born under Gemini, it means you're easygoing and adaptable, but also indecisive and flaky. If Gemini was rising when you were born, you're going to be gregarious and extroverted." She raised her eyebrows. "I'd be happy to cast your star chart and fill in the gaps."

"I'll keep that in mind. So what's the curfew about? I saw a sign."

"It depends who you ask. The mayor and the governor say it's performative politics, and the feds say it's a full-blown insurrection."

"What's your spin on it?"

"They're trying to keep protesters away from the federal buildings. They've been tagging them. Nobody will harass you if you stay out of the Civic Center." Monta's brow furrowed. "Are you carrying your passport, I hope?"

"Why would I do that?"

"You're a brown guy on the streets of LA. If you can't

prove you're a citizen, you might just wind up in a Salvadoran concentration camp." She waved a hand. "Can you tell me anything else? About the thrift store, and what the owner was planning for Flynn?"

"Not yet. But things are happening. I'll know more next week," he said, and walked out.

SIXTEEN

S LATER WALKED BACK TO the GTO and got on the freeway toward Glendale. It was slow going with Friday traffic and the wet roads. When the rain came, half the drivers in LA sped up to get through it faster, and the other half slowed way down because it was so unfamiliar.

When he finally pulled up at Svetlana's building, he climbed out and stretched. He never came here in the dark. The structure looked abandoned save for the feeble light leaking out the narrow high windows. The front entrance looked different now, like it was new and functional. It had a heavy door that probably opened. Before it had been nailed shut. The fire marshal had been on her case to make it usable, and she'd likely turned it into an exit.

The real entrance was in the alley, and he walked onto the side street and around to the back door. A bright floodlight was aimed downward from overhead. He looked up into the camera, and the door lock snapped open. Stepping into the antechamber, he waited for the tech to scan him for weapons, and eventually the inner door clicked open.

When he walked in, Svetlana was perched on a stool in front of a computer monitor that sat on the workbench that lined the room. Its surface was littered with electronics and cables and plastic parts interspersed with other monitors, a stool in front of each.

In her fifties, Svetlana always wore bright colors over her bulky frame, today in a green and orange print blouse and a red skirt. She swiveled around to greet him.

"You're working late," she said, in her flat Slavic accent. "And you have another new old car."

"It's a borrowed car."

"Also a strange car." She raised her eyebrows. "It shows no engine heat."

"There is no engine. It was modified to be an EV." He frowned. "You monitor the street in infrared?"

She shrugged. "Only the cars that park in front of my building."

"Are you always here in the evening?"

"Sometimes. I like to get deliveries when there are fewer people on the streets. I have a vendor arriving at ten."

It made sense. Everything she built for him was shady, and a lot of her business had to involve illicit stuff.

"There's a room with a camera in it," Slater said. "A consumer job. I want to know how to make it stop working for a short time without actually unplugging it."

"Do you know the manufacturer's name?"

He recited it. "But I don't know the model number."

"Let's find it."

She swiveled to the monitor and tapped at the keyboard. The screen was just a blur from where he stood because she had a privacy filter on it.

"Look at these," she said finally.

Slater stepped sideways to stand behind her shoulder so he could see the images on the screen. He pointed to it. "Bottom left. That's the exact model."

"Let's see how it works." She clicked around, scanning the screen. "Not a complicated device. Video is sent to remote servers. No onboard storage."

"Is it hardwired?"

"Only for electricity. Video is transmitted wirelessly. Only on local Wi-Fi, not on the cell network." She swiveled to face him. "You could disrupt the Wi-Fi signals in the room. Nothing will be recorded while it's offline."

"Great. I already have your signal jammer."

"That device disrupts many frequencies. Using it on this camera is like using a chainsaw to cut the bread for your soup. I have something more elegant for you."

She slipped off the stool, and walked to the door in the side wall, and held her wrist to the reader. The lock snapped open and she disappeared inside.

He looked around the workshop, at the cluttered workbench, the jumble of circuit boards and wire and plastic housing. She made effective tech but the place always looked like chaos.

When Svetlana came back, she handed him a little green plastic box. It felt heavy. One end had a USB port, and there were prongs that folded out to plug into a wall socket.

"It looks like a phone charger," he said.

"Unfortunately the port doesn't work. But when you fold out the prongs, it turns on a Wi-Fi jammer. It will stop everything within fifteen feet from connecting. It can run for up to an hour. But it only affects Wi-Fi. Most cell signals will still work."

"This is perfect. There's tons of these kicking around."

"Hiding in plain sight," she said. "If you see a red light, it means you need to recharge the battery. Just plug it into a socket. It won't interfere with Wi-Fi when it's connected to the electricity."

"Will the person in charge of the camera know why

there's a gap in the video recording?" Slater said.

"It will just tell them the camera was offline for a few minutes." She shrugged. "Most of this miraculous technology that we are subjected to barely functions. The software is riddled with bugs. Batteries die after a few months. Internet providers supply half the city with one cable and no redundancy. No one is surprised when it doesn't work properly or breaks down."

"Except your stuff. It always works for me."

"Some of my customers have a low tolerance for failure."

He waggled the device. "How much?"

"For a good customer, two dollars."

Slater dug out his wad, and peeled off the C-notes, and handed them over. She tucked them into her bra and gestured to her monitor.

"This consumer camera has a lamp on the front that will tell you it's not connected. Green or blue means it's working. Strobing orange means it's disconnected."

"Thanks for your hard work," he said.

She threw up her hands. "I know nothing but work."

When he walked out to the GTO, the rain had stopped, but the windshield was dappled with raindrops, and he started the wipers. Traffic was better on the drive to his house, and he parked in front of the garage door, and went in the front.

Only the Pacer was in the garage. He hit the button to roll up the door, then stepped under it and parked the GTO next to the wall charger. Pike had had it put in for his future EV. Lifting the cable off the rack, he pulled down the GTO's license plate and plugged it in. From somewhere up front came a happy-sounding chime. Presumably that meant it was working. It was, he saw—the readout on the box for the wall charger said 38A.

Climbing the stairs to the bedroom, he ditched his clothes and had a shower, then put on clean jeans and a fresh shirt and went up to the kitchen. He filled a glass with water, then opened the cupboard with the booze. Just to look. He pushed his damp hair back and slammed the water. Of course he wanted to get into the bourbon, but that didn't fit with his booze rules. He still had stuff to do. He closed the cupboard again. At least he knew it was there, knew it was waiting for him.

He walked through the big empty room and stretched out on the sofa. It wasn't raining but the French doors were speckled with raindrops. That freaking roof had better not leak, he thought idly. Flat roofs did that, and fixing them was a bear.

<hr>

STARTING AWAKE WHEN HE felt fingers on his cheek, Slater grabbed the wrist and struggled to focus his eyes. It was Pike, on one knee next to the sofa, a silly grin on his face. He released his grip.

"I startled you," Pike said.

"I was in dreamland," he said, his tongue thick. "On the freeway. I kept falling asleep at the wheel, and I'd snap awake. But I was already asleep."

Pike chuckled. "That's a highway hypnosis type dream. You've been on the road."

"Apparently you can wake up inside your dreams."

"Lucid dreaming? I've never had much luck with that."

"Of course you've tried it."

Pike leaned in, running a hand into his hair, and mashed their mouths together, and caressed his chest. Eventually he pulled back.

"So I'm having a bit of cognitive dissonance," Pike said. "There's a fifty-year-old muscle car plugged into the EV charger in the garage."

"It's a resto-mod. This guy found it at an auto wrecker. Someone had taxed the engine, but the body was in good shape, so he dropped in EV parts."

"Interesting. And where's my rig?"

Slater sat up. "Honesty is the foundation of any healthy relationship."

"You say that like you memorized it from a book." He shifted onto the sofa next to him. "And like you know I'm not going to be happy if you tell me the truth."

"I loaned it to a guy named Jason. It's fine. I took a photo of his license."

"Who the hell is Jason?"

"I met him in a twelve-step meeting."

"Why would you give my car to a random stranger?" Pike demanded. "You don't trust anybody. You don't even trust me."

"I didn't give it. I swapped it. For a motorcycle." He waved a hand. "It's temporary. He wants his bike back."

"And then you swapped the bike for the GTO?"

"The GTO is a loaner. It's too cold to ride the bike that far."

"What kind of bike?"

"A Sportster," Slater said. "It looks fairly new. It's fuel-injected."

"Those haven't been carbureted in twenty years. I didn't know you had a motorcycle license."

"Technically, I don't."

Pike groaned and rubbed his eyes. "This just gets better. At least that bike is worth more than my vehicle, if it's running. How do you know the bike's not stolen?"

"It's a small town. You can't pull stuff like that for very long and get away with it."

"I guess if he gets into a high-speed pursuit with the highway patrol in my rig, I'll be able to watch it on TV."

"He's not that guy," Slater said. "People in the meeting know him. He's long-term clean."

"Clean—that means you went to an NA meeting."

"My target was there. I'll tell you about it, but can we strap on the old feed bag first?"

"The rain is supposed to be done," Pike said. "We can walk down to Sunset."

They went down to the street, and Slater saw that the Continental was parked at the curb farther up the street, glistening wet and cloudy blue and beautiful in the dark. On Sunset they found a place with some tables along the sidewalk. They'd fired up the heat lamps for the wet night.

When the server stepped over, Pike ordered a burger.

"A salad for me," Slater said.

"Which salad?"

"Just put in all the vegetables."

She nodded. "Can do."

Once she'd walked away, Pike said, "You've been dining in small-town eateries."

"I know you've been there. There's just so much grease."

He chuckled. "So why were you going to NA meetings?"

Slater told him about finding the water bottle, and talking to Candy.

"Who's the guy that took you into the park?" Pike said.

"His name is Zeke. He spends a lot of time in the back-country. Decent guy. A little odd. He thinks there's some spirit in the desert. An intelligent species that's out there, but we can't see it."

"That idea is one of the explanations for aliens," Pike said. "That they're a nonhuman intelligence living in some parallel overlay to our reality. They're right here, but somehow concealed from us."

"Zeke said he can feel them."

"Vibes don't count as science, and it's not part of somebody's religion, so what's left is the occult. Mysterious stuff that you need extra tools to detect."

"Zeke didn't claim any special tools."

"If he picks up vibes, that's a tool."

The server set down their plates, and Slater jabbed his fork into his salad. After he'd bitten into his burger, Pike spoke.

"A lot of the UFO stuff is like that. One theory goes that besides not being able to detect them, it's possible that we don't even have the capacity to understand them."

"That's starting to sound like a religion," Slater said. "'This is too much for you to grasp, peasant, so just do what I tell you.'"

"With religion you have to believe something that has no evidence. Zeke's vibes are his evidence. The saucer-heads use the analogy of an ant colony next to a freeway. The ants might be able to detect the freeway through sound or vibration, but they'd have no way to conceptualize the scale of it, or what it was for, or who built it. Maybe we're like the ants, and there's all this other stuff going on that we can't even fathom."

"You're a damn saucer-head," Slater said.

He laughed. "I do like reading about it. The paranormal and the unexplained."

"I have enough trouble just figuring out what's going on right in front of my face."

When they got back to the house, Pike unlocked the front door, then stepped into the garage.

"You have to show me the resto-mod."

Slater grabbed the garage door opener from the Pacer, and gave Pike the keys to the GTO.

"I love that it's under the license plate," Pike said, and disconnected the charging cable.

"That's where the gas cap was. It keeps the lines of the fenders clean."

They both climbed in, and Pike drove around the neighborhood. The wet streets were quiet now. He stopped at a light, and when it turned green, he punched it and raced up the block.

"The acceleration is amazing."

"Right?" Slater said. "It's kind of insane."

"It's because you're not dumping more fuel into an engine and waiting for it to burn, you're sending more electrons to a motor. It happens way faster."

"I like that it doesn't have the nanny technology, like 'ding, ding, buckle your seatbelt, comrade,' and 'beep-beep-beep, you're going to bump into a wall.'"

"I don't mind all those sensors," Pike said. "But this does feel like a happy medium."

He turned onto their street and pulled into the garage. Once they'd climbed out, Pike plugged it in.

"Good to know the charger works," Pike said, looking at the wall box. "It's pulling thirty-eight amps."

"Is that a lot?"

"It's just about the max for the circuit." Pike waved to the Pacer. "If you take a step back, and look at where we're at—you have three classic cars here now, and I have zero cars of any kind here now. Can you see how it feels like things aren't trending in a healthy way?"

He put his hands on his hips. "I'll get you your whip back."

"What if I get an EV? There's no room in here."

"Rats." Slater gestured helplessly. "I think I need to sell the Pacer."

"Despite its extreme beauty?"

Stepping toward it, Slater looked it over. "Lo, those curves. And that glass. It's too much for me. Like eating doughnuts for every meal, or three fingers of bourbon for breakfast. I don't think I can handle it long-term. It came into my life like a dream. As ephemeral as a fleeting blossom. Maybe it's time for the dream to fade."

Pike nodded. "That sounds like progress."

As they climbed the stairs, Slater spoke. "You should read to me. I want to find out what happens to Prometheus.

Surely he's not still chained to that fricking rock."

"I guess we'll find out."

Reading the classics had become their thing, and right now they were deep into the *Theogony*. It was a modern translation that laid out all the background so they could understand what was going on.

Slater got settled at one end of the sofa, and Pike grabbed the book from the coffee table, and leaned back on him. As he found the page, Slater wrapped an arm around his belly.

"When Heracles came across Prometheus," Pike read, "he shot an arrow to kill the eagle tasked with attacking him each day. Heracles then released Prometheus from the chains that bound him."

"Finally," Slater said. "Heracles is a total badass."

"It would take a lot of chutzpah to go against the will of the king of the gods."

"Can you imagine being attacked by an eagle every damn day?"

"That would get annoying fast," Pike said. "But the chains sound kind of hot."

"If that's your attitude, I feel like I should hook you up."

Pike turned to look at him sidelong and closed the book. "Bring it."

They got up, and Slater took the book from him, and set it on the coffee table. "You realize we read approximately one sentence."

"This will be more fun. You've been away."

They headed down the stairs, and Slater grabbed a pair of handcuffs from the bedside drawer. As Pike stepped close, he wrapped an arm around his neck, notching his throat into the crook of his arm. Slater growled in his ear.

"Don't you fucking move."

Pike grasped his arm with both hands. He knew how to break out of the hold, and he could have easily done that, but he didn't, breathing hard now. "I should take my shirt off first."

Slater let go of him, and ditched his shirt and his jeans as Pike did the same. Once they were naked, he grabbed Pike's wrist, then the other, and pulled them behind his back. He clicked on the cuffs and spun him around.

Pike was totally hard. "This is so hot."

"Shut the fuck up."

He squeezed his cock, and caressed his chest, then shoved him backward. Losing his balance, Pike flopped onto the bed and laughed. Slater straddled him, savaging his mouth and his jaw, and pressed his woody into his thigh. He could feel his swelling cock beneath him.

Reaching for the lube, he stroked Pike's cock, then lowered himself onto him, wincing at the intensity of it. Gradually he got into it, shifting back and forth. He met Pike's gaze, and could see that he was close. Winding up, he slapped him hard across the face.

"Fuck," Pike shouted.

Slater slapped his other cheek.

"Fucking hooligan," Pike said through his teeth, and then came, straining into him.

Slater grabbed his own cock, and stroked himself for a few seconds until he came too, then climbed off and flopped beside him.

"I'll unhook you," he said. "Just give me a second to catch my breath."

"I don't even care. That was so fricking hot."

Sitting up, Slater kissed him, and pushed his nose into his sweaty hair, inhaling his heady scent.

"You're fricking hot. I love you so hard."

SEVENTEEN

▱▱▱▱▱▱▱▱▱▱▱

SLATER HAD SET HIS alarm for early, and he'd stuck to his ration of the rotgut bourbon last night, so he woke with a clear head. Pike got up with him, and trudged upstairs, and made coffee.

After they'd eaten together, Slater stuffed some clean clothes into his satchel and carried it down to the garage. The screen in the GTO said it was charged to two hundred and forty miles. That was more than enough to get back to Flynn's place.

When he was a few blocks from the house, his phone buzzed. It was Pike.

"You forgot your jacket," he said, when Slater picked up.

"I'll definitely need that to ride the bike."

He made a quick turn onto the boulevard. In front of him on the pavement was a dark bundle, sprawling into the street from the gutter. Twisting the wheel, he managed to swerve and avoid hitting it. It was a body, he saw.

"Fucking royal fuck."

Pike was still on the line. "What happened?"

"There's a dude lying in the middle of Alvarado. I'm

163

not sure if he's dead or alive."

"Should you call the cops?"

"It's right next to a homeless encampment. He spilled out of there. They can figure it out."

"I'll bring your jacket downstairs."

When he pulled up to the house, Pike was on the street, and handed him the jacket through the window, a smile on his face, and sweet words for him. It still blew his mind how upbeat the guy was, how he managed to be calm and cheerful when the world was on fire.

———◆———

SLATER MADE GOOD TIME on the drive back to the desert, as he'd left well before traffic. Pulling into the yard at Flynn's place, he saw Jason's bike was where he'd left it. He backed the GTO up to the charger and plugged it in, then took his jacket and his satchel and knocked at the door of the casita.

"I'm glad you're back," Flynn said as he pulled it open. "I can make my meeting."

Slater handed him the keys. "It still has about a hundred miles' range."

"Right on. Make yourself coffee if you want."

He had time for that, he decided, watching Flynn leave. He looked around the kitchen. There was an old-school espresso pot on the sideboard, and he loaded it up with water and ground beans from the bag, and set it on the stove, and soon had a steaming mugful of joe.

Stepping out the front door, he stood in the sun to sip at it. He felt a little spacy, tired from the early morning. Maybe he had some of that highway hypnosis Pike had talked about. Closing his eyes, he turned his face to the bright sun, willing it to wake him up, to snap him out of it.

Once he'd slurped the last of the joe and got ready to leave, he realized he couldn't lock the casita's deadbolt.

Instead he twisted the thumb lock on the inside door handle before he left. Zipping up his jacket, he pulled on the helmet, and climbed on the motorcycle.

On the stretch of open highway on the way to Twenty-nine, he noticed a vehicle pull up close behind him. What was this moron up to? Tailgating a motorcycle was pure stupidity. The left lane was wide open. Nevada plates, he realized. This was the same Range Rover that had pulled into that gas station.

There wasn't a lot of traffic—there'd be no witnesses if the driver decided to take him out. A collision would barely scratch the grill of the lumbering three-ton Rover, but no way would Slater and the beautiful bike survive it. Twisting the throttle, he felt the surge of acceleration as the bike responded and leaped ahead. In the mirror he could see the Rover receding.

The dirtbag would catch up eventually, but he'd seen a road sign yesterday along this stretch: the hospital, the county offices, and most significant right now, the sheriff's station were together in a cluster.

The Rover was gaining on him when he came to the sign. Braking hard, he made the turn, and rolled up the driveway. The Rover pulled in behind him. As he stopped in front of the sheriff's station, the driver rolled to a stop several yards back. He must have realized where they were, knew it was risky to mess with somebody in front of the cops.

Slater kicked down the stand, and climbed off the bike, and stood facing the Rover's windshield. There were two men inside. The driver looked to be the same cue ball from the gas station. Neither one of them moved to get out of the vehicle. Slater put his hands on his hips. Were they going to wait for the deputies to notice them?

A moment later the Rover made a sharp U-turn, and cruised down the driveway, and turned onto the highway, and roared off.

"Can I help you?"

Slater turned to see that a deputy had stepped out of the office. In the familiar tan-and-green uniform, she had her dark hair tied tightly back. He flipped up the visor on his helmet to show her his eyes and meet her gaze.

"I was looking for the permitting counter."

"The county offices are right next door." She gestured farther up the driveway.

"Thanks." He raised a palm and then swung his leg over the bike.

She'd either bought it or didn't care, and walked over to one of the prowl cars parked out front, and climbed in.

Flipping the visor down, he started the bike, and waited for the prowl car to roll down the driveway and pull out onto the highway. A minute later he followed, and rode to the thrift store, and parked along the side. The orange Wrangler was here again. Walking in, he saw Luanne was over amid the racks of clothes on the side marked WOMEN, and called a greeting to her.

He went back to the stock room and through the swinging doors. There had been boxes in here yesterday, but today there were more of them, a dozen cartons piled three high along the wall next to the back door. They weren't marked, and they were all identical, and looked pristine. This definitely wasn't janky donated used stuff. It had to be about Knox's wholesale side hustle.

He could hear Knox's voice, and stepped over to the office door. Knox was sitting at his desk. The guy was so weird. He was wearing pristine black patent-leather oxfords, but the kicks didn't mesh with the nebbishy washed-out jeans and the rumpled plaid shirt. Those looked like they'd come directly off the racks up front.

"Gimme a second," Knox said into his phone, and looked at Slater. "It's after ten."

"I'm here, aren't I?"

He scoffed. "I'm on a call. Tell Luanne she needs to train you."

Slater raised a hand in acknowledgment, then pointed at his feet. "I dig those stomps."

When he walked into the shop, he saw there were a couple of customers here now, digging through the racks. Luanne was picking clothes off the floor and putting them on hangers. He walked over to her.

"I remember you," she said, straightening up.

"Is that your Wrangler parked outside?"

"That's the boss's. I'm in the ratty beat-up Chevy."

"Knox said you should train me."

Her eyebrows shot up. "So you're the new guy."

"John Slade."

"Well, it's not brain surgery, John. It's mostly about picking things up off the floor. I don't know why people insist on doing that, pulling stuff off the hangers and just dropping it."

He pulled a hanger from the rack. It had a gray print shirt on it. "No price tags?"

"Some items have them. The more expensive stuff. But everything that's not marked is eight bucks. Unless it's flimsy and small."

She stepped over to another rack and held up a pair of lamé booty shorts, and then a hanger with a loop of pink fabric on it.

"What's that, exactly?" he said.

"A tube top." She stretched it on her hands and held it up to her breasts. "Stuff like this, and the hot pants, that's five bucks. Swimsuits too. Jackets and coats are twelve."

"Got it."

Luanne put the tube top back on its hanger and waved at the big room. "I call all this secondhand interesting things."

"I'm not sure how much of it is actually interesting."

"Think about the acronym that makes. Secondhand

interesting things." She raised her eyebrows. "s-h-i-t, John. That's what it is. It's all shit."

Slater nodded. "That tracks."

She laughed. "I'm just saying don't take it too seriously. It's not Rodeo Drive in here."

"Are prices negotiable if people ask?"

"Nobody's going to haggle over an eight-dollar shirt."

The ding of a bell sounded from the direction of the till.

"That's important," Luanne said. "We're needed at the register."

He followed her as she ambled toward the front. Luanne wasn't limping, exactly, but her steps fell heavy.

A woman had piled some clothes on the counter, and Luanne greeted her as she stepped behind it. Slater watched as she tapped numbers into the till. It looked easy enough to operate.

"That's twenty-seven total," she said, and stuffed the woman's cash in the register. "Do you need a bag, honey?"

"I can just carry them," she said, and scooped it all up, and walked out.

"Most people pay cash?" Slater said.

"We get both. This thing is for card payments." She tapped a little box with a screen and a cable attached, and showed him how to use it.

Stepping out from the counter, Luanne scanned the room. "There's nobody's here right now. Come into the back."

He followed her through the swinging doors. Knox's office door stood half closed. Luanne pointed to a set of blue lockers.

"You can put your stuff in there, but you have to bring your own padlock."

Slater pulled off his jacket and hung it in an empty locker, briefly feeling the pocket to make sure Svetlana's

Wi-Fi jammer was still there.

"We call that the loading dock." Luanne gestured to the back door with the crash bar. "You might get donations dropped off. Usually people come in the front first. If they have a lot of stuff, tell them to pull around here to unload."

"You just take whatever?"

"Unless it's obviously not saleable." She scoffed. "One guy tried to donate a bunch of used tires. Books and vinyl records are fine. Kitchen stuff if it's not cracked or chipped. If it's clothes, you have to spray them."

From a shelf next to the lockers she grabbed a spray can, one of a dozen with the same label, and handed it to him. In big letters it claimed it was sanitizer, but that seemed awfully vague. It was likely an insecticide. He popped off the cap and sniffed the nozzle.

"That's the smell of every thrift store I've ever been in," he said.

"You know it's totally toxic." She took the can from him. "There's some latex gloves here so you don't get it on your skin."

Knox pulled open his office door. "Don't be teaching him your bad habits. Telling him it's toxic." He eyed Slater. "You don't need gloves. Just assess the clothes, spray the ones that aren't ripped or stained, and hang them on the racks. We don't take underwear."

"What if they're ripped or stained or underwear?" Slater said.

"The dumpster is right outside." He pointed to the back door, then stepped back into his office.

Luanne rolled her eyes. "Let me show you the crockery and the books."

As she was explaining that part of the store, they heard the bell ding up front, and they both walked up to the counter. Luanne had him ring up the sale, and stood nearby, watching him work. The guy paid with a card, and

Slater managed to get the transaction to go through.

"It looks like you can handle it," Luanne said, once the guy left.

The place seemed to get busier around midday, and Luanne spent time chatting with the customers. Slater walked the floor and ran the till when Luanne wasn't up front. He hadn't planned to actually work here, but Knox was still in his office when he checked. Until the guy left, he wouldn't have the opportunity to rifle his office.

As he was ringing up a sale, Luanne walked up, her purse slung on her shoulder. She waited for the customer to leave before she spoke.

"I'm going to the supermarket to buy a sub and a fruit cup. Fresh bread and sweet, sweet melon."

"You don't get food delivered?" Slater said.

"Oh, honey, they only deliver junk food around here. I put on five pounds just driving past a burger joint." She glanced over her shoulder, toward the back of the store, and lowered her voice. "Working in this place makes me feel grubby. Like I need to eat something clean. I have some cheese I've been saving up."

He frowned. "In your handbag?"

She held his gaze. "It doesn't really need to be refrigerated."

"Hey, smoke 'em if you've got 'em."

"Are you going to be OK here on your own for a while?"

"I will," Slater said.

"If you need any help, ask Knox." She waved and walked out.

Standing behind the counter, he folded his arms and looked around the room. He could still smell that spray.

A woman with smoker's wrinkles and wearing a stretchy black top approached the register, and held up a hanger with a white shirt on it. "How much is this?"

"Eight dollars."

In her other hand was a puffy jacket with ratty fur around the hood. She lifted it up. "What about this?"

"That one's eight dollars," Slater said.

She frowned. "Are you sure? It's a winter jacket."

"Why would I lie to you about that? If it was a few inches longer, it'd be twelve. But that one is eight."

"I'll take them both."

Slater rang it up and took her cash. As she was leaving, Knox walked up.

"How's it going?"

"Like Luanne said, it's not brain surgery. The foot traffic is pretty consistent." He frowned. "Did you change your shirt?"

This one was solid gray, and before it had been blue plaid.

"Why not? I have a whole store full of clothes. Listen, John, while there's a lull, do you know how cash registers work?"

"I've been running this one all morning."

"It keeps track of all the sales. At the end of the day you can take out the float. It's always the same amount. What's left is the cash you made."

"You want me to do that?"

"We do it after closing," Knox said. "The thing is, this morning I made some sales and didn't punch them in. I just stuffed the cash in the drawer. It was a lot, so I have no idea what's in there. Can you do a count, and pull out whatever's not the float, and bring it to my office?"

"How much is the float?"

"One fifty. Leave the small bills." He turned and walked toward the back.

Thinking about it, that was an odd task. If Knox wasn't sure of the take, he'd definitely count the lettuce himself. The only explanation was that Knox was running a gimmick—testing him.

A man with thick gray hair approached the counter and draped a jacket on it. Once Slater had rung up the sale, the guy walked out. He pulled out the cash tray and set it on the counter. Leaning in, he looked in the back of the drawer. He could see the handgun Flynn had mentioned. Grabbing it by the handle, he pulled it out and looked it over. It was a bulky .45. Knox had probably chosen it to be intimidating.

Digging out his hankie, he wiped his prints off it, and tucked it back in the drawer, then started counting the cash. On top of the float there was almost twelve hundred dollars. They hadn't sold nearly that much in eight-dollar increments today. Cash sales might have been two hundred. He found an elastic band, and rolled up the cash, and wrapped the band around it. Scrabbling in another drawer, he found a sticky note and wrote $1,182, and stuck it on the wad.

Once he'd put the cash tray back, he slammed the drawer. A few people were perusing the racks but nobody looked like they'd imminently need to check out. Slater carried the roll of cash back to the stock room, and into Knox's office, and set it on his desk.

Sitting up, Knox chuckled. "You rolled it up like a drug dealer."

"What's the point of having a cash register if you don't record all your sales?" Slater said.

He gestured dismissively. "I was in a rush."

"You know I could have kept half of that, and you'd never know."

He raised his eyebrows. "Did you?"

Slater scoffed and walked out. If that was a test, what was the follow-up was going to be?

Only one customer was on the floor when he walked through to the front counter. A few minutes later a couple of guys walked in. One was pasty and blond, with an annoying military haircut. His tight T-shirt displayed his impressive pecs. The other guy was wearing a sweatshirt with a sports team logo and had his Black hair in a sharp fade. That was a military haircut too, he decided. He knew there was a Marine base near here. Both these jarheads were buff and totally fuckable.

The one in the T-shirt nodded in greeting as he stepped in, mopping his brow. "It's getting hot out there."

Slater gave him a pointed once-over. "It's getting hot in here."

He chuckled. "Where's the men's stuff?"

"You know gender is a construct, right?"

His eyes narrowed. "Where's the clothes that look like what you're wearing?"

He gestured to the room. "All of that side."

A while later the guy in the sweatshirt came to the register, a pile of clothes in hand, and set them on the counter. The one with the pecs waited by the front door, idly perusing the table lamps.

"The sign says most stuff is eight dollars."

"Let's see what you've got." Slater picked up a T-shirt, then another. "These are almost the same. You sure you want them both?"

"They're nice shirts."

"If you say so. Let's call it two for eight on those."

He tapped that into the register, then held up a pair of pale-green short shorts in a sheer nylon fabric. They were probably meant for running.

"These are a little hoochie." Slater met his gaze. "Four clams."

The guy laughed. "If they're hoochie, they should cost double, not half."

"You want to try them on? I can do a fit check for you. Assess whether they make you look like a hoochie daddy."

"It feels like you're flirting with me."

"We can hook up after my shift, if that's what you're asking." He jutted his chin toward the other guy. "That set of tits you walked in with is invited too."

His brow furrowed. "That's not going to happen."

Slater held up a tank top from the pile. "This doesn't even have arms. Five on that one."

"I thought I'd need it," he said, watching Slater tap at the register. "I heard it's going to get warm this summer. I just got posted here."

"When it's hot in the desert you need long sleeves and long pants," Slater said. "Light and loose but covered up. And a hat with a brim."

"That's what he said." He jabbed his thumb toward the other guy. "He's from New Mexico. I didn't want to believe it."

"That's seventeen." Slater watched him dig out his wallet. "Where's home?"

"The Mississippi Delta," he said, and handed him a twenty.

"Home of the blues."

"You know it."

Slater handed him his change. "Do you know a musician named Ernesta?"

"Not personally, but I know who she is."

"I saw her in a bar last week."

"She's definitely a Delta girl."

"It gets sweaty down there, doesn't it? Save the booty shorts for the Delta."

EIGHTEEN

A WHILE LATER LUANNE RETURNED, flashing a smile as she stepped into the thrift store.

"How did it go?"

"People came in, people left," Slater said. "Some of them bought stuff."

She chuckled. "You didn't get overwhelmed?"

"Not yet."

"I can staff the register if you want to do floor duty."

"Meaning pick stuff up off the floor?" Slater said.

"You catch on quick."

He stepped out from behind the counter. "I see secondhand interesting things, Luanne. So much secondhand interesting things."

There was a lot of stuff on the floor, with an equal number of empty hangers on the racks. At least they didn't need to be sorted, he thought as he hung stuff up, although different racks had different kinds of clothes, all shirts or pants or jackets.

As he worked, he heard Luanne calling, "John … John."

Slater looked up as she approached him, suddenly

remembering that was him.

"Are you wearing earbuds," she demanded, "or are you deaf?"

"I must have spaced out. What's going on?"

"There's a donation coming in at the loading dock. Can you deal with it? I'll stay on the register."

He walked into the stock room and pushed on the crash bar on the back door. It had a little stop attached at the bottom, and he kicked it down to prop it open. A dusty SUV was parked right outside, and a guy with shaggy hair was opening the lift gate. He pulled out a bulky black leaf bag. It was almost full, and loosely tied at the top. It looked heavy.

"It's all clothes," the guy said, and heaved it onto the concrete pad outside the door.

"Nothing ripped or stained?" Slater said.

He scowled. "It's good stuff, you ingrate." He slammed the lift gate and walked around to the driver's side.

As the vehicle pulled away, Slater opened the top of the bag. He could feel eyes on him, and he looked around to see a woman standing over by the wall of the building, next to the dumpster. Bone-thin, she had her hair tied up, and looked a little grubby. It was hard to tell whether she was homeless or not. When he eyed her, she gestured to the bag.

"Anything good in there?" she said, her voice low.

"How would I know? I just got it."

"Can I look?"

Knox's voice came from inside. "Who's out there?" A moment later he stepped out the door and glared at the woman. "You know you're not supposed to be around here, sugar for brains. Go on, get the heck away from my place."

The woman didn't move, and jutted her chin. "Yeah, yeah."

Knox scoffed and eyed Slater. "Don't let her in—ever."

Once he'd gone back inside, Slater turned to her. "It's basically impossible to cuss someone out when you don't use cuss words."

She laughed. "He's an idiot."

"What did you do to get banned from this place?"

"I may have neglected to pay for something. Boss man thinks I'm some kind of felon."

"Isn't felony shoplifting like a thousand dollars now? You'd need a semitruck and four hours' hard labor to take that much out of this place."

"I was looking for a jacket. It gets cold at night."

Slater glanced behind him into the stock room. Knox was nowhere in sight. He pulled open the leaf bag. "Maybe there's something here."

She stepped over and quickly dug through it, eventually pulling out a suede jacket with fluffy white wool lining. "Look at this thing."

"Keep your voice down. Do you need anything else?"

"The rest is all men's clothes." She pulled it on. "Does it fit me?"

Two of her could fit in that jacket, he saw, but he said, "Close enough. Listen, did you ever meet a guy named Ferret around here?"

Her expression didn't shift. "I know what a ferret is, but I never met anybody with that name."

"OK." He heaved up the bag. "Stay warm."

Stepping inside, he set the bag next to the rolling rack with all the hangers and went through it. There were pants and shirts and a couple of suits, all neatly folded, none of it stained or damaged. It all smelled like laundry detergent or fabric softener. He started putting the stuff on hangers, then carried them out into the shop, and hung them on the racks with similar items.

Luanne stepped over. "Did you spray them?"

"I think the guy already washed them. They seem fine."

She clicked her tongue. "Don't let Knox hear you say that. If he asks, you sprayed them."

"Got it."

"Can you take the till? I'm going on floor duty."

He walked over to the counter and found a guy looking into the glass display case under it. Definitely a teenager, he was wearing a backpack, and had thick dark hair. As Slater stepped behind the counter, he pointed to a laptop in the case.

"How much is that?"

"Let's find out." He turned to the shelves and lifted the beckoning cat statue. The key was there, like Flynn said it would be. Once he'd unlocked the case, he pulled out the computer, and turned it over, then set it on the counter. "It's not marked."

The kid lifted it to look at the label on the bottom. "I can't afford it anyway. It's the new one."

"You need it to edit your vandalism videos for social media?" Slater said. "Or film yourself for the eat-dishwash-er-soap challenge?"

He scowled and set it down. "I need it to get through high school, you dick."

A woman stepped over. Still in her thirties, maybe, she was wearing jeans and a light jacket. "What's going on?"

"It's too new," the kid said.

"It doesn't actually look new to me," Slater said. "Everything in here is secondhand interesting things."

The kid waved a hand. "Trust me, it's less than a year old."

"Secondhand interesting things," Slater said. "It makes an acronym."

The woman's brow furrowed. "What are you talking about?"

Slater eyed the kid. "Secondhand interesting things. What's the acronym?"

"S, H ..." He laughed. "I get it. Everything in here is that."

"How much money have you got?" Slater said, eyeing the woman.

"Not enough. You can put that away. What have you got that costs less than three hundred?"

He jutted his chin. "Show me the money."

She frowned but pulled out her wallet and dug out a sheaf of twenties. There was a C-note at the bottom, he saw.

"That one." He reached over to pull it out, then handed the kid the computer.

"Are you serious right now?" he said. "It's worth ten times that."

He tapped 100 into the register, and put the C-note in the drawer, then rolled it shut. "What about the charger? I don't see one in here."

"I don't need it," the kid said. "They're universal now."

"Who knew?" Slater turned to the woman. "I can give you a receipt, but if you have any trouble with it, don't bring it back here."

She nodded. "That works."

The kid pulled the laptop open. "I won't have any trouble. It's basically new."

"If anybody asks," Slater said, "you didn't buy it here."

"I can work with that." The woman stuffed the receipt in her bag. "Listen, thanks."

Slater saw Luanne walking toward the front, moving slow in her lumbering gait. He lowered his voice. "Either put that thing away or blow."

He folded it closed, and tucked it under his arm, and they walked out the front door. Slater lifted the beckoning cat and put the key back under it.

A while later his phone buzzed in his pants. Jason from program. He picked up.

"I've taken care of my issue," Jason said. "We can swap back."

"I'm in Twentynine right now."

"I'm nowhere near there."

"Not a problem," Slater said. "I can come to you. Just tell me where."

"We can meet halfway." He named two roads, and Slater wrote it down on the sticky pad.

"It's called Two-Mile Road," Jason said, "but it's only a mile north of the highway. It'll take you half an hour."

Once he'd ended the call, he found the crossroads on a map, and memorized the route. It was easy, with just one turn from the highway. Walking back into the racks, he found Luanne.

"I have to clock out."

"Oh, sweetie, we're still open for another hour."

"It doesn't seem that busy. You'll be fine."

"You should tell Knox."

Walking into the back, Slater stuck his head in the office door. "I'm leaving. I've got stuff to do."

Knox frowned. "That's not actually how having a job works."

"Luanne's got you. It's closing time soon."

He grabbed his jacket from the locker, and went out the back door, and walked past the orange Wrangler. It wasn't new but it looked like it had just been washed. That seemed pointless out here when it was always so dusty. Pointless like wearing patent-leather oxfords to sit alone in an office.

The wind had picked up, and he took a deep breath of the unscented air, and flapped his arms in the breeze before he pulled on his jacket. With any luck that cloying smell wouldn't linger in his clothes. Pulling on the helmet, he climbed on the bike, and kicked up the stand, and headed toward the highway.

The road he turned onto was dirt, but it was maintained, not bumpy and rutted like farther out, where his land was. There were no structures on the corner when he rode up, but he knew it was the right place—Pike's SUV was pulled over to the side. He rolled past it and kicked down the stand, then climbed off, and pulled off the helmet. Jason was next to the SUV, zipping on a pair of black chaps.

"I'm digging the leathers," Slater said. "Are you sure you're completely straight?"

He laughed. "You flatter me."

"I could do a lot more than that to you."

"How was the bike?"

"Riding that thing is a blast," Slater said, and handed him the key.

"I know it is."

As he took Pike's key, he saw a black Navigator rolling up the road. It slowed down and pulled in behind the SUV.

"Friends of yours?" Slater said.

"They must have spotted the bike." He took a deep breath. "You should go. Just drive away. They're going to fuck me up."

"Are they armed?"

"They don't roll that way. It's too risky."

"So let's teach them some manners."

They watched as two guys climbed out of the Navigator.

"Seriously?" Jason said.

"There's only two of them."

One was the baldy with the mustache, the one who'd accosted him at the gas station. He could see the aggression in his eyes. Slater knew that look—he was fixing to throw hands. The other guy had a hard face, blotchy, like he'd spent too much time in the sun, his hair in a crew cut. The pair of them strutted toward them.

"Play it cool until they make a move," Slater said under his breath, "then *bam*."

"Right."

The guy was bigger than he remembered, half a head taller and built thick. Slater took a breath and spoke in a genial tone.

"Hey, Stardust. I know you—you were flirting with me at that gas station."

He scowled. "No, I wasn't."

"That's how I remember it," Slater said. "I guess we can agree to disagree."

"I don't know you, *cholo*. You need to stay out of this."

"Cool it, baby. You can't control other people. You can only control your own emotions. You need to look at yourself in the mirror and admit that you're the problem. Just say it: 'I'm the asshole.'"

His jaw tightened, and he wound up to take a swing. The guy knew how to brawl, but Slater knew this type. He relied too much on his bulk. That made him slow.

Slater ducked and lunged at him, throwing his weight at his belt. The guy lost his balance and stumbled backward. As Slater punched at his jaw, the guy tried to grapple with him, and Slater elbowed him in the dick. He yowled and twisted away.

As he pulled back to take another swing, the guy landed a glancing blow to his cheek. Before he could deliver the punch, a black biker boot appeared in the periphery and struck hard on the side of the guy's face, snapping his head sideways. He twisted and dropped to the ground.

Standing erect, Slater stepped back. Baldy lay there unmoving. His head was in a natural position, he decided. That meant his neck hadn't snapped, despite the flying kick that had taken him down. He was just out cold.

Jason was standing next to him, Slater realized, his long hair a wild mess. Fists balled, he was breathing hard, staring down at the guy. The other goon was stretched out too, with bright red on his upper lip, and smeared on his cheek, and trickling at the side of his mouth. He hadn't seen any of that interaction, but it must have gone down fast.

"I can't believe you rinsed them both," Slater said.

"It wouldn't have happened without your help."

"All I managed was a dick-punch."

He gingerly touched his cheek with a finger. It was sore but it wasn't bleeding.

"We should go," Jason said. "They're going to come around soon."

The bald one had been driving, and Slater squatted and dug in the guy's front pants pocket, and pulled out a key fob. He held it up, dangling from his finger.

"Want to slow them down?"

"Oh, hell, yeah."

He threw the key overhand into the landscape next to the road. A branch on a creosote bush jerked and recoiled as the fob sailed through it.

"Why did you call him Stardust?" Jason said.

"The Stardust casino in Vegas. His rig had Nevada plates."

"I don't really do Vegas."

Crouching next to the other goon, Slater pressed two fingers to his neck. His pulse felt regular enough. He rolled him onto his side, into the crash position.

"You want to get him a pillow and a blankie too?" Jason said.

"He's bleeding." Slater stood erect. "You don't want him to drown in his own blood."

Jason scoffed. "I'd be just fine with that outcome."

"Well, I don't have the bandwidth to face a manslaughter rap right now."

"You didn't have to stay. You didn't have to help me."

"I don't know what their beef is with you," Slater said. "I don't really care. But I know you're a decent guy. You've been straight with me from the start. And I know you're trying to be a good father."

Jason nodded. "You really should beat it." Walking over to his bike, he took a second to bundle up his hair, then pulled on the helmet.

Climbing into the SUV, Slater waited for Jason to ride past, then made a wide turn to avoid running over the goons. As he headed back toward the highway, he pulled the rearview down to look at his face. His cheek was red and swollen. It might bruise, but the skin wasn't broken.

NINETEEN

T HERE WAS STILL AN hour or two of daylight, but Slater needed to eat. He drove Pike's rig to Flynn's place and pulled into the yard. The GTO was parked next to the casita. He got out and rapped on the door.

When Flynn pulled it open, he frowned. "What happened to your face?"

"Someone came at me."

He looked past him into the yard. "Where's Jason's bike?"

"Jason wanted it back."

"Did that happen at the thrift store? You got into a fight?"

"Can we eat before the debrief?"

"I'm actually headed to a meeting," Flynn said. "We can eat after that if you want to come with."

"On Saturday night?"

"That's the easiest night to fall off the wagon."

"Is there any food here?"

"I've got beef jerky, and string cheese. There's some of those vacuum-packed boiled eggs."

"Fuck that." Slater huffed. "You're driving."

He followed Flynn out to the GTO and climbed in the passenger side. On the way he told him about the thrift store.

"Knox was in his office the whole damn day," Slater said. "I didn't have a chance to poke around. I'll have to go back."

"The thing about counting the cash in the drawer is odd. He never made me do that."

"I think he dangled the unaccounted cash in front of me to see if I'd rip him off. It makes me think he's got something else planned."

"Whatever he was trying to do to me, he'll do to you, don't you think? He'll set you up to be the patsy in some scheme." Flynn glanced over at him. "So who punched you?"

"That incident is not connected to the thrift store," Slater said.

"Is it a secret? Some insurance code of ethics that you can't break?"

He groaned and leaned back on the headrest. "I've got a lot on my plate."

Flynn rolled into the church parking lot and pulled into a stall. "There's Jason's bike."

"I should have copied the key," Slater said. "I could jack that beautiful thing and just go. Ride it into the sharp red edge of dawn and never look back."

He laughed. "You're not that guy."

He was making assumptions about him, but he didn't need to point that out. Slater had basically jacked Knox today, selling that kid the laptop for a C-note. But then Knox had been hurling abuse at a homeless woman. It seemed ugly to dunk on somebody who was already on the skids.

"Save me a seat," Slater said as they climbed out.

He stepped over to a Joshua tree growing at the side of the lot and looked it over. It was healthy. It likely got some water here. It was going to flower soon, with a stark white panicle growing up high among the spikes. They only did that in years when the conditions were right. It was such an odd plant, with its elegant blades and the wild contorted branches.

Walking into the meeting, he sat with Flynn at the side of the room. The same woman as a couple of nights ago was at the table up front. Gwen. It felt messed up that he remembered her name. He was getting way too caught up in this world, way too entangled with Flynn.

On the other side of the room Jason met his eye, and frowned, and tapped his cheek.

Slater flashed his palms and shook his head, a tacit *I've got no idea how that happened.*

Gwen went through the routine stuff, then asked who wanted to share. A woman in the circle put up her hand and talked about trying not to break down at work. Just listening to her graphic story felt intense. After she spoke, Jason raised his hand.

"Somebody helped me out today," he said. "There was some stuff I had to deal with on the side of the road. He didn't have to pitch in, but he did anyway. The guy said he could tell I was trying to be a good dad. That meant a lot." He looked around the circle. "I can feel it in these rooms. The strength that comes from being part of a group. It makes my life better. I hope I can do that for others too."

Slater briefly clapped for him along with everyone else.

Leaning toward him, Flynn spoke under his breath. "That's the gestalt thing I was talking about. He's feeling it."

After the meeting, people got up and walked around, clustering in small group conversations. Flynn stood there talking to a couple of people. Waiting for him, Slater got up and arched his back, then rotated his shoulders. Dani came over and touched Slater's arm.

"I'm glad you're coming back," she said.

"Like Gwen said, it works."

"Are you already working the thirteenth step with Wheels?"

"I value Wheels for his car," Slater said. "Not for his step work."

Dani giggled. "It just seems like you two got awfully chummy awfully quick."

Flynn turned to them and greeted Dani, then eyed Slater. "I'm ready to go."

Gwen stepped over to them, a smile on her face. "Gentlemen."

Slater glanced over his shoulder. "Where?"

She chuckled. "You're funny. Are you coming for fellowship?"

"We can't tonight," Flynn said. "But have fun."

As they walked out to the parking lot, he saw that it was nearly dark out, the gray of dusk fading to black.

"I overheard that other guy hit you up for a fellowship outing too," Slater said. "Is it because it's Saturday night, or they're just always social?"

"I think they're concerned about the thirteenth step." He sighed. "It doesn't really matter. Where do you want to eat?"

"I don't know. I'm sick of deep-fried."

"There's a pho place."

"Sold," Slater said.

They climbed in the GTO, and Flynn drove to the place, and they got a table by the wall. Once they got into the food, Flynn gestured with his chopsticks.

"So are you sleeping at my place tonight?"

"I want to," Slater said. "Unless you've got another date."

"I'm not that guy."

"You could be. With absolutely zero effort."

Flynn laughed. "You think I'm hot."

"It's not an opinion. It's objectively true. You're a snack, son."

"Somebody told me I was a Mojave 11. I asked Monta, and she said in LA I'd be an 8. In WeHo maybe a 6."

"I'm not sure grading yourself like a box of apples is all that helpful," Slater said, pushing his bowl aside. "It's simpler than that. You're a smoke-show. Lean into it."

"People who think they're hot tend to act entitled."

"You don't need to do that. Just be content with the hotness. Not being a dick makes you even hotter."

Flynn watched him for a moment. "Who are you, man?"

"I gave you my business card."

"You know what I mean."

———

AFTER THEY'D EATEN, FLYNN drove them to his place. Once he'd bolted the door, he stepped close, and kissed Slater, and nibbled his ear.

"Are you not getting tired of this?" Flynn said.

"That never happens."

Flynn stepped back, a wry grin on his face, and unbuckled his belt. Ditching his jacket and then his shirt, Slater stooped to untie his boots.

"Leave the jeans on," Flynn said.

"You like the look?"

Naked now, he stepped close, and holding his gaze, unbuckled Slater's belt, and pulled his fly open. He pushed him toward the bed, and Slater stretched out on his back. Flynn was already hard, and straddled him, and pulled out his junk. Lowering his weight onto Slater's body, he savaged his neck and his face. Eventually he pulled up.

"Can I ride you?"

"Get a condom," Slater said.

He reached for the bedside drawer, and pulled one out, and spent a minute stroking Slater, and kissing him, until he was rock hard. Slater didn't mind somebody else doing most of the work, and this guy was into it.

Flynn rolled the condom on him, then shifted position and sank onto him, grimacing and biting his lower lip. Eventually he settled into a rhythm, rocking back and forth, massaging Slater's pecs. Caressing his torso, Slater stroked his cock with the rhythm of his movement. When Flynn came, yelping and craning his head back, it sent him over too, and he thrust up into him.

Eventually Flynn climbed off and stretched out. His breathing quickly sank into the rhythm of sleep. Slater couldn't do that himself, not yet. Rising, he tossed the condom in the trash, and buttoned his fly, and pulled on his shirt.

"Are you going somewhere?" Flynn said.

"I'll be back."

He'd brought clean clothes this time, but not booze, and in the melee on Two-Mile Road he'd forgotten his bottle in Jason's saddlebags, along with his toothbrush and his laundry. Stepping out of the casita, he climbed into Pike's rig, and drove to a liquor store, and found a pint of cheap bourbon.

There was a snack aisle, and he walked the length of it, finding some toiletries at the end. He grabbed a bottle of mouthwash. That would cover the smell of the sauce.

If Flynn figured out that he was boozing, it would initiate some unpleasant twelve-step activity—an intervention, maybe, or at minimum a lecture. No way was he going to get into that.

Once he'd pulled into the yard at Flynn's, he killed the engine, and sat in the dark, looking at the warm light glowing through the curtains of the casita. Cracking the pint, he guzzled his nightly ration, coughing a little, and relished the heady burn. It had been a long day. He took another snort, then capped the bottle and tucked it in the back seat. He could feel the delicious warmth in the pit of his stomach.

Opening the mouthwash, he swished his mouth with it, then cracked the door open to spit it out on the dirt. His tongue felt tingly from the minty stuff. Thinking about it, this was exactly the behavior that people in the meetings had been talking about. Hiding their drug use, keeping secrets about it, telling lies. Was he really that freaking boring? Was he just another junkie?

"Damn it," he muttered, and climbed out. Inside he found Flynn awake, propped up in bed, looking at a sheaf of paper in a manila folder.

His brow furrowed as he looked up. "Where did you go?"

"Basic hygiene." He held up the bottle of mouthwash.

"I'm reading about Ferret. This is really stomach-churning."

"Is that the autopsy report? You went into my satchel." He raised his voice. "What the fuck?"

"You did leave it here."

"That was a dick move."

"Settle down." Flynn folded it closed. "It feels weird to see my name on this."

"Did you see the photo of the defect in Ferret's eye?"

"I remember he had that. I always wondered whether he could see normally or not. I never asked him about it though. Why did they photograph it up close?"

"Because it was distinctive, dead boy." Slater pulled his shirt off, then his boots and his jeans, and climbed in the bed with him.

Flynn killed the light then shifted close. "What time do you start at the store tomorrow?"

"I'm not even sure. I think it's ten or eleven."

"Have you never had an hourly job before? The shop opens at ten."

"I guess I'll swing by around then."

Flynn laughed and shoved an arm under his neck. "You should set an intention to wake up in your dreams tonight."

"How do you do that?"

"Just say it to yourself. 'I'm going to wake up in my dream.'"

"What about setting up one of those mile markers?"

"You mean a checkpoint. The easiest one is to read something, then look away, then try to read it again. If it's different, or you can't reread it, you know you're dreaming."

"And what's the benefit of doing this?" Slater said.

"Our minds are limited by focusing too much on this reality. The dream state is less limited. You can achieve a lot more. Focusing too hard on the waking world is like wearing blinders."

"Focusing on the dream world isn't going to pay my phone bill."

"That's like somebody who says 'I'm not going to change my oil because it's expensive.' You let it go long enough and it'll cost you a lot more."

"You drive a car that doesn't even have a crankcase."

Flynn chuckled. "The dream world is like the staging area for the waking world. You try things out. Act out scenarios to see how they might work. Then you bring one version into waking reality. If you can get more aware of what's happening in the dream state, maybe you can make the waking world more effective. More in line with what you want."

"It sounds like I'd have to grind all night in addition to grinding all fricking day," Slater said. "Can't I just sleep?"

"Just try it out. See what happens."

Slater took a breath. This guy was a handful.

———◆———

IT WAS STILL NIGHT when Slater woke to a hazy face looming over him in the dark. He grabbed at the throat.

"The fuck are you?"

A hand grabbed at his wrist and pulled him off.

"Stop it. You know me. What are you dreaming about right now?"

He did remember this guy. "A bowl," he said, his tongue thick. "A soup bowl. But it's not for soup."

Flynn chuckled. "Go back to sleep."

TWENTY

T WAS LIGHT OUT when Slater woke, roused by the sound of metal utensils and crockery. Someone was doing something in a kitchen. He gazed idly out the window as his mind swam up to consciousness. That palo verde was filling out, its flowers vibrant yellow. Desert flora was intense like that. The flowers were huge. It had to be that hybrid for landscaping, not the one that was native to the Sonoran Desert.

Slater remembered where he was, and sat up, and rubbed his eyes. Flynn stepped around from the kitchen and grinned at him.

"You're awake." He handed him a mug, and slurped at the other one, then climbed onto the bed. "Do you remember that I woke you last night?"

He sat back and sipped at the java. It was strong and tasty. "Now that you say it, yeah, I do."

"You were so out of it. You didn't know what planet you were on. I thought you were going to merc me."

"Why did you wake me up?"

"To ask you what you were dreaming about."

"What did I say?"

"You were dreaming about a soup bowl." Flynn chuckled.

He thought about it. "Not a soup bowl. One of those plates with a recessed part in the middle." He gestured with a finger to outline the shape. "Like a flat bowl. You can put soup in it, or pasta."

"I know what you mean." He grabbed his phone and tapped at it, then turned the screen toward him.

Slater peered at the image. "That's it. The plate of my dreams."

"It's called a rimmed deep plate, or a soup plate."

"It was more than that. Part of some process. Not only an object. The plate is just what was at the surface."

"It's so great that you remember that." Flynn set his phone down. "The dream world can't be translated directly into the waking world. In the field they say it's ineffable. You can't describe it in words, so you need symbols. An intermediary language."

"So what does the soup plate symbolize?"

"What does it mean to you?"

"You sound like a freaking shrink right now," Slater said.

He sat back. "Well, I had some success last night. I dreamed I was in Union Station. Do you know the part that used to be the ticket hall?"

"Sure."

"It was full of cars. Chockablock, like when they do stacked parking. I was looking for someone, walking between the rows. I was able to get lucid for a minute."

"What did you do when you were lucid?"

"I tried to remember the place," Flynn said, "and study it. I knew I was dreaming because I read the sign on the wall, and I couldn't read it the second time I looked."

"What did it say?"

He frowned. "I can't even remember now."

"Were you able to manipulate the dream?"

"One of the techniques is to try to change the lighting. Like flip on a light switch, or turn up a dimmer. I found a wall switch, but it was blank, so I couldn't change it."

"Why not?" Slater said. "Dreams are so malleable. Couldn't you just will it to happen?"

"I think that kind of interaction is locked in a deeper part of my mind. To get to the next level, I have to get through that."

Slater looked at his phone. "I need to get up."

Draining his mug, he rolled out of bed, and washed up, and got dressed. Flynn was still in bed with his coffee, looking at his phone.

"You said Knox was a Jesus freak. Does he work Sundays?"

Flynn met his gaze. "He'll be there."

As he pulled on his jacket, he felt it to make sure Svetlana's jammer was still in the pocket, and walked out to Pike's car.

The diner was dark when he pulled up in front, and the hours posted in the door said it didn't open until the afternoon on Sunday. There was a supermarket in the same strip mall, and that was open. He went in and bought some apples and bananas, and ate them on the drive to Twentynine.

His phone said it wasn't quite ten when he pulled up at the thrift store, and when he walked up, he found the front door locked. He pounded on the glass with the heel of his fist, then cupped his hands to peer inside. The lights were on. He walked around back and tried the door. It was locked, and he pounded on it too.

The sound of movement came from inside, so he stepped back, and the door flew open. Knox was standing there, a hand on the crash bar. He looked different—his halo of dark hair was oiled and combed, and he was wearing a dark-blue suit with a pastel plaid shirt. The look he was working was years out of date, but maybe it was appropriate where he was going. He had on another pair of ostrich-leather boots, these ones in powder blue.

"Was that you banging on the front door too?" Knox said, scowling at him.

"I don't have the key. If you want me to work, you actually have to let me in."

"Go on." Knox waved him inside. "You can open up."

"Where's Luanne?"

"She'll be in after church."

Slater raised his eyebrows. "Don't you go?"

"I go to a real church. Hers is one of those misguided ones. Like those Catholics you're so fond of." He paused in his office doorway. "I'm headed there soon. You'll be on your own for an hour or two."

"I'm sure I can handle it," he said, and walked away.

"Hold up," Knox called to him.

When Slater went back to his office door, Knox handed him a pair of keys on a ring.

"That's the front and back doors. In case you have to leave when you're here on your own." He held his gaze. "Don't leave."

"Whatever you say, boss."

Tucking the keys into the pocket of his jeans, he hung his jacket in one of the lockers, then walked to the front of the store. The sickly sweet smell seemed muted today. Maybe he was getting used to it.

He unlocked the deadbolt on the door, then did a circuit of the floor. Just a few things needed to be picked up. Luanne must have done most of it yesterday.

Slater was among the clothing racks rehanging a shirt when Knox walked in, and jabbed a thumb toward the stock room.

"I'm going to church."

"OK."

"My daughter is doing a reading."

Slater frowned. "You don't want to miss that."

Why was the dude talking to him about it? It felt like he didn't really want to go.

"Do you have kids?" Knox said.

He waved a hand. "I'd only damage them. There's enough misery in the world."

"My daughter is really good at math, and my son is really interested in fashion."

"You say that like it's a bad thing."

Knox waved an arm. "They'd be a lot happier if it was the other way around."

"You mean you'd be happier. I bet if you let them be who they are, they'll be just fine."

"That's not how the world works, John."

"Aren't you going to be late for church?"

He straightened up. "I'll pray for you."

Slater frowned. "Don't waste your time. I'm not super-stitious."

Turning toward the stock room, he scoffed. Slater heard the back door slam. He walked to the till, and found a Sharpie, and wrote on a piece of cardboard: BACK IN 15. Once he'd taped the sign inside the glass of the front door, he flipped the bolt to lock it.

He strode to the stock room and pushed the crash bar to open the back door. The Wrangler was gone. Pulling the door closed, he went to his locker and fished Svetlana's jammer from his jacket pocket. The green plastic box looked innocuous, considering what it was capable of. He pulled out the prongs and felt them lock into place. A lit-tle LED lamp between them flashed green, just once, and stayed dark.

With the device in hand, he went into Knox's office.

The fact that the guy hadn't even closed the door wasn't encouraging—it meant he didn't likely have anything valuable or private inside. But he had to look.

Slater eyed the camera on the shelf. Just as Svetlana had promised, an orange light slowly strobed on the front. It had been kicked offline. Setting the jammer on the desk, he went over to the safe and tried the handle. It was locked, of course. No way could he get into that without tools.

Sitting in Knox's desk chair, he opened the laptop. It was password protected. He wasn't going to get into that either without help. He folded it closed and then rolled open the desk drawers, one at a time. There was mostly stationery, and grubby office tools that someone had probably donated—an electric pencil sharpener, an antique hole punch, an actual dip pen. In the bottom drawer was a trio of skin magazines, rumpled glossy pages with images of naked women. It wasn't overly raunchy stuff, but a religious nut never would have bought these. Someone had donated them. They looked thoroughly and repeatedly perused. Slater set them back in the drawer and absently wiped his fingers on his jeans.

Next he swiveled to the file cabinet. It looked old, and it didn't have a lock. Rolling open the upper drawer, he rapidly flicked through the paperwork. This was all bills, and tax stuff, and bank statements. In the lower drawer was more of the same, but then he found a folder labeled WHOLESALE. It was a thick stack of invoices issued by Retread Me. Slater spent a minute looking through them.

Every invoice was for a different customer. Some had a business name and an address, and others only a personal name. The ones with addresses were all over Cali, but mostly in LA and behind the Orange curtain. The business names implied they were retailers.

The weird thing was that the only line item on all of them was "used clothing," but in every instance the dollar amount was a huge round number. The smallest was four grand, lots of them were six or eight grand, and some as high as fifteen.

Maybe Knox was reselling some primo high-fashion couture that people donated. But these numbers implied there had to be a lot of it. With the regular schmattes hanging on the racks, even if he was selling them retail, he'd need to move a thousand pieces to invoice somebody for eight grand. It just didn't wash. This wasn't about the thrift store's inventory. Something else was going on.

He spent a minute photographing a stack of the invoices, flipping through them one after another. Eventually he heard pounding at the front door. Shuffling all the paper into the folder, he put it back where he'd found it, then rolled the drawer closed.

Grabbing the jammer, he walked out, and as he was crossing the shop, folded the prongs down to switch it off, then tucked it in his pocket. He pulled his sign down as he unlocked the front door.

A curvy woman stood outside, scowling at him. "You're not supposed to be closed."

"We're not closed," Slater said. "Come on in and savor the secondhand interesting things."

"It's hot out there," she said as she walked past him, as if that was his fault, and headed into the women's section.

Stepping behind the counter, he swiped through the photos he'd just taken of the invoices. Most of them were legible. He sent a link for the images to Andy, then sent him a text:

> What do these businesses have in common? They're not really buying used clothing. What are they really paying for?

As he tucked his phone away, a customer walked in. She was wearing a stretchy top and had smoker's wrinkles, her gray hair bound tightly behind her head. She greeted him as she went by. Walking into the men's section, Slater picked up some stuff from the floor and rehung it. When he heard the bell ding at the counter, he headed over to ring up the sale, and watched the woman walk out, happy with her purchases.

His phone had buzzed in his pants a while ago, and he pulled it out to check. It was a text from Andy:

I'll look into it.

He glanced to the door as a woman stepped inside, then had to do a double-take. Most of the customers who came in looked local, and none of them were visibly afflu-ent, but this one was different. Maybe still in her twen-ties, she was working a look: cut-off jeans and an airy print shirt, a floppy hat, and high-top leather boots.

The boots were actually appropriate for walking around in the desert brush, but that particular pair had never seen the backcountry, or even a dirt road. Her makeup looked too complicated and precise for a day in the wilderness. Ignoring him, she walked past the counter into the store.

On his phone he looked through more of Knox's invoices. A couple of the buyers sounded like shoe stores, and one of them was in LA, on Melrose Avenue. He knew that stretch was about trendy retail fashion. Andy was good at this kind of analysis. The guy would come up with something he wasn't able to see.

Slater slid his phone into his jeans as the woman in the floppy hat approached.

"Can you tell me about these belts?" She set them on the counter. "They're the same. Were there a lot of them before?"

"I'm not sure. I haven't worked here very long."

She made her eyes wide. "You seriously don't know the inventory in your store?" Picking up the belts, she looked them over. "I can't really make this part of my look if a bunch of basic people are running around wearing it."

Slater put his hands on his hips. "You're looking for one-of-a-kind pieces."

"That's why I come out to the middle of nowhere."

"And you want stuff that's cheap but not basic."

"That's why I come to thrift stores, Einstein." She huffed. "You know what—I don't want these anyway. They're too dark to show well on video." She set them on the counter again.

"You're an influencer."

She smiled. "You've seen my work."

"You definitely seem familiar."

She dug a business card out of her hip pocket and set it on the counter. "Just scan the QR code. You can watch all my videos, and see how I use my instrument."

Slater glanced at it. It bore no text, just the broken mosaic square of the inscrutable code. When he flipped it over, the back was blank. He eyed her. "What kind of music do you play?"

She frowned. "My instrument is my body." She gestured up and down her torso. "Was that not clear?"

As she walked away, back toward the clothes racks, he dropped the card in the trash.

The impatient customer who'd banged on the door came to the register with half a dozen pieces. She seemed calmer now that she'd been able to shop. He started to ring it up.

"Can I get a discount because you kept me waiting out in the hot sun?" she said.

"Why not?" He lifted one of the shirts. "How about I comp this one?"

"I appreciate that."

He held up a long skirt that was the deep red-purple of amaranth flowers. It seemed to have an outsize gap in it. He pulled up the flap of fabric. "I'll comp this one too. It looks damaged."

"It's a slit skirt. It's supposed to look like that."

"Lucky for you, it's also free."

After she'd paid and walked out, he rolled his neck, then took a deep breath.

TWENTY-ONE

A FEW MINUTES LATER, THE influencer came to the counter with a straw hat in hand.

"How much is this?" she said. "It's not tagged."

"It's two ninety-nine," Slater said.

"Great deal." She set it on the counter. "The sign says most stuff is eight bucks."

"No, I mean two hundred ninety-nine. You don't recognize the designer?"

She frowned. "Who is it?"

"I'm not in the education department, toots. If you don't know what you're looking at, you should probably put it back. Leave it for someone who's better informed." He slid the hat away from her, closer to the cash register.

She gasped. "You can't keep this from me. It was on the shelf."

Slater folded his arms. "Like I said, it's two ninety-nine."

"I don't pay retail. I'll give you fifty for it, plus exposure on my social media channels."

"I don't actually need exposure." He pursed his lips for a moment. "You know what? You seem savvy." He glanced toward the back of the store and lowered his voice. "One fifty, final offer, cash only. And I can't give you a receipt. My boss would kill me for letting it go that cheap."

"Done." She dug in her bag and produced the cash. Setting her own hat on the counter, she put the straw one on her head. "Thanks, sucker."

Slater watched her walk out, then tapped 10 into the register, and put a sawbuck in the cash drawer, and pocketed the rest. He didn't need to be running a clip joint, but it wasn't really thievery. More like a tax on hubris. Knox got his eight bucks, and the customer left happy. Value was subjective anyway.

Grabbing the floppy hat and the belts she'd dumped, he carried them over to the racks, and put the hat on a shelf with an array of others. As he was hanging up the belts, Knox stepped out of the stock room and called to him.

"I'm back."

Slater waved a hand in greeting, then picked up a couple of shirts from the floor. Someone dinged the bell at the till, and he walked back to the counter and rang up the sale.

As he was running her credit card, a guy stepped in the front door, wearing running shorts and a gray hoodie, a red bandana over his face. People who were worried about viruses usually wore medical masks. Maybe the bandana was for the dust.

He handed the customer her credit card, and she gathered up the stuff she'd bought and walked out. The man in the bandana was standing near the entrance, looking at the display of table lamps. His chest was heaving—he was breathing hard. Something about this guy made the hair on his neck stand up.

"Hey," Slater called to him. "No face coverings in the store."

He didn't pull down the bandana, but stepped toward the counter, and pulled out a blade. It had a thick hilt.

That wasn't for camping. It was a weapon. Slater stood up straighter and instinctively flashed his palms.

"Don't move," the guy growled, and waggled the blade. "Give me the cash."

"I can't do both. If you want me to get the cash, I'm going to have to move."

"Give me the cash," he shouted.

Slater took a slow step, and opened the register drawer, and lifted out the cash tray.

"Give me that."

"Hold your horses. I keep the big bills in the back."

Setting the tray on the shelf behind him, he leaned down, and reached into the drawer, and grabbed the heater. Turning, he leveled it at him.

"What the hell? Where's the big bills?"

"I lied about those, babe."

He growled in frustration, then waved the knife. "You're not going to shoot me. Your finger isn't even on the trigger."

Raising his arm to aim straight up, Slater fired. The deafening blast came with the simultaneous metallic *plink* of the bullet punching through metal. He was glad the thing was actually loaded.

The guy ducked a few inches and froze. At the same time came the clatter of the blade hitting the concrete floor. Slater could see a dark stain spreading on the front of his shorts.

Slater waggled the handgun. "Are you going to wait around for the cops, or are you going to spread out? Go on, get the fuck out of here."

His own voice sounded weird, like he was underwater. The gunshot had messed up his hearing. Bandana turned, and hustled toward the door, and shoved his way outside.

"Idiot," Slater muttered, and pulled out his hankie to wipe his prints off the heater, then tucked it in the drawer.

As he set the cash tray in, he worked his jaw to unclog his ears.

Knox strode up from the back. "What the heck was that?"

He rolled the drawer closed. "A guy pulled a knife on me. He wanted me to empty the till. I popped one off to encourage him to move along. He didn't get anything."

"You shot at him?"

"I shot at the ceiling."

Knox looked up. "What the heck is wrong with you? I'll have to get a roofer out here now. It'll be summer monsoon before you know it."

"Dude," he said intently. "You didn't get robbed today. You're welcome."

"You brought a gun to work with you? Into my store?"

"It's your rod, boss, not mine."

"You fired the .45?" Knox demanded. "How did you know about it?"

"It's sitting in the cash drawer. That makes it pretty hard to miss."

He watched him for a moment. "Did you get a look at his face?"

"He was wearing a bandana over it."

Knox briefly looked toward the door. "He just took off?"

"Not before he dropped his knife." Slater stepped around the counter, and picked it up, and looked it over, then handed it to Knox. "Any blade this long is totally illegal."

"I know that. It means I can't sell it in here." Holding the handle with two fingers, as if it might be contaminated, Knox let the point dangle, and looked at the floor. "Did he spill his soda or something?"

"He pissed himself when I fired that round."

"Well, that's nasty." He wrinkled his nose.

"Are you going to report it?"

"I'm not, and neither are you. Don't call anybody. Just forget it happened."

"That suits me."

"You need to mop that up," Knox said, gesturing to the puddle before he walked away.

As Slater went back behind the counter, a woman walked in the front door, a red shirt stretched over her curvy frame, and stepped toward him. "I heard a gunshot."

"It did kind of sound like that," Slater said. "Some burnout dropped a bottle of soda. It was loud." He leaned over the counter and pointed to the puddle on the concrete.

She glanced down. "I could have sworn it was a shot. I live out east. In Wonder Valley. I hear gunfire a lot."

"The glass bottom must have hit just right." He puffed out his cheeks and mimed an explosion with his hands.

"I haven't seen you here before."

"I'm new. The name's John. Are you a regular?"

"Nancy. I work next door. Is Knox around?"

"He's in the stock room. You can go on back."

"We're not really what you'd call friendly." She raised her eyebrows. "Good luck, John."

He watched her walk out, and checked his phone. There was a text from Andy:

> At first glance they're all skate shops and shoe stores. Some of the personal names show up in that world too. Maybe Retread Me is selling high-end kicks? Lots of those cost several grand. I'll dig some more.

A while later Knox walked up. "I need you to load a truck." He waved for him to follow.

They pushed through the swinging doors into the stock room. The back door was propped open, with bright daylight flooding in. Slater could see the side of a white vehicle parked outside. A guy stepped in the doorway and greeted them. He had a weathered face, and thick black hair, and he was buff, wearing a pair of tight chinos. The guy was totally fuckable.

"Dizon, this is John," Knox said. "He'll load up for you."

"Let me open the van." The guy stepped out.

Knox held up a finger, watching him go, then stepped close to Slater and lowered his voice to just above a whisper.

"Put all the boxes in his truck except one. It has a pen mark on the side. A blue squiggle. Try to hold it back without him noticing."

As Knox went into his office, Dizon paused in the doorway. "Do you need a hand?"

"I have to do it myself," Slater said. "Insurance liability."

He waved and stepped outside.

Looking at the stack, he saw there were twelve boxes in all. He picked one up. It wasn't heavy, so he set it down and lifted two at once. Neither one had a pen mark on it. He carried them to the back door and into the daylight. The van was parked with its side door right here, and he loaded them in, sliding them against the bulkhead.

He grabbed two more and loaded them, then on the next trip saw the pen mark. Dizon was still outside. Slater lifted the box, and set it up on top of the blue lockers, then grabbed more of the boxes and went outside. Eventually they were all in the van, and he rolled the side door closed.

Dizon stepped around from the driver's side. "That's all ninety-six?"

"I was counting cartons," Slater said, "not what's in them. There were twelve."

"That sounds right." Dizon went inside, and over to Knox's office.

Slater walked through the swinging doors into the shop. A few minutes later, Knox came out to the register.

"Did it work?"

"He didn't notice the missing box," Slater said. "I'm sure you know that already. I left it in back. On top of the lockers."

He chuckled. "You're not worried about cheating the guy?"

"Is that what happened?" He scoffed. "You cheated him, not me. I'm working for you."

"Go pull it down."

Walking into the back, Slater grabbed the box and set it on the floor. Apart from the blue pen mark, it was pristine, and sealed with packing tape. He glanced into the store. Knox hadn't followed him back here, and he wasn't in sight, but his voice was audible, somewhere up front. A customer must have waylaid him.

Pulling off the packing tape, Slater folded back the carton's flaps. Inside were shoeboxes. He pulled one out and lifted the lid. Andy's insight was right—it was a pair of fugly tennis shoes. Digging out his phone, he snapped a photo of them, then closed up the carton and moved it to where the stack of them had been.

As he walked into the shop, he saw that Knox was chatting with a woman, the pair of them standing amid the clothes racks. When he got to the counter, he sent the photo to Andy with a text:

Are these in that several-grand price range?

Knox stepped over to the register, a weird grin on his face.

"How would you feel about a little extra work off-site? You'd have to keep it quiet."

"That means it's not on the level. It depends on how likely it is that I'll wind up in the hoosegow," Slater said.

"That won't happen."

"I can't even consider it unless I know exactly what I'm in for."

He stepped back as a guy piled a couple of shirts on the counter, and waited while Slater rang him up. When the guy left, Knox spoke again.

"You know there's nobody in most of the Mojave. It's empty godforsaken sand."

Slater took a breath. The desert was a wide array of complex fragile ecosystems, with a riot of flora and fauna. There were major political battles over preserving them and regular skirmishes over water rights and mining claims and solar power plants. But he didn't need to point that out.

"OK," Slater said.

"There's no people, but there's trains."

"I know there's a rail line at Amboy, and one farther north at Kelso."

"Those places aren't even towns. There's nobody in them. A fudge-ton of stuff rolls from the ports in LA to the rest of the country. Dozens of trains every day loaded with shipping containers."

He folded his arms. "That makes sense."

"The trains are two miles long," Knox said, "and there's only one person on board. Right up front in one of the engines. So if something falls off the back of the train, nobody's going to see it because it's literally miles away."

Slater narrowed his eyes. "Are you talking about a damn train robbery?"

"That's not what it is. If somebody leaves valuable stuff unsecured, why shouldn't I help myself?"

"Have you done this before?"

"I know what I'm doing," Knox said. "I've seen enough of you to know you're no stranger to this kind of thing."

"You mean I'm just crooked enough to rob a train."

"It's not robbery. It's liberating unprotected cargo from a careless handler."

"Explain how the job works."

"We'll do that on the way out there. It's a long drive."

Slater shook his head. "Not good enough. I need to know the risk involved. The broad strokes, at least. Do you disable the train, or do you do it while it's rolling?"

"I've done a lot of research on this, John, and I have experience. There's a good chance it's going to happen soon. Can I count on you?"

"Only if I get way more details."

Knox huffed and stood up straighter. "In time. Can you close up later? I've got family stuff to do today. Did I tell you Luanne called in sick?"

"I wondered where she was. Sure, I can close up."

Knox walked toward the stock room, and a few minutes later, Slater heard the back door slam. A customer came to the register, and once she'd walked out with her newly acquired secondhand interesting things, he scanned the store. Nobody was in here. It was still hours until the posted closing time, but that wasn't his problem. He flipped the bolt on the front door, then went out the back way, and climbed into Pike's SUV, and headed for LA.

TWENTY-TWO

T HE HIGHWAY WASN'T ANY busier than usual, but once Slater was down in the Coachella Valley and on the freeway, he remembered there was traffic coming back from the deserts on Sunday. But it only slowed down a few times, and he skipped some of it closer to the metropolis using the express lanes. As he exited the freeway in his neighborhood, he saw a jacaranda that was starting to flower, an airy riot of bright purple floating above the street. It felt early for that, but it had been warm.

When he pulled to the curb in front of his house, it was still daylight out, the sun low in the west. He grabbed his jacket and his satchel from the back seat.

Upstairs he found Pike lounging on the sofa, with music on, reading a book. It was the one Doris had given him.

"How's *The Razor's Edge?*"

Pike set the book on the coffee table and got up. "Doris was right. It's engaging."

Embracing him, Slater ran his hands on his back, and savored the warmth of his body, and lingered in a kiss.

When he pulled away, he reached for the book.

"So chumps are getting slashed left and right?"

"It's not that kind of razor." Pike chuckled. "More like an indictment of the way we do things. Materialism and snobbery."

"I get it. They have it, and we don't."

"Isn't this house paid off? That actually makes you one of the haves."

"It doesn't feel like it," Slater said. "I've been working retail for the last few days. These dogs are barking."

Pike kissed him again, and when he pulled back, Slater dug out his car key.

"Your wheels are back and intact. I even gassed it up. I'd tell you there's no new scratches on it, but that would be meaningless. There's so many there's no way to know that none of them are new."

"You gave the Sportster back?"

"Jason said he'd sorted out his issues."

Pike's brow furrowed, and he touched Slater's cheek. "What happened here?"

"One of Jason's associates got a little pushy."

"It's like trouble finds you. It swirls around you, and sticks to you. Like the jacaranda blossoms messing up the street."

Pike mouthed his neck, and Slater tilted his head back, relishing the intensity of it.

"Wait till I stick you." He pressed his nose into his hair. "I'm going to mess you up. Rock-hard and deep inside you. I'm going to make you scream."

"Big talk," Pike murmured.

He pulled back, and met his gaze, and raised his voice. "I'm not playing around. I am going to destroy you."

Pike chuckled. "I can't wait. Do you need to eat?"

They heated up leftovers in the kitchen, and carried them out to the deck, and sat at the patio table. It was starting to cool off at the end of the day, with golden sunlight on the hills and long shadows below.

"Are you back for good?" Pike said. "And what did you mean about working retail?"

"I have to go out there again in the morning." He set his fork down and told him about the last few days, about Flynn and Knox and the thrift store. "I think my target is robbing trains out in the desert."

"I know that happens," Pike said. "Where the rail lines are away from the highways it would be easy. They only have a couple of workers on board."

"This guy said the train crew is only one person now, and the trains are two miles long."

Pike pushed his plate away. "That would make them easy pickings. As long as they're not rolling too fast."

"I don't really care what happens to the trains. If the railroad couldn't afford to get robbed, they'd hire guards."

"That doesn't make it OK, but you're right. It's like shoplifting. Sometimes it's cheaper to let it happen than to pay more salaries to stop it. The railroads probably have some tech measures to deter it. Stronger locks, maybe."

"The thing is, I do care what happens to this dirtbag," Slater said. "He tried to put my client's ex in the frame. He got the guy so twisted up that he's legally dead."

"That's extreme," Pike said. "I can't believe you found the dead guy at a twelve-step meeting."

"I had to go to so damn many of them," Slater said. "I think I get it now. Why people go. It makes me think I'm resistant to it so that I can keep doing what I do. So that I don't have to be honest about it like those patsies are."

Pike tilted his head back and guffawed, and slapped the patio table, rattling the cutlery.

"Why is that funny?" he demanded.

"It's not. I'm just so happy to hear this. It sounds like a breakthrough."

Slater frowned. "I'm not going to go sit in those rooms, and I'm not going to quit drinking. So you can smash that pipe dream."

"The point is, you're thinking about it. That's freaking great."

"I don't really have a choice." He folded his arms. "I had to sit there and listen to those dopers."

"So what are you going to do about your case?"

"Ideally I want to bench Knox, and let Flynn get back to his life."

"The railroads have their own police. I know they'd be interested in a train robber."

"I can't just tell them about the guy," Slater said. "Nothing will happen. They're not going to investigate him because of a tip from some nobody."

"Maybe you can tip them off about when and where he's going to hit the trains, and they can intercept him."

"Even then, they'd just discount it as gossip. You're talking about corporate security guards? Are they armed?"

"They're real police," Pike said. "It's a quirk from the Old West. They work for the railroad companies, but they have full law enforcement powers. They can arrest and detain people, and they train in the same academies, and take the same oath. I know a railroad police guy in Albuquerque. I can talk to him. He might have some ideas for you."

Slater watched him for a moment. "That thing Doris said. That I married my father."

He laughed. "I'm not trying to baby you, forty-niner. I'm helping you out. But only if you want the help. It's just an introduction."

"It's probably worth talking to them."

Rising, Pike lifted the plates. "I'll do it at my desk."

Slater grabbed the other dishes, and followed him inside, through to the kitchen, and listened to Pike's footfalls descend the stairs. His phone had buzzed a minute ago, and he set the dishes on the counter, and pulled it out to check. It was a text from Andy:

That pair of shoes retails for 800 clams. But they're collectible, so the street value is 3G to 5G. There's more. Drop by.

Dialing his number, he held the phone to his ear and waited for Andy to pick up.

"I can't come over," he said. "What did you find out?"

"Several of those places are shady," Andy said. "A couple of them do pop-ups, but it's … more like they're moving around to evade oversight."

"What kind of oversight?"

"You can't run a store without a business license and … getting set up to pay sales tax. It takes a minute for the … city and the state to figure out who's not doing that. By that time they've … moved on."

"That's good intel. Anything else?"

"One of the shops is run by a guy who ran a … different business before," Andy said. "A few years ago he got charged with … receiving stolen property."

"So he's a fence. What kind of stolen property?"

"High-end accessories. Those designer purses and … belts that cost a few grand. Do you need more … detail on him?"

"That's enough," Slater said.

"Are you going to pay me?"

"Don't I always pay you?" He scoffed and hung up on him.

He was tired from the drive, and the food in his belly was making him groggy. He walked back into the big room and lay on his back in the middle of the broad empty floor. The hard wood surface felt good. It would get uncomfortable eventually, but right now he could feel it straightening out his back.

It made sense that Knox was selling to lowlifes. He was

a damn gonif—those invoices were about trying to make stolen goods appear legit. Keeping records like that meant the income looked clean. He could claim people donated the valuable stuff, not that he'd stolen it from shipping containers on a train.

<hr>

SOMETIME LATER PIKE'S VOICE made him start awake.

"What are you doing?"

He sat up and mumbled. "Just thinking."

It was dark out now, and Pike's frame was silhouetted in the light from the kitchen.

"Have you got enough room in here for that?"

"I can't believe Doris thinks we should fill this with furniture. How boring is that?"

Pike extended a hand and pulled him to his feet. "Let's sit."

Over at the lounge furniture, he turned on a lamp, and dropped into a chair, and Slater sat opposite on the sofa.

"You talked to the railroad po-po?"

"It turns out their station for the rail lines that run through that part of the Mojave is in Barstow," Pike said.

"That makes sense."

"If you can detour through there on your way back out, I can set up a meeting."

"I'm down for that," Slater said. "It'll have to be early."

"Let me text the guy." He spent a minute tapping at his phone, and eventually looked up. "Also, I looked at the resale value for the Pacer. There's definitely a market for them."

Slater frowned. "You really want that garage space freed up so you can get your EV."

"If you're going to sell it, why dawdle?"

"The most important part is to find someone who'll be a good steward for a fine automobile. I have to vet them."

"Maybe you can do that when they look at the car."

"There is somebody I wanted to show it to in the high desert," Slater said. "I'll do that tomorrow."

"You're going to drive the Pacer to Barstow and then Twentynine? There's a lot of miles between garages on those desert roads if you break down."

"Duarte says it's in top condition. Plus it's not that hot yet. It'll be fine."

Pike looked at his phone. "There it is. You have a meeting first thing. The railroad cop's name is Torres. I'll text you the address."

"It means you think I'm legit," Slater said.

His brow furrowed. "What are you talking about?"

"You wouldn't make the intro if you thought I was a flake, or if you thought I didn't have a real case."

"I know it's real. I've seen you work. From the day we met." He raised his eyebrows. "You stole a horse to come and rescue me."

"I rented that horse."

"And I didn't need rescuing. But you don't have to doubt my belief in you."

"Thanks, Pop."

Pike chuckled and stood up. "You've got an early morning, and there was talk of someone getting destroyed."

He followed him downstairs to the bedroom, and they both got undressed. Pike stretched out on the bed, stroking himself. Once Slater had ditched his jeans, he stepped over and climbed up, massaging his chest. Pike squeezed his cock.

"You're ready. I'm going to lie on my belly."

"So I have to do all the work," Slater said, and sat up as Pike turned over.

"You love it."

Grabbing the lube, he straddled his pelvis, and started to slowly press into him. Pike whimpered and shifted position, and he pressed deeper, lowering his weight onto him.

Shoving his arms under Pike's shoulders, he pulled himself close. He started to thrust, then built up to pounding him. Burying his nose in his hair, inhaling his heady scent, he came, and a minute later pulled back, and climbed off.

Prodding Pike to roll over, he shifted down the bed and took him into his mouth, massaging his belly and his chest. Pike ran a hand into his hair to guide him, and soon climaxed.

Slater rolled onto his back, listening to Pike's breaths gradually slow. He woke when Pike got up and padded to the shower. Forcing himself out of bed, he went upstairs and poured his ration into a tumbler. He couldn't afford to overdo it. There was a lot of driving to do tomorrow. Taking a gulp, he carried the glass over to the French doors and looked out at the dark hillside and the glittering city.

Maybe this was his inertia. Flynn's was being legally dead, and Slater's was slamming this rotgut, not willing to change anything. He drank to make everything else bearable. He probably needed to face up to that, the way Flynn and the saps in program were. It would be so easy to quit, just to put the glass in the sink and walk away. But that wasn't going to happen. Not now.

He slammed the rest of the heady elixir and went downstairs. Pike was getting into bed, and he climbed in next to him, and mouthed his neck.

"Why do you do this to me?" Slater murmured.

"Is the wet hair annoying?"

"It's you. You drive me crazy. You're so damn beautiful. I can't stand it."

Pike kissed him, and lingered in it, then stretched out.

"Do you remember your dreams?" Slater said.

"Sometimes. I don't write them down or anything."

"I told you my target does lucid dreaming."

"It might be fun if you could direct your dreams," Pike said, "and it would be great if you could short-circuit the nightmares."

"He says the dream world is like a staging area for waking reality."

"That idea is totally New Age. That you create reality yourself."

"Is it true?" Slater demanded.

He laughed. "How would I know? It's an interesting idea. Like the guy who took you into the backcountry. He thinks there's some other intelligence overlapping our world. I kind of get that. It feels like there's more going on than what we see."

"To me it all kind of sounds like somebody's religion."

"The difference is that the New Age is all about your own experience. You literally create your own reality. Religions have symbols and texts and priests to organize the world for you."

"The degenerate thrift store guy said he'd pray for me."

Pike groaned. "Small towns. It's Jesus and firearms."

"He's actually got a gat too."

"Apparently the way to spark lucid dreaming is to tell yourself you're going to wake up inside your dream."

Slater tapped his temple with a finger. "Done. Let's see what happens."

He hit the light on the bedside table, and in the darkness Pike wrapped an arm around his torso, and notched his knees behind Slater's. This was the best feeling there was.

———◆———

SLATER REALIZED HE WAS looking at his palm. He turned it over and looked at the back of his hand, then held up the other one. They looked symmetrical. Was this real? He needed to read something, he remembered, and looked around. He was standing on a boulder, so he checked the other side, then looked behind him, assessing the options for an alternate route. Zeke said there was always another way.

His phone, he remembered. There'd be text on his phone. He looked at the screen and read through it. It was hard to concentrate on the words. Something about Rupinder the Younger. But he couldn't retain it, couldn't absorb what it meant.

Looking away, he made sure his footing was stable. One wrong step and he'd tumble and bust his ass on the crumbly gritty pink granite. He was supposed to read it again, he remembered. He looked at his phone, but the text wasn't there anymore. With that, the whole thing slipped away.

TWENTY-THREE

THE ALARM ON SLATER'S phone buzzed on the bedside table, and he sat up to kill it before it woke Pike. It was still dark outside. This, he knew, was real. He got dressed in the low light filtering in from the street, then went upstairs to the kitchen and toasted half a bagel, not bothering to sit down to eat it. He munched on an apple too and then headed down to the garage.

At the back, past the cars, was his gear cabinet. It was built to look like a cheap sheet-metal office supply box, but it was really a gun safe, made of thick hardened steel, bolted to the floor, with a multipoint lock. Like Svetlana's Wi-Fi jammer, it looked innocuous, but it was more than it seemed. Hiding in plain sight. He didn't have any firearms but this was where he kept all the illicit tech he got from her.

Once he got it open, he unplugged a couple of vehicle trackers. Matte-black boxes about the size of a phone, they used local cell towers to calculate their position, so they didn't need an external antenna or a view of the sky, and he could plant them out of view under a vehicle. They had much longer battery life than anything that picked up the weaker GPS signals from space.

He tucked both of them into his satchel. The plan was still coalescing, but his vague intention was to plant one on Knox's stupid Wrangler. That way Slater could keep track of him if he did wind up helping him rob a train. The second one would be useful if Knox took a different vehicle on the job.

Pausing at the bulky red tool chest, he rolled open the drawer where he stuffed all the vehicle paperwork, and dug around, and found the title for the Pacer. He put that in his satchel too.

Hitting the button to roll up the garage door, he climbed into the Pacer, and set his satchel on the floor of the passenger side, and backed into the dark street. As he watched the garage door roll down, he shifted into Drive. He loved the sound of this beautiful beast's engine, smooth and light but not tinny or cheap.

The city was still quiet, and he headed east on the freeway, then north toward Barstow. As he started the ascent up the Cajon Pass, he realized he wasn't going to be speeding on this long incline. But the engine wasn't straining either. It could handle this, but it had to be at a steady sedate pace.

Rounding a curve, in the gray morning twilight he saw a freight train ascending the pass. The tracks weren't far away, and the string of double-stacked containers stretched as far as he could see. It made sense that the rail line paralleled the freeway. There weren't that many ways to get from the metropolis through the mountains and up into the desert.

The train was moving slow, even slower than the Pacer, and eventually he passed the engines with their bright lights. As he got farther up the grade he saw the back end of another train. Knox was right when he said there were a lot of them. There couldn't be more than twenty minutes between this one and the one behind it.

As he rolled through the empty desert north of Victorville the sky started to get lighter, and the pink glow on the horizon turned gold. When the sun finally broke into the sky, he killed the headlights and pulled on his sunglasses.

The diner where Pike had told him to meet the railroad cop was on the main drag, and when he rolled into the parking lot, sure enough there was a cop SUV parked out front. Painted as a prowl car, it had a light bar on top and the railroad's logo on the door.

When he walked inside, a guy in the dark navy uniform was crossing the floor, from the counter toward the booths along the side wall. His black Latin hair was slicked back, and he was beefy, with a great butt. Eminently fuckable, Slater decided.

Another uniform was parked in a booth, and the guy sat with her on the same side, leaving the opposite bench empty. They were waiting for him. The woman looked Anglo, he decided, as he walked over. Her brown hair was pulled back in a knot, and she was wearing a lot of eye makeup. As he stepped up, Slater read their name tags. The guy's said TORRES, and hers was SWIFT.

"I'm Ibáñez," he said.

Torres flashed a smile and introduced himself. "Sit down. This is Swift."

Slater slid in across from them and flipped his coffee cup over. Eyeing Swift, he tapped his own collar.

"You've got more bling than him. Are you the ranking officer?"

"I'm his CO, if that's what you're asking." Swift frowned. "How do you not see my rank?"

"Why would I care about what's on your damn uniform?" Slater said.

The server stepped up and poured coffee for him. "Something to eat?"

"Just the joe."

As she walked away, Swift spoke. "I'm confused. Are you not law enforcement?"

"Not even close."

"This request came through law enforcement." She picked up her phone and tapped at it. "Zebulon Pike."

"People just call him Pike." He lifted his cup. "We're embroiled in a multidimensional narrative complex."

Swift's eyes narrowed. "How nice for you. Why don't you tell us what you want?"

Slater slurped at the java. "I have a shortcut for you to catch a train robber."

"Who's going to rob a train?" Torres said.

"I can lay that all out, but to clarify, you need to catch him in the act, don't you? I can tell you in advance when it's going to happen. All you have to do is show up and snap on the cuffs."

"Why would we believe your info is valid?" Swift said.

"You can believe whatever you want. If you don't show up, he's going to get away with it. I'm pretty sure he's done it before."

"How are you involved?" she said.

"I'm stooging for the guy," Slater said. "I just started at his legit business, and now he wants me to help him rob a train. If you're not going to intervene, I'll blow him off. But if you want the bust, I'll lead you right to him."

Torres waved a hand. "When and where is this going to happen?"

"Soon. He hasn't told me specifically where yet, but it has to be out here somewhere. The guy is based in Twenty-nine Palms, so I'm thinking Amboy or Kelso."

"Those are two different lines," Swift said.

"I thought you policed both of them."

"The thing that makes the most sense is to intercept the suspect after the robbery," Torres said, "with the goods in hand, before he gets on the road. The company will document the pilfered containers at their transit point when they get unloaded, so we'll have that evidence when we need it. At this end we can just focus on the perp."

"Don't get ahead of yourself," Swift said, then eyed Slater. "No disrespect, but why should we help you?"

"Are you even listening?" Slater demanded. "I'm not asking for your help. I'm offering you a bust. Won't that get you a fat year-end bonus or something?"

"The thing is, I don't know you," she said.

Torres eyed her. "The captain in Albuquerque says Pike is OK. That means this guy is OK."

Swift heaved a sigh and folded her arms. "I guess we can hear you out."

"I'm going to need a yay or nay well before this goes down," Slater said. "I'm not going to help rob a train if you're not going to nail this knucklehead."

She raised her eyebrows. "We'll let you know."

"How many officers are you going to commit to this?" Slater slurped at his coffee and watched as they exchanged a look. "OK, how many of you are there at this station?"

Swift shifted in her seat. "We have a team."

"There's six of us," Torres said.

"So you can't really handle this kind of operation. You're actually wasting my time." He gestured to Torres. "You're wearing the sidearm and the badge and the fuck-me boots, but what do you even do all day?"

Torres furrowed his brow. "What about my boots?"

"We can handle it," Swift said. "If we need to, we can get local law enforcement to assist."

"It makes me think that if you do it, you'd be making the bust personally," Slater said.

Torres nodded. "That's likely."

"So when will you get your act together and decide what you're doing?"

"Once you give us the details," Swift said. "We need advance notice. As much as possible."

"I'll pass that along as soon as I know."

"We'll need a body count," she said, "and a description of all the vehicles, and a full rundown of the weapons."

"It's just going to be me and him, so I'm thinking one vehicle. I'll get the details on it. There won't be any weapons. If he wants to pack a rod, I'm going to bail."

"Good man," Torres said. "Those things aren't safe."

"You're wearing one."

He waved a hand. "That's different."

Slater scoffed. "How do I know you won't forget about this arrangement and throw me in the jug too?"

"There's enough people who know you're an informant," Torres said. "Both of us, and our captain in Albuquerque, and Zebulon Pike. Even if you get pinched, you won't slip through the cracks."

"I hope that's true. How can I contact you?"

"I'll give you my cell number."

Slater dug out his phone, and thumb-typed the number as Torres recited it, then texted the guy his name.

"I sent you a text," Slater said. "Can you check?"

He frowned. "Why?"

"To ensure that the lines of communication have been correctly established," Slater said intently. "I'm putting a lot of trust in you yahoos."

Torres pulled out his phone. "I see it. Slater is your first name?"

He sat back as the server set down two plates of food, pancakes and bacon and hash browns. Swift picked up her fork, shifting her focus to the grub.

Draining the last of his java, Slater jabbed a finger at each of them in turn. "Do not burn me on this." Rising, he walked toward the door.

"Oh, OK," Swift called after him. "Buh-bye, now."

Stepping into the bright daylight, he pulled on his sunglasses. It felt like amateur hour. These idiots should be thrilled to get such a juicy tip, but they were acting like he was inconveniencing them. They were more interested in their pancakes.

He paused next to the prowl car. If there were only six of them, they didn't likely have many of these. It might be useful to know where it was on game day. Glancing back at the restaurant, he saw that nobody inside would have a view of the vehicle. Nobody was in the parking lot either, and there was only intermittent traffic on the street.

Opening the Pacer, he fished a vehicle tracker out of his satchel, and wiped it down with his handkerchief. He walked around to the driver's side of the prowl car and squatted at the rear wheel well, holding the device with the hankie, and with a fingernail clicked on the recessed power switch along the side. Reaching in above the tire, he moved it over the rough surface. There was a satisfying tug as the magnetic ribs quickly found purchase.

Slater stood erect and glanced around. No one was watching him. He got in the Pacer and looked at his phone. The tracker was already showing up in Svetlana's app, with a green circle on the map for its estimated location. As he watched, the circle shrank a little, surrounding the diner and part of the road out front and a couple of nearby businesses.

He looked up the address of the railroad police. Their station was near the tracks along this main road. Firing up the engine, he drove over to it.

It was a squat utilitarian building in a dusty yard with a radio mast next to it. Parked beside the structure was another prowl car, a marked SUV with the railroad logo, the same as the one at the diner. If there were only six of them, this could be the other half of their entire fleet.

Slater rolled up next to the vehicle and looked around.

There were no windows on this side, and no cameras in view. He waited a few minutes to see if someone would notice him and step outside, but nothing happened.

Digging out the other tracker, he wiped it down with his hankie, then climbed out, and squatted beside the prowl car's wheel well, and planted it. As he stood up he tucked the hankie away and looked around again. Nobody was nearby, and he got back into the Pacer.

Spying on cops was risky, but he was taking a risk too, collaborating with Knox. He needed to have as much information as possible going into this.

TWENTY-FOUR

T HE DRIVE TO TWENTYNINE was through miles and
miles of the Mojave. Once in a while the landscape
was studded with Joshua trees, and in other places it
was just the creosote bushes. Everywhere had that idiosyncratic desert light and the craggy dark mountains always in
the distance.

It was mid-morning when Slater pulled into the pumps
at Rupinder the Younger's place. He gassed up the Pacer,
then stepped inside. Rupinder was working the till, and
smiled in recognition.

"It's the classic car guy."

"Can someone else mind the store for a minute?" Slater
said. "You should come outside."

Her brow furrowed. "Why?"

"Bring your driver's license."

She stepped into the back, and briefly spoke to someone, then followed him out. She was taller than he'd
thought. Until now he'd only seen her perched on the stool
behind the register.

"Oh, wow." Rupinder stopped and looked over the

Pacer. "Maroon and cream. It's so beautiful. You mentioned this, but you didn't tell me you actually had one."

Slater handed her the keys. "Take it for a spin."

"I'd love to. Are you coming with me?"

"I'll wait."

"You're very trusting," she said, "letting me drive away in your car."

It wasn't about trust. She needed to forge her own bond with the vehicle. He didn't need to be crowding up that space. But he didn't say that, and instead gestured to the store.

"If you don't come back, I can always burn down your place."

Her eyes narrowed. "Don't do that. I won't be long."

Rupinder climbed into the car and pulled out, not overrevving it. She knew how to handle the classic engine without it being explained. That was a good sign. He knew she'd be a worthy steward.

As the Pacer rolled away, he stepped out of the shade of the canopy over the gas pumps, into the bright sunlight, and pulled off his sunglasses. With his eyes closed, he turned his face to the sun, willing its blazing heat to energize him.

A few minutes later Rupinder returned and parked in a stall at the side of the store.

"It rides like a dream," she said, climbing out.

"I haven't had it for long, but my mechanic tells me the previous owner kept it in good shape."

She looked at the vehicle. "Thanks for letting me check it out."

"It's for sale."

"That's crazy. Why?"

"I already have a car that I've been neglecting. A '73 Continental."

"The Mark IV?"

"You know it."

"You're like a drug dealer," Rupinder said. "Bringing this here, and getting me to drive it." She lowered her voice. "Your first taste is free."

Slater chuckled. "The Pacer is the best dope ever."

"What do you want for it?"

"What are you driving now? I'm going to need wheels."

"You want to swap cars?"

"It depends on what you've got."

She gestured to a little black pickup, parked a few stalls down, along the side of the shop. "The '99 Frontier."

Slater stepped over to it. It was scratched and dented, but he liked that it was small, and that it only had one row of seats. Like Pike's rig, he could park this on the street and never worry about it getting jacked or sideswiped.

"It's not a classic quite yet," he said, "but it's close. How's it running?"

"Mechanically it's fine. Obviously it needs a paint job."

Slater met her gaze. "This rig plus fifteen grand and the Pacer is yours. I've got the pink slip with me."

She looked back at the Pacer. "You think it could be my everyday ride?"

"You're the only one who can decide that. I know you know the value in it, and I know you'll take care of it. If you couldn't handle it, I wouldn't be here."

She pursed her lips for a moment. "The Frontier plus ten grand."

"Normally I'd negotiate, but I want it to go to a good home. If you can sign over the Frontier, we can do this now."

Rupinder chuckled. "Come inside."

Stepping over to the Pacer, he grabbed his satchel and tossed some stuff from the glove box into it. He checked in the back seat, then lifted the hatchback to make sure there was nothing else he needed to keep.

Inside the shop, a guy with a heavy gray beard was

working the register, seated in front of the wall of tobacco products, and gave Slater the once-over as he walked in. He was dressed in the uniform of desert rats through the decades, in jeans and plaid, along with a dark-blue turban. This was a family business, and the guy was an elder, so he needed to greet him, Slater knew. He nodded and mumbled "Hello." Rupinder exchanged a few words with him in another language, then waved Slater into the cramped office behind the counter.

"My uncle," she said. "He's curious about what we're up to."

Slater sat adjacent at the little desk. It took a while to fill out the paperwork, and then Rupinder set up a bank transfer on her laptop.

"Do you want to check whether the money came through?" she said.

"I'm sure it will. If not, I know where to find you."

"If there's any hiccups, come and talk to me before you burn the place down."

"Deal." He gathered up the paperwork. "I'll need the keys."

She stood up. "Let me get my stuff out of it."

Outside, Rupinder opened the door of the pickup, and grabbed a grocery bag, and loaded all the stuff from the glove compartment into it. As she worked, Slater stepped over to the Pacer and put his palm on the roof.

"Good-bye, sweet prince. You've been good to me. I know you're in good hands now."

Eventually Rupinder slammed the door of the Frontier and handed him the keys. "I hope I've made the right decision."

"You can always sell it and buy another pickup." He raised his eyebrows. "But don't. It's too much fun."

She laughed. "That sounds like good advice."

"The former owner had a name for it," Slater said,

gesturing to the Pacer, "and gendered pronouns. Do you want to know what they were, or just start with a clean slate?"

"Of course I want to know."

"He called it Milton. *He* and *him*."

"Got it."

Climbing into the Frontier, Slater started the engine. It was high-revving, and caught right away, and sounded healthy. Backing out of the stall, he pulled onto the highway, forcing himself not to look back at the Pacer.

On the drive to the thrift store he got used to how the Frontier handled, how it responded, how it was geared. It didn't even need a wheel alignment. Even gearheads and serious car whacks tended to neglect that.

It felt like he'd been rolling for days, but it wasn't even opening time yet, and there were no vehicles parked at the store. Slater used the keys Knox had given him to go in the front door, and he left it unlocked, in case there were any early birds. There was lots of clothes on the floor. Rolling his shoulders to warm up, he set to work hanging things up. He didn't need Luanne to think he was slacking.

A few customers wandered in, and he rang up a string of sales as the morning wore on. At one point it got quiet, and he stepped out from the register to look around. Over by one of the wall mirrors a guy was holding a gray T-shirt to his chest. He looked buff, despite the baggy jeans, but he also looked awfully young.

Stepping closer, Slater called to him. "How old are you?"

He frowned. "Seventeen. Why?"

"No reason."

The guy held up the shirt, and a similar one in his other hand. "Do you know either of these bands?"

"The bands don't matter. Both those shirts are way too big for you." He walked over to the rack, and flipped through the T-shirts, and found a black one. "This is it."

"It looks small."

"It's exactly your size."

"You think? Can I try it on?"

Slater handed it to him. "Knock yourself out."

The guy pulled off his shirt, revealing his hairless torso, and pulled on the black T-shirt.

"It feels a little tight."

"It's long enough to tuck in," Slater said, "and it looks great. You've got the pecs. Why hide them?"

"I'm not really used to putting my body on display."

"It's like driving a nice car. Do you throw a sheet over it, or do you let people see it?"

"How much are these?"

"The one you're wearing is four dollars. The oversize band shirts are twelve."

"I need shorts for summer too."

Slater pointed him to a nearby rack, and they both flipped through the options. The guy pulled out a pair of baggy cargo shorts.

Slater held up a finger. "No."

"Why not?"

"They're so long they don't even qualify as shorts. Are you going to be working construction this summer?"

He frowned. "I'm going to Parker to float on the river."

"Then you don't need cargo shorts." He pulled out a pair of gray short shorts and handed them over. "These are better for the water."

Turning to the wall mirror, he held them up to his waist. "They seem a little sleazy."

"They're not sleazy unless you can see your butt cheek below the hem. Try them on."

Farther along the wall was a curtain on a rail that served as a changing booth. The guy went over and pulled the curtain, and came out a minute later wearing the gray shorts.

"I don't think they expose any of my butt."

"That means they're appropriate wherever shorts are appropriate."

"Do you think girls like guys in clothes like this?"

"I'd say they probably appreciate being able to preview the merch," Slater said. "And everybody is more attractive when they're comfortable in their clothes."

The guy scoffed and turned to the mirror, tugging at the front of the shorts. "How do you manage that?"

"You have to own it. Lean into it. Even if the clothes aren't totally comfortable, you have to make them look comfortable."

Watching himself in the mirror, he flexed his arms, showing his biceps. "I don't really have swagger."

"Being confident doesn't mean acting like a dick," Slater said. "It just means you don't focus on your clothes. Let other people focus on them."

He met his gaze in the mirror. "How do I not focus on the clothes?"

"Don't mess with them. Don't adjust the fit. Just own it. If you want to relate to women, lots of them understand that firsthand. Think about the stuff they have to wear."

Turning sideways, he looked at himself in the mirror. "So you think women like confidence, but not dick swagger."

"What do I know, man? I work in a thrift store."

The guy stepped back into the changing booth, and Slater walked up front. A minute later the guy set the gray shorts and the black T-shirt on the counter.

Tapping at the register, Slater said, "Eight bucks even."

"For both?"

"That specific shirt is four, and the shorts are four."

Nodding, he pulled out the cash. As he left, Luanne came in, walking past him.

"He looked happy," she said, approaching the counter.

"He's going to Parker to float the river this summer."

"Must be nice. How's business?"

Slater waved a hand. "People come, people go."

She chuckled and stepped behind the counter, picking up a little plastic box from the shelf. "I thought I'd lost these." She popped it open, revealing a jumble of colorful blobs of jelly. "I'd offer you one, but they're medicinal."

"THC or CBD?" Slater said.

"I'm not on weed, honey. They're for my arthritis." She popped one in her mouth.

"Do they work?"

"Not miraculously, but they help."

Knox appeared, dressed in pleated blue chinos and a plaid shirt, and stepped up to the counter. Pleats didn't really work when your waist was bigger than your hips, but Slater probably didn't need to point that out. He'd dispensed enough fashion advice today.

TWENTY-FIVE

"**S**LADE—I NEED YOU IN back," Knox said.

Slater followed him into the stock room and then his office. He noticed his shoes as Knox closed the door behind them. The were orange alligator leather, with square toes, and totally out of sync with the rest of his look.

Knox sat at his desk and waved him to the guest chair next to it. His eyes bright, the guy seemed antsy, swiveling in his chair like he'd had too much caffeine.

"The job is going to be tomorrow."

"What happens, exactly?" Slater said.

"It's simple. We drive out to the rail line, and remove some cartons from a sea can, and load them in the vehicle, and drive back."

"Who's we?"

"Just you and me, bud."

"What vehicle?"

"My Jeep," Knox said. "I saw you ride up on a motorcycle. That won't work."

"How do you know which train and which container?"

"You don't need to know that."

"You know I can bail on this at any time, right?" Slater said. "Give me the dope."

He huffed. "I have a friend at the port."

"And he tells you what train it's loaded onto, and gives you the container number? How does he know what's in the container?"

"He can see the customs manifests. It doesn't always work out. I can't get into just any sea can. It has to be one of the upper ones. They stack them two high on the train. Plus it has to have a basic lock. Some of them have harder locks nowadays."

"How do you get into the container?"

"A rotary saw. That'll be your job."

"You need to show me how to run it before we get out there."

Knox nodded. "We'll do that."

"Is the train moving?"

"We hit it when it's stopped. The stops are scheduled. I don't have access to that information, but I've been watching, and almost every train stops for half an hour or so near Kelso. I'm not sure why. Maybe it's about congestion on the line. There's so darn many trains."

"How far from Kelso?" Slater said.

"A few miles." He frowned. "Does it matter? They stop just east of a little siding called Lisbon. They don't use it for anything anymore. There's nothing there."

"Lisbon is west of Kelso," Slater said. "Maybe eight or ten miles."

His eyes narrowed. "That's a very specific thing to know."

"It's a very specific place to be." He waved dismissively. "I've spent time in the Mojave Preserve."

"So you know the terrain. There's no roads along the rail line, but there's some four-wheeler trails."

"Those are called double-tracks. You drive out on one of those from the pavement at Kelso?"

"Once you're away from the paved road," Knox said, "there's nothing but trains. Nobody goes out there to camp or anything. Railroading is a super profitable business. You can haul as much as a hundred semitrucks and pay a salary to one person. It's like a license to print money."

"It's almost like they deserve it," Slater said. "Like you'd be foolish not to rob them."

He threw up his hands. "Exactly."

Asking him the container number, even the train number, would be too suspicious, he knew. "When will this train be stopped at Lisbon?"

"Right around 10:20. We'll leave here at 8."

"You and me and your car, and a two-hour drive each way. What's my cut?"

Knox chuckled. "You don't get a cut. You get a salary."

"That doesn't seem fair. What are you stealing, anyway?"

"I'm not stealing. I'm seizing an opportunity. Levying a tax. It's none of your business what I'm taxing."

"That's not going to work," Slater said. "Is it opioids? Missile launchers? Plutonium pellets? Anything like that is way too risky for me."

He leaned toward him. "There's zero risk. Nobody's out there. Nobody's on the train. It's just going to be parked there. We drive up, open the can, unload some boxes, and drive away."

Slater raised his eyebrows. "What's in the boxes, boss?"

He growled in frustration. "Tennis shoes. Those stupid expensive ones that are wrapped in plastic in the store so you can't even try them on."

"What are you planning to pay me?"

"I'll give you a thousand dollars for the day's work."

He laughed and sat back. "That's definitely not worth the risk."

Knox waved a hand. "So what do you want?"

"Five grand."

He shook his head. "No darn way. Impossible. I'll give you fifteen hundred."

"Three grand," Slater said, "with fifteen hundred up front, and fifteen when we get back."

Knox sat staring at him. "With that attitude, you might just end up like the last guy."

"I heard he was dead. Were you responsible for that?"

He raised his eyebrows, a tacit challenge. Slater could feel his heart start to pound. But he couldn't punch this guy in the face right now, no matter how much he was asking for it.

"Have you got somebody else lined up who can help you on short notice?" Slater said. "Maybe Luanne? She could probably run a rotary saw if she doubled down on her arthritis medication."

"Fine," Knox said through his teeth.

He rose and stepped over to the safe, shielding it with his body. Slater heard the keypad beep as he tapped in the combination, then heaved open the door. A moment later he stepped to the desk with a wad of C-notes, half a rack or so, and counted out fifteen of them.

Slater riffled through them, then set them on the desktop and sat back. "These are new, and sequential. That's not going to work. I need small used bills."

He scowled. "Money is money."

"You can take these to the bank and swap them for twenties if you need to. I can wait."

Scoffing, Knox scooped up the bills and went back to the safe, and returned with a bundle of cash bound with a blue elastic band. Pulling it off, he counted bills off the stack, and when he got to five hundred, handed Slater the rest of it.

"That's fifteen."

They were all twenties, he saw, and used, and not sequential. He tucked the wad into the front pocket of his jeans.

As he wrapped the elastic band around the five hundred, Knox held his gaze. "You're committed to this now. No backing out."

Slater jutted his chin. "Show me the saw."

They both got up, and Knox tossed the bundle of cash into the safe and locked it. As he stood erect he tapped at his phone.

"See this? That thing in the middle is the lockbox."

Leaning in, Slater studied the screen. It was an image of the end of a shipping container, the heavy corrugated metal painted tan. An oblong box was mounted at the seam where the doors met, connected to the handle that controlled the locking cams at the top and bottom.

"We cut vertically through it," Knox said. "Right down the middle. You line up the blade with the doors. It doesn't take long. Once you're through it, you can just pull the doors open."

He walked into the stock room, and pushed on the crash bar, and stepped outside. Following him, Slater winced at the bright daylight and pulled on his sunglasses. Knox pointed a key fob at the Wrangler, and unlocked it, then went to its rear door. It was hinged at the side, and he pulled on the spare tire, swinging it open. Sitting in the back was a rotary saw. It looked a lot like a concrete saw, with a two-stroke engine, but it had a different kind of disk blade.

"Do you know how to use one of these?" Knox said.

"Basically." He grabbed the handle and lifted it. It wasn't as heavy as it looked, and the engine was similar to lots of gardening tools that he'd used. He pointed to a lever on the side. "Is this the choke?"

"It's a decompression valve. You open it until you get it running, then close it for more power. Cutting through steel, you need lots of torque."

Knox grabbed a pair of work gloves from the back of

the vehicle, and handed them to him, then took hold of the saw and carried it over to the dumpster that sat next to the building. He pointed to the heavy steel box welded onto the side of it.

"Imagine this is the lock on the sea can."

"Isn't that for the garbage truck's forks?" Slater said, pulling on the gloves. "You want me to wreck the dumpster?"

"Who cares? It belongs to the trash company. You're just going to put a little slice in it." He handed him the saw. "Once you get it running, throttle it up before you make contact. You have to be on full throttle to get through the steel. Don't wimp out on me, now."

Setting the saw on the ground, Slater opened the valve and pulled hard on the start cord. It started up on the first pull. When he closed the valve, the sound of the puttering engine deepened.

"Let it run for a few seconds," Knox said, talking over the noise of the engine, "then crank up the throttle."

Slater lifted the machine and throttled it up, eliciting a loud angry buzz and oily exhaust fumes. He aimed it at the side of the dumpster. Myriad sparks flew as the blade bit into the steel, but the blade guard kept the bright spray mostly away from him. It only took a few seconds to cut through the slot on the side of the dumpster. He pulled it back and let off on the throttle. Knox waved at his own neck with his fingers, a tacit *Knock it off.*

Once Slater had killed the engine, Knox gestured to the dumpster. "You obviously know what you're doing. It'll take a little more work to get through the lock on the sea can, but you get the idea."

"What are you going to be doing while I'm cutting into it?"

"I'll be there." He frowned. "You're not afraid of heights, are you?"

"No more than most people."

"Well, I get vertigo. That's why you're going up the ladder."

"What ladder?"

Knox took hold of the saw, and walked to the back of the Wrangler, and pulled out an aluminum prop ladder. Slater heard it click as it locked into place when Knox folded it open. It had just a few rungs. He carried it over to the side of the building, and propped it at an angle, and gestured to it.

"I know how ladders work," Slater said.

"Try it out. Get comfortable."

He stepped on the bottom rung, then climbed two more.

"Right there," Knox said. "You'll be on that rung. The lock on the upper can will be right where your chest is."

As he turned to look at him, Knox gestured to his own chest.

"So you need the ladder to get up to the lock," Slater said.

"The cans are eight and a half feet tall. The end of the rail car goes about halfway up the lower can. The car has a handy little platform at the end. That's where you prop the ladder. There's plenty of room to work."

Slater hopped backward, landing in a crouch on the hard earth.

"You cut through the lock," Knox said, "and pull open the doors, and we're in."

"Are you sure the stuff you want will be right inside?"

"The whole container is the same product. I'll take as much as I can get." He folded the ladder and carried it to the back of the vehicle.

"How much will fit in the Wrangler?"

"Thirty or forty boxes. I'm not greedy." He slammed the vehicle's back door. "I can't really drive a cargo van out to where the trains stop. I need the high clearance and the four-wheel drive. There's a couple of sandy washes to get through. Plus it's less suspicious to be on the back roads with a Jeep than with a van."

"I guess it's clear enough."

"Get here before eight," Knox said, "in case there's anything we need to figure out."

As he walked to the crash door into the store, Slater glanced at the ugly raw gash he'd made in the dumpster, the newly exposed steel glinting in the sunlight. He followed Knox inside and walked up to the register. Luanne was behind the counter.

"How's business?" Slater said.

"It's all secondhand interesting things, honey."

A woman walked in the door and called a greeting.

He watched as she stepped in among the clothes racks. "Well, people seem to love it."

A while later, when Luanne was on the floor and there were only a couple of customers, Slater walked out the front door and around the building. The crash door was closed. Digging out his phone, he took a photo of the Wrangler, then a close-up of its rear license plate, then went to the windshield to get a photo of the VIN. He took a moment to check the screen to make sure they were all legible. Why hadn't he brought another vehicle tracker? Putting the ones he had on the prowl cars meant he had no way to keep track of this rig.

Walking around to the side of the building, he paused and dialed Torres's number. The idiot had better answer him.

"Hey, Slater," he said when he picked up.

"The job is on for tomorrow morning," he said, his voice low.

"Yikes. That's soon."

"Can you handle it?"

"What details do you have?"

"It's just two of us and one vehicle. I'll text you some

photos of the rig. I didn't get a train number, but he said it would stop for half an hour or so at 10:20 a.m. just east of an abandoned siding called Lisbon. It's a few miles west of Kelso."

"I know where Lisbon is," Torres said. "We call them historic sidings, not abandoned. I'm not sure that's enough to go on."

"Well, that's what I've got. You need to tell me whether you can handle this before eight in the morning."

"I'll make some calls. You never actually told us who the suspect was."

"I'll text you what I know about him."

"Is he going to be armed?"

"He won't be, and if he is, like I said, I won't be there. But I'll give you a heads up if he insists on packing."

———✦———

AFTER SLATER AND LUANNE closed the shop, he drove to Flynn's place. There was no sign of the GTO, and when he knocked on the door of the casita, there was only silence.

Climbing back in the Frontier, he drove to a diner to eat. While he waited for the chow he sent the photos he'd taken of the Wrangler to Torres. He added notes about Knox—his name, and the name of the thrift store, and what he looked like. Even though he'd gone through the details on the call with Torres, he thumb-typed what Knox had told him, the schedule of the train and where they were going to hit it.

When the fries came, they were greasy, but at least they were hot. The fruit salad was mostly mushy bland canta-loupe with a couple of soggy grapes. He really needed to get out of this town.

It was dark when he got back to Flynn's place. The GTO was here now, parked nose out. When he knocked, Flynn waved him in.

"Were you at a meeting?"

"Good guess," Flynn said, and dropped into the lone lounge chair. "So what's going on with Knox? Did you get into his office? What did you find out?"

He sat facing him on the end of the sofa. "I know definitively now that he's a grifter. Did he try to get you to do anything shady? Like robbery or cheating his wholesale clients?"

"Just the thing about robbing the safe."

"I think he's trying to manipulate me into a similar position."

Flynn frowned. "How?"

"He wants me to help him steal stuff."

His phone buzzed in his pants, and he pulled it out to check. It was a text from Torres:

Operation approved. See you there.

That was very good news. He sent a terse acknowledgment then tucked the phone away.

"Steal what?" Flynn said. "Is there a way you can turn that into him getting arrested?"

"Things are evolving." He rubbed his eyes and rested his head on the back of the sofa.

"It doesn't seem like that. I feel like I'm stuck. Like I'm not accomplishing anything. Just treading water. I need something to happen."

Slater didn't open his eyes. "Inertia is an illusion."

"What's that supposed to mean?"

"Give me a day or two. Things are about to change."

Flynn didn't speak for a minute. "You look wiped out."

"I've been up since way too early, and on my feet all day at the store. I don't know how Luanne does it. Maybe there's speed in her arthritis gummies. Or her purse cheese is synthesizing meth. Did you know she keeps cheese in her handbag?"

"Are you too tired to get busy?"

Slater lifted his head and met his gaze. It was a mistake to be sleeping with this guy, he knew that. He needed to keep his dick out of his cases. But that ship had sailed.

"Never," he said.

Flynn chuckled, and they both rose, and got undressed. He pushed Flynn onto the bed, and climbed up, pushing his knees apart, and started to smoke him. Flynn quickly got hard, and shifted to take Slater into his mouth. When Flynn came, his body spasmed, and Slater followed a moment later.

They both lay there, sweaty and spent, and as his breathing slowed, Slater quickly drifted into sleep. Sometime later Flynn woke him.

"Do you want to get under the covers?"

"I need to get my bag."

Slater got up, and pulled on his jeans, and stepped outside. The night air felt cold on his bare torso. Unlocking the pickup, he pulled the pint of bourbon out of his satchel, and guzzled from it.

The moon was out, over in the west, almost half full now, fatter and brighter than it had been last week. He stood watching it, and took another slug, shivering involuntarily at a gust of cold air. Those freaking railroad cops had better not screw this up.

Tucking the bottle away, he went back inside and climbed into bed with Flynn.

———·———

SLATER WOKE, AND IN the low light, he saw a face looming next to him. He knew this person, he decided.

"What are you dreaming about?" Flynn said.

His tongue felt thick. "I get a glimpse of it sometimes. It's just … nothing. Completely empty."

"What's the feeling that goes along with that?"

"It makes me …" Slater hesitated. "It gives me awe. It's so … naked. Honest."

"What are you seeing?"

He closed his eyes. "What?"

"What is it that's empty?" Flynn said.

"I am," he mumbled, and flipped over, and willed himself back to sleep.

TWENTY-SIX

WHEN SLATER WOKE IN the morning, Flynn was sitting up in bed.

"What were you dreaming about just now?"

"You are relentless, son."

"What was it?" Flynn said. "Think. While it's still fresh."

"I was trying to get at somebody. There were metal bars between us." He traced them in the air with a finger. "I was shouting and rattling the bars."

"Who was on the other side?"

"No idea."

"Do you remember me waking you last night?"

Slater eyed him sidelong. "Maybe."

"Do you remember what you said?"

"Enlighten me."

"You told me you got a glimpse of it sometimes, and I asked what, and you said it was you. That you were empty."

Slater narrowed his eyes. "That sounds far-fetched."

He chuckled and got out of bed. "Do you want coffee?"

When he came back with a mug for him, Slater sat up and sipped at it.

"You said lucid dreaming was about manipulating dreams," Slater said. "If they're about constructing your waking life, what's wrong with just letting it happen? If there's already a process in place?"

Flynn sat next to him with his own mug. "Wouldn't you rather have some say in it?"

"It's like ordering a sandwich. I don't need to know where the lettuce grew, or how the bread got baked."

"I want to be more aware of it," Flynn said. "I want to influence the parts I can influence. Like the emptiness you saw. You said it made you feel awe. Don't you want to explore that more?"

He slurped at his coffee and didn't reply. It was way too early for shrinky stuff. Eventually he got up and got dressed.

"Are you going to the thrift store?" Flynn said. "When exactly is Knox getting you to steal stuff for him?"

"It might be happening today. I'll let you know tonight."

"You've thought all this through, right? You're not going to let him fuck up your life like he did mine?"

"You don't need to worry about me," Slater said, and walked out.

He drove the pickup to the thrift store. The peppy little engine was a lot of fun. He might have to hang on to this for a while. Pike wouldn't even get steamed since this whip could be left on the street.

The Wrangler was parked at the back of the shop, and he pulled up nearby, and let himself in the back door. Knox was standing in his office. The guy was dressed for the backcountry, in washed-out jeans and a long-sleeved plaid shirt, a ball cap, and scuffed work boots rather than his usual flashy dress shoes.

"You're on time," Knox said.

He looped a strap around his neck. It was a pair of spotting binoculars, Slater saw, and Knox let them dangle at his belly.

"What do we need to do?"

"My contact said the trains are on time today. I just need to get Frances and we can roll."

Slater frowned. "Who's Frances?"

"My .45. In the register." He raised his eyebrows. "The one you fired the other day when you put a hole in my roof."

"You can't take a heater."

Knox frowned. "You don't actually get a vote. I'm running this operation."

"You said no one would be out there. If the cops happen to drive by, or somebody on the train crew shows up, do you really want to get into a gunfight with them? Use your head."

"There's not going to be anybody there."

"So then you don't need the rod. You know there's a big difference between burglary and armed robbery, right? Years and years of your life in stir."

"You actually look like the guy who'd know all about that," Knox said. "Still, I think I'll take the chance."

"If you're rolling strapped, I'm going to bail."

He huffed. "You're being paranoid."

"Ticktock. Let's go."

"Darn you." Knox glared at him for a moment, then picked up a pair of license plates from the desk. "We need to put these on the Jeep. Grab a screwdriver."

There were some tools on the shelves next to the lockers, he knew, and went over and found one. Following Knox out the back door, he pulled on his sunglasses, then dropped to one knee at the front bumper of the Wrangler, and unscrewed the tag. When he pulled it off, Knox handed him the replacement.

"Where did these come from?" Slater said.

"We need to be stealthy."

"I know why you're doing it. I'm asking about the source."

"It doesn't matter."

"It will if you pulled them off a stolen vehicle. You know prowl cars have automated plate readers, right?"

Knox didn't respond to that. Walking around to the back, Slater swapped the rear plate, and Knox took the original set and walked toward the crash door.

"Put the back seats down," he called to him as he stepped inside.

Slater opened the side door. There was a flat of plastic water bottles on the back seat, and he shifted them to the ground until he got the seat folded down, then lifted the water in again. As he walked around to fold down the other side, Knox stepped outside.

Opening the vehicle's back door, Slater saw the rotary saw, and the half ladder, and the gloves he'd used yesterday. There were two pairs, and he picked them up and turned them over.

"What are you looking for?" Knox said.

"Gloves. These will work." He tossed them in and stepped back.

Knox closed the door. "Can you drive a stick?"

"I can."

Digging in his front pocket, he tossed Slater the key fob, and went to the passenger side. Slater climbed behind the wheel, and adjusted the mirrors, and pulled into the street.

"You need to turn on Amboy Road," Knox said.

"I know the way."

Once they were rolling through the desert landscape, Slater spoke.

"Tell me about the dead guy."

"His name was Flynn. He stole from me."

"Like that homeless woman did? He took some of your secondhand interesting things?"

"He stole cash. Somehow he got into my safe and robbed me of three hundred grand."

That was a lot more than Flynn said he'd taken, he knew, but the cops would have no way to verify Knox's claim.

"That seems like a lot of jack to have lying around a thrift store."

"I have other business interests," Knox said. "It hit me hard. It was months ago and I'm still scrambling to keep on top of things."

"Did the cops investigate Flynn?"

"He's dead, so it doesn't even matter. Nobody can hold him accountable. That screwed things up for me too."

"Selfish of the guy to up and die on you," Slater said.

"Tell me about it. So why do you go into the Mojave Preserve?"

"It's the open desert. There's a lot less scrutiny than in the national park."

"What are you doing that you don't want scrutinized?"

"The wilderness is a good place to conceal things."

"Like a body," Knox said.

"Theoretically, sure. I've never done that."

"You just drive out on a Jeep trail?"

"You mean a double-track," Slater said. "I walk away from the double-track. Almost nobody ever walks more than ten minutes from where they can park a vehicle. Twenty minutes' walk reduces that to absolutely nobody."

"You could only hide stuff you could carry."

"That's how it works."

"So it has to be cash, or jewelry, or gold coins. Are you a jewel thief, John?"

"You don't spend a lot of time with other lowlifes, I'm thinking, or you'd know it's bad manners to ask something like that."

"Other lowlifes." Knox scoffed. "You make it sound like I'm a lowlife."

Slater looked over at him. "We are headed to rob a train right now."

"You're the lowlife," Knox said intently. He jabbed a thick finger at him and raised his voice. "You. Riding around on a motorcycle, and talking all anti-church."

Slater frowned. "Who says I'm anti-church?"

"When you trash-talked my painting. Trying to tell me the lord was Catholic. And you said you weren't religious."

"I said I wasn't superstitious. That includes religion. It doesn't mean I'm going to car-bomb your church. We all have to tolerate that stuff. One of my shrinks called it the social contract. We put up with it the same way we tolerate sewage plants and uncontrolled wildfires and billionaire CEOs."

"Church never hurt anyone."

"Tell that to my ancestors who got garroted by the Inquisition."

"I don't go to that kind of church," Knox said. "You should check it out. There's some Mexicans who come."

"Dude." Slater raised his voice. "I'm Jewish."

"Seriously? A Mexican Jew? That's a new one."

Slater's instinct was to serve up a kovac or throw a punch, but it wasn't safe right now. He'd wind up rolling this stupid car. Instead he gripped the wheel hard and focused on the road.

He knew the marketing spiel was inevitable with Jesus types, and he tried to tune it out as Knox got into it. Pike had explained that reacting to it was a mistake. Pushback served as a win for them, since it reassured them that they were safe and righteous in their insulated little group. Reacting to the marketing confirmed that the rest of the world was against them.

Eventually Knox took a break.

"You know what's most grating about Jesus freaks?" Slater said. "There's never any doubt. Just absolute confidence in this story that has no evidence. The ancient Greeks would have called that hubris."

"You called me a lowlife, and now I'm a freak."

"You did just give an extended sales job for your religion."

"The ancient Greeks don't matter. They're all in hell. Nobody who lived before the time of Jesus can get into heaven."

Slater scoffed. "More hubris. The payback for that was nemesis. The gods' retribution. It's not an arbitrary punishment either—it comes in proportion to your arrogance. The Persians invaded Greece and thought it would be a cakewalk because they had a bigger army and more ships, but the Greeks rinsed them because they were smarter about it. *Bam,* hubris gets paid back with nemesis."

Knox looked over at him. "It sounds like you managed to take some correspondence courses while you were in prison."

They crossed the tracks at Amboy, rolling past the oddball volcanic cinder cone and its debris field of black lava rock, and headed farther north. Eventually they got close to Kelso, and just before they reached the rail line, Knox pointed out a dusty double-track.

"This is it," he said. "Turn in here."

The track was rough and rutted and barely visible, but he turned onto it and drove as fast as the surface allowed. At least the track was clear of brush as it snaked along the rail line, never straying more than a dozen yards from the tracks.

Slater slowed to roll through an arroyo. The rail line went over it nearby on a low bridge. It hadn't flowed in a while, judging by how it looked, and there wasn't enough loose sand to merit using the four-wheel drive. The Wrangler easily climbed up the other side.

Ahead of them Slater spotted a glimmer in the landscape. As they crested a rise he saw that it was the bright headlight of a train that loomed in the distance, headed toward them.

"Is this the one?" Slater said.

"Not yet."

They heard a loud rumble as it got closer, and then it started to roll past them. First were the engines, painted red and orange, and then the endless string of double-stacked containers in myriad dull colors.

"See how they're set up?" Knox said. "That little platform at the end of the car. You stand on it and set up the ladder."

He could see now why it had to be the upper container. Each rail car was like a well, built for the containers to ride as close to the tracks as possible. The lower one sat deep in the frame of the car, its doors inaccessible until it was lifted out.

"It's not moving very fast," Slater said.

"Maybe thirty or forty. It doesn't matter. The one we're after is going to be stopped."

Eventually the end of the train passed. A few miles later a line of shrubby trees appeared. They'd been planted in a tight row flanking the tracks, with another row on the far side. They were some kind of dryland juniper.

He could see why they'd planted them. This stretch was drier than anywhere they'd been so far, with next to no local vegetation or soil crust. Trees would keep the sand from drifting over the tracks. Eventually the trees ended, and the landscape had more flora again, creosotes and even some yuccas.

Knox was looking at his phone. "This is the spot."

TWENTY-SEVEN

"**T**HIS IS LISBON?" SLATER eyed the tracks, but there was no sign of a siding.

"That's a little farther," Knox said. "Right here we'll be halfway along the train when it stops. Pull up behind the greasewood."

Desert rats called them that, but Slater knew it as a creosote. He parked the Wrangler next to it. The sparse bush wouldn't hide the vehicle from the train crew or from a camera, but it would make it less obvious.

They both climbed out, and Slater stretched, rolling his shoulders and arching his back.

"It won't be long now," Knox said. "Get ready to jump in. If the train stops before I spot the sea can, we'll drive farther, toward the end."

"So you don't know where in the train it's positioned."

"I only know that it's somewhere on the next one, and it's on the top."

Slater felt the rumble of the approaching behemoth before he saw it, and soon the loud engines rolled by. Knox was watching intently, intermittently looking through the

259

binoculars farther down the train.

The serial numbers were stenciled on the side of some of the containers, he saw, but every one of them had it stenciled on the end doors. There was enough room between the cars to get a look at them as they passed.

Dozens of cars rolled by. It felt like the train was slowing down. It definitely was, Slater realized. There was no doubt about it now. Eventually it slowed to a crawl.

"No sign of my can," Knox said. "Let's go."

They climbed in the Wrangler and Slater drove alongside the train. It came to a full stop with the squeal of metal and the hiss of air brakes. Knox rolled down his window, intermittently peering through the binoculars. They passed dozens more cars before Slater spoke.

"Is it possible this is the wrong train?"

"It's the right one," Knox snapped. "I just have to find it." Then he slapped the dash and raised his voice. "That's it. The green one. Stop next to it."

Slater pulled up parallel to the rail car, but not too close, as the double-track was a few yards from the rails. As they clambered out, Slater looked in both directions along the line. This had to be at least a mile from the engines. He couldn't see the back end of the train from here either. And there was no sign of Torres or any other cops.

Moving fast, Knox had the back door of the Wrangler open. They both pulled on the work gloves, and Knox handed Slater the ladder, and grabbed the rotary saw. At the end of the rail car were three rungs to step up to the platform. That made it easy.

Slater climbed onto it, and folded open the ladder, and propped it against the lower container. Knox handed up the rotary saw, and he set it on the deck to pull the start cord. It caught on the first try, and he closed the decompression valve, and heard the throbbing of the engine deepen in tone, building power.

He climbed a couple of rungs on the ladder, until the lockbox on the doors of the upper container was within reach. Revving the saw to full throttle, he squinted as he pressed it into the steel.

Sparks flew upward and downward in bright streams. This was way more steel than on that dumpster. It took a minute, but eventually the blade got through the box, bisecting it top to bottom. It looked like a clean cut. He flipped up the latch on the right-hand door, and twisted the handle, and tugged on it. The mechanism was free of the lock, and he could see the vertical bar rotate the cams at the top and bottom. But why wouldn't it swing open?

The ladder, he realized. He couldn't pull it open with the ladder and his own weight propped against it. Idiot. Hopping down, he shifted the ladder against the left door, then heaved on the right, and pulled it open a few inches.

"Yes," Knox hissed. He was standing on the ground watching him work. "Give me the saw."

Once he'd killed the engine, he handed it down to him, and went back to the open door, pulling it wider. Cartons filled the entire space, right to the top, and he climbed a couple of rungs and pulled one out.

Knox followed him onto the platform and cackled as he took hold of the box. "I did it. This is the stuff."

He heaved it toward the Wrangler, and it landed on the ground with a *snap*. At first Slater thought it had split open, but it looked intact. It was just the sound of cardboard striking sand. The box wasn't heavy. Logically it should survive being tossed a few yards.

"Come on." Knox waggled his hands for another box. "Let's do this."

Slater pulled out another, handing it down, and got into the rhythm of reaching for the next as Knox tossed it. They'd shifted a dozen or so when the train suddenly lurched, with the loud *clank* of myriad metal parts being pulled taut. Slater grabbed the container door and managed not to lose his balance on the ladder.

"What the heck are they doing?" Knox said, bracing himself on the lower container. "It's not supposed to be moving yet." He waved for another box.

Slater handed him one, and watched him toss it. The Wrangler was slowly starting to drift away.

"We should get off," Slater said.

"Keep working."

They shifted a few more cartons as the train gradually accelerated.

"At some point it won't be safe to jump," Slater said.

Knox ignored that and waved for another box. They heaved out more of them as the train gradually got rolling faster.

"I'm going to walk back to the vehicle and come pick you up," Slater said finally, hopping off the ladder. "Don't wait too long."

He growled in frustration. "Pick me up before you stop for the boxes. We'll collect them together."

Stepping to the edge of the little platform, Slater crouched and then jumped. He hit the sandy earth on his feet but lost his balance, pitching forward. His hands landed hard, and he tumbled sideways. He didn't scrape his palms, as they were protected by the gloves, and he managed to keep his face away from the ground.

As he got to his feet, he rolled his wrists, then swatted the dust off his shirt and his butt. At least he hadn't messed up his wrists or torn his jeans. Walking back toward the vehicle, he could just see it, a boxy orange shape in the distance. It was at least half a mile away. The end of the train rolled past him, and the lumbering noise of the heavy beast gradually receded, replaced by the stillness of the desert. He glanced behind him, but there was no sign of any vehicle.

Where the hell were Torres and Swift and the other

cops? Had they blown him off? Right now was the time to make the bust, with the pilfered cartons scattered along the tracks. It didn't get any more red-handed. Digging out his phone, he saw that there was no cell signal out here. He should have thought of that—he had a satellite receiver for this kind of situation, but it was sitting in his garage, hundreds of miles away. He couldn't call Torres or even check on the vehicle trackers he'd put on their prowl cars. Tucking the phone into his jeans, he roared at the empty landscape: "Fuck."

One of the cartons he passed had landed on a corner, splitting open the packing tape. He paused to flip it over and pry up the cardboard flap. Inside he could see the logo on one of the smaller boxes. This was definitely a pair of bougie tennis shoes.

Eventually he got to the Wrangler, and took a minute to load the cartons they'd tossed down before the train had moved. Climbing in, he drove back along the line, passing another dozen boxes at increasing intervals. Some of them sat in the middle of the double-track, and he navigated around them.

Where was Knox? The train had gradually been accelerating, and it had to be going at least twenty when Slater jumped. If Knox waited too long he'd break something.

Finally Knox appeared ahead, trudging toward him, carrying the folding ladder. As he got close he could see that his left sleeve was ripped and hanging loose, his arm bloodied. He stopped the vehicle next to him and climbed out. The guy was glistening with sweat and breathing hard.

"Get back in," Knox said. "We need to pick up the boxes."

"You're bleeding. Do you have a first-aid kit?"

"That can wait."

"You have to wash the dirt out of it at least." Slater took the ladder from him and stepped around to the back to toss it in, then grabbed a bottle of water from the flat.

"Hold up you arm."

Knox extended it, wincing with the effort. The outside of his forearm was scraped and gashed. It looked gory, but it had to be superficial, as he wasn't bleeding that much. Once he'd rolled up the tattered sleeve, Slater poured water on the wounds and brushed away the dirt and gravel. Knox flinched and groaned, gritting his teeth, but he didn't complain. Once he'd rinsed the skin again, he stepped back.

"That's about all I can do."

"Let's get the boxes. I'll drive." Knox waggled a hand for the keys.

Slater grabbed a bottle of water and cracked it as they both climbed in. Knox made a three-point turn. Headed back along the rail line, he drove too fast for the road, bouncing them both around and making the cartons in back tumble and slide. Slater gave up trying to drink from the bottle and braced an arm on the dash.

Knox rolled to a stop just past the first carton they came to, and Slater climbed out.

"Hustle," Knox called to him.

Once he'd loaded it in back, he got in, and Knox punched it before he'd even closed his door. They picked up more of the boxes and eventually came to a spot where the tire tracks ended.

"This is where we started," Slater said. "We got them all."

Knox got the vehicle turned around. "Did you count them?"

"I didn't, but I'd guess you got thirty or forty."

He laughed. "I'd call that a success, despite the injuries."

As they drove back east, Slater looked in the side mirror now and then. There was no sign of the cops ahead or behind. That idiot Torres had blown him off. That meant Slater had helped this yutz commit a felony robbery, and

264

he was going to get away with it.

Eventually Knox nosed the Jeep up onto the pavement at Kelso and headed south, picking up speed.

"I'm home-free now," he said, and whooped. "What a buzz."

Slater looked out the window at the dusty landscape rolling by, finally able to guzzle water from the bottle. Why had he trusted those idiot duffer cops? If some deputy on patrol pulled them over now, and figured out what they'd done, he was going to jail too. Having the wrong tags on the car was a red flag for patrol cops, and he was the one who'd actually made the switch. It was like he'd painted a target on himself and said "Come at me."

It was infuriating that Torres hadn't even bothered to tell him they weren't going to show. If any of those railroad losers came looking for him to ask about this, he was going to acquire a serious case of forgetfulness. No comment, no statement—he wouldn't even give them the time of day. He'd handed Knox to them on a platter, with accurate dope about the train and the time and the place, and somehow they had better things to do. They could damn well figure it out without him.

On the drive back to Twentynine, Slater intermittently watched the side mirror, but there was no sign of deputies or prowl cars or almost anybody else, just the odd vehicle headed the other direction. He really wanted to punch Torres in the face right now and wipe off that smarmy grin.

When they pulled up at the thrift store, the place looked open, with a couple of cars in front. Knox parked outside the back door.

"You need to unload," he said. "You can stack them along the side wall of the stock room."

"You need to put some peroxide on your arm, and wrap it up."

Knox scoffed, and unlocked the crash door, and propped

it open. As he went in, Slater pulled open the back of the Wrangler. He started moving the boxes inside, two at a time, piling them along the wall. After a couple of trips he saw that Knox was sitting at his desk, wrapping a roll of gauze around his arm.

When he stepped through the door a couple of trips later, he heard a distant scream. It came from up front. In the store. As he set the boxes down, Knox came to his office doorway.

"Did you hear that?" Slater said.

"It sounded like Luanne."

"Are you going to check on her?"

He nodded toward the shop. "Why don't you go?"

Before he could take a step, Flynn pushed through the swinging doors. His eyes were hard. Down at his side he held a handgun. Slater had seen that piece before. It was Frances, the .45 from the till.

Stopping a few paces in front of Knox, Flynn lifted the weapon, and held it at waist level, aiming it at his chest.

TWENTY-EIGHT

"**F**UCK, MAN," SLATER SAID. "What are you doing here?"

Flynn didn't take his eyes off Knox. "I'm not going to let him do to you what he did to me."

Knox stood there, eyes wide. "You're dead."

"That's what Luanne said before she hit the deck." Flynn briefly glanced at Slater. "I think she fainted. She didn't hit her head. It was more of a slow-motion type thing. She'll be fine."

"I should have known you'd pull some crap like this," Knox said. "You left me completely exposed."

"You tried to get me arrested," Flynn shouted.

Knox eyed Slater. "This guy is crazy. Let's rush him, Slade, and grab the weapon."

"That would definitely be an elegant solution for you." Slater put his hands on his hips. "I rush him, he shoots me and gets popped for murder, and you can keep doing all the degenerate bunco that you do."

"He's pointing a gun at me," Knox said. "You need to do something."

"How about you pay me the rest of what you owe me?

After that, maybe I can convince him not to ventilate you."

"He can't just shoot people," Knox said, his brow furrowing.

"You can't just rob trains either, fool, but here we are." He jutted his chin. "Go on. Fifteen hundred. No C-notes, and nothing sequential."

Knox eyed them in turn, then growled and went back into his office. Looking at Slater, Flynn threw up his free hand, a tacit *What the hell?* Slater rolled a finger in the air—*Just go with it.*

"Does he have another bang-bang in there?" Flynn said, stepping into the office to watch him. He raised his voice. "If you try to draw down on me, I'll definitely get in the first shot."

"There's no gun," Knox said. He pulled out a stack of cash with a blue elastic band on it, and showed it to them with his fingers spread, then tossed the bundle through the doorway to Slater. "Now take the gun away from him."

Stepping into the office with them, Slater pocketed the cash, then turned to Flynn, and waggled his fingers for the weapon.

"What are you doing?" Flynn demanded. "He can't get away with this."

"I know."

He hesitated, but then huffed, and flipped the weapon around, and handed it to him. Slater took hold of it and aimed it at Knox.

"Truth time, toots," Slater said. "Why did you try to put Flynn in the frame?"

Knox frowned. "Don't point that thing at me. You work for me, remember?"

"Our business is concluded." He waggled the weapon. "I asked you a question."

"I don't know what you're talking about."

"Liar," Flynn shouted.

Moving closer, Slater smacked the side of Knox's head with the weapon, then backhanded him on the other side. His finger hurt as Pike's chunky class ring bit into his skin. Knox instinctively held up his arms but knew better than to fight back. He'd drawn blood, Slater saw as he stepped back. A thick drop of it slowly descended his cheek from his temple. Knox pressed his fingers to the side of his head and glanced at his bloody fingertips. The expression on his face was more surprised than angry.

He stood up straighter. "You can't just pistol-whip me."

"You need to squawk, baby. If not, I will happily blow your head off. I have a witness right here who'll explain that it was self-defense."

"I like that plan," Flynn said. "He rushed you. You had no choice but to fire. It was him or you."

Breathing hard, his face red now, Knox glared at Slater. "Judas."

Slater lifted the weapon again and stepped toward him.

"Stop it." Knox held his hands up, and when Slater paused, he leaned back against the side of the desk and took a breath. "There were too many questions about the tennis shoes. Who knew that some of those darn things had serial numbers in them? One of the retailers said the heat was on, and they were going to have to give the police something. That meant they were going to trace the shoes back to me. So I needed somebody else to take the fall for taking them off the trains."

"That's what this was all about?" Flynn demanded. "You were stealing that stuff from trains?"

Knox raised his eyebrows. "I'm pretty sure it was you stealing from the trains."

"Asshole," Flynn shouted.

"So your plan was to get Flynn popped for passing the stolen cash," Slater said, "and then you were going to finger him as the train robber."

He shrugged. "Or as the fence. Either way. I was waiting for the right opportunity. For when I needed it. But then he went and died on me."

"Do you have any idea what I've been through because of you?" Flynn said.

"It's not about me, Flynn." Knox held his gaze. "You can't blame your problems on other people. You need to get right with Jesus."

"Fuck that," Flynn roared. "You set me up, and you're going over for it."

A loud chirp came from Slater's jeans. He touched the outside of his pocket but didn't bother to pull out his phone. He knew what it was. Svetlana's software. It was loud for a reason—it was a warning. A proximity alert for his vehicle trackers. The only ones he was running right now were on those two railroad police hoopties.

Eyeing Flynn, he could see the raw burning hatred in his eyes, his lip curled in disgust as he glared at Knox. Slater snapped his fingers, and Flynn looked at him.

"Do you trust me?" Slater said.

"That would be no."

"Fair enough. But whatever happens in the next couple minutes, do not make any moves. Just keep your mouth shut and let this play out. You're a bystander. Think freeze tag."

"What are you talking about?"

"Just do what I say," Slater said. He stepped toward Knox and handed him the heater. "This belongs to you."

"What the fuck?" Flynn shouted.

Slater stepped back. "Take a breath."

His eyes wide, Knox looked at the weapon in his hand. "This day just gets better and better. Thank you, Jesus." He aimed it at Flynn. "I wish you'd spent more of those C-notes. You'd be in jail right now, or maybe for-real dead, not fake dead. And I'd have an explanation for all the shoes." He waved the weapon at Slater. "And you, John. I

270

can't believe you're this stupid. Who's the lowlife now?"

"It's still you," Slater said flatly.

"No," he shouted, and shook the gun. "It's you. You're the lowlife. You're not leaving here alive. You realize that, don't you?"

"And lo, he shows his true colors," Slater said. "They're as fugly as all your nasty shoes."

"Fudge nuggets," Knox shouted. "You know what? I'm going to take back that fifteen from your carcass after I plug you. After I plug you both. I'll claim you tried to rob me."

From the office doorway came a woman's voice. "I wouldn't do that."

Turning toward her, Slater instinctively flashed his palms and stepped back, toward the wall. It was Swift, in uniform, her arms extended with her weapon aimed at Knox. Behind her were several other guys in uniform, spread out in formation, sidearms drawn.

Swift jutted her chin to Flynn. "Step aside, son."

His palms already in the air, Flynn stepped back, giving her a clear line of sight to Knox.

"Drop the weapon," Swift said, her tone intent.

Knox set the heater on his desk. "Officer, thank god you're here. These hooligans were trying to rob me."

"He's lying," Flynn said.

Holding up his bandaged forearm, Knox made his eyes wide. "They assaulted me. You can see the extent of my injuries."

"Everybody out of the office," Swift said.

Knox showed his palms and stepped toward the stock room. "Why are you pointing that thing at me? I'm defending myself here."

"Cuff them all," Swift said.

One of the uniforms holstered his sidearm, and stepped over to Knox, pulling his arms behind his back. The other one pulled Flynn's arms down to snap on the cuffs, then grabbed Slater's. He hated that sound, the ratchet click, hated the finality of the bracelets going on.

Stepping into the office, Swift retrieved the .45, and popped out the mag, and cleared the chamber.

"Were you going bear hunting?" she said, and looked around the office, then stepped out again.

From the back door, Torres stepped inside, and pushed his sunglasses up on his head. "Hey, fellas. How's it going?"

Knox turned to him. "Officer. Thank god. Your subordinate here interrupted a robbery. I'm very grateful. If you could just uncuff me."

"Is this your vehicle?" Torres said, gesturing outside.

"I don't know anything about that. I loaned my Jeep to these two this morning. I have no idea what they did with it."

"That's not what the cameras on Kelbaker Road say." Swift raised her eyebrows. "We almost missed you because the plates didn't match your vehicle."

"He cold-plated the Wrangler this morning," Slater said. "The original tags will be here somewhere. Look in his desk."

"I wasn't on Kelbaker Road," Knox said. "It must have been these ungodly lowlifes."

"There's not a lot of vehicular traffic out there," Swift said. "We spotted you eventually. Ibáñez drove northbound, and you drove back. Photographic evidence puts you at the scene."

Knox frowned. "Who's Ibáñez?"

"There's a dozen cartons in the back of the Wrangler," Torres said, "and more inside, I see. It all matches what was pilfered from that train this morning."

Eyeing one of the uniforms, Swift jutted her chin. "Document what's in the vehicle. Photos and an inventory."

"This is part of it too," Torres said, and waved at the

cartons stacked at the wall.

"I do not consent to a search of my vehicle or my store," Knox said.

Torres scoffed. "It's too late for that."

They didn't even need a warrant, Slater knew. He'd been in the process of unloading the Wrangler, so its door was hanging open, and so was the one to the shop. It was easy for them to see what was in the vehicle and to walk right in.

"Let's get him processed," Swift said to the other uniform, and they led Knox out the back door.

"John," Knox called back. "Tell Luanne to call my wife. This is all a silly mistake. She needs to bail me out."

Once Knox was gone, Slater jutted his chin at Torres. "Are you going to unhook me?"

He gestured for the other cop to uncuff him, and as he stepped behind him, Slater held Torres's gaze.

"In different circumstances, this could be hot. But you'd have to do all the work."

Torres's eyes narrowed. "Pike said you were a lot of man."

"You talked to Pike?" he said. "Why did you do that? He's not my pop."

"He was concerned about your welfare," Torres said. "It was actually kind of sweet."

When the cuffs came off, Slater rubbed his wrists. He knew he couldn't be angry with Pike. Calling Torres was ham-fisted, but he probably just wanted to make sure Slater didn't get benched along with the dirtbags.

"What about this one?" the uniform said, gesturing to Flynn.

"He's not part of this," Slater said. "He just walked in."

Torres nodded, and the cop uncuffed Flynn, then went out the back door.

"You did it." Flynn was massaging his wrists, a wry grin on his face. "You took out Knox."

"He did that to himself." He frowned at Torres. "Where the hell were you, anyway? I expected a little action out there at Lisbon."

Torres waved a hand. "We staked out the wrong train. It took a little while to figure out, but we got you eventually. On the highway camera." He looked behind Slater toward the swinging doors. "It's all over, ma'am. Thanks for your cooperation."

Luanne stood there, wisps of hair hanging loose, her eyes bright.

"I just saw Knox leave in the back of a patrol car," she said. "He's the suspect the police were looking for? Not one of you two?"

"Knox was robbing trains," Slater said. "That's where all the boxes of shoes came from. He tried to get me to help him."

"I wondered about that. All those shoes coming and going. It didn't make any sense. They were always brand-new."

Slater stifled a groan. Why had she said that? Now she was part of it too. Torres was going to make sure she got interviewed and deposed and cross-examined in court, just like Slater would be. They'd waste her time just like they were going to waste his for the next half decade.

"I can't believe you're alive, Flynn," Luanne said. "What happened?"

Flynn ran a hand through his hair and exhaled audibly. "It's a long story."

"He's been roughing it," Slater said. "Way out in the desert. He was at a prospecting camp until today. When he got back to town, his wallet and his ID were missing. The junkie they found in the park must have robbed his place and taken them. That guy had a tattoo on his arm that looked like Flynn's, so the coroner assumed it was him."

She watched him for a moment, absorbing it, then eyed

Flynn. "Well, welcome back to the world of the living."

"Are you feeling OK?" Flynn said. "You kind of passed out when I came in."

As he stepped over to talk to her, Torres spoke to Slater in a low voice. "Is any of that true?"

"Dude." Slater waved his arm. "Why would I lie?"

www.ingramcontent.com/pod-product-compliance
Lightning Source LLC
Chambersburg PA
CBHW011321310726
48973CB00011B/3003